THE HOLY OAK HAUNTING

THE BRADDOCK & GRAY CASE FILES

H.P. BAYNE

BAYNE
INDEPENDENT
PUBLISHING

Cover art by H.P. Bayne using art licensed through depositphotos.com

CHAPTER 1

Halloween 1971

A trio of garbage-bag ghosts danced in the old oak tree as Raiya Everton eased shut the front door and slunk across the wooden porch. One of the boards needed to be replaced, and Raiya expertly skirted it as she crept onto the steps leading to the front garden.

It was dark, near midnight, but Raiya's mother was a light sleeper. One creak would have her down here in a flash, and Raiya would be doing extra chores for weeks.

The country property was in the rural area surrounding the town of Holy Oak, far enough to render this a lonely place for a sixteen-year-old girl to call home. Raiya had her driver's licence but no car, and on her father's wages—and with his proclivity to spend much of his earnings on gambling—she wasn't likely to get one anytime soon.

For now, she was reliant on schoolmates if she wanted any kind of social life. Schoolmates, not friends. Not yet.

But maybe soon. Hopefully.

Small towns didn't readily roll out the welcome mat for

outsiders, and Raiya was most definitely an outsider. Not only did her family move here just last month—leaving behind the perfectly friendly community of St. Stephen's—but she was considered weird by nearly everyone. Her little sister, she suspected, was partially to blame. While she'd denied it, Raiya was certain Mags had told others exactly how weird Raiya was.

Mags might have been in the wrong in telling, but she wasn't wrong in substance. Raiya was weird. Even she knew it. People who saw and sensed the things she did were unusual even in places many times the size of Holy Oak.

So when Becca Symes and Louise Penske invited her to come with them to a Halloween party at Becca's boyfriend's house, Raiya quickly said yes—even as a niggling in the back of her head warned her to be careful.

A heavy swath of trees encircled the property on nearly every side, leaving Raiya uncertain as to whether Becca and Louise were awaiting her as promised. It wasn't until she'd jogged most of the way down the driveway that she caught sight of headlights from a stopped vehicle.

Raiya paused, slowing. She didn't want to seem overeager, but besides that, something else was bothering her. Something she couldn't put a finger on.

She realized what it was as she reached the road. This wasn't the car belonging to either Becca or Louise. Everyone knew this car. The sleek, black, two-door Chevy belonged to Becca's boyfriend, Cary Holdfast.

Raiya wasn't allowed to be out with boys, certainly not at this hour without having so much as sought permission. The rule set by her old-fashioned parents seemed a stupid one to Raiya, but it wasn't like she'd ever before been in a position to challenge it.

This wasn't good. Bad enough she had snuck out to go to a party —a party that apparently didn't exist. After all, if Cary was here—and he wasn't likely to have loaned his precious car to anyone—he couldn't very well be at home, could he?

Raiya saved the question until the passenger door swung open to reveal a beaming Becca.

"What's going on?" Raiya asked.

"Get in," Becca exclaimed. "We're going to have a gas."

Raiya hung back. That niggling feeling was now nearer a full-on writhing serpent in her brain. "What about the party?"

"Forget the party," Becca said.

"I don't know ..."

"Don't be a square," Cary said, flashing his own grin. His seemed more a put-on than Becca's. "Party's cancelled. We've made better plans. This is going to be way cooler. You in or out?"

Out, Raiya thought to herself. Aloud she said, "In, I guess."

"Right on," Cary said. Then to Becca, "Scoot forward so she can get in. I wanna jet."

Becca did as asked, but Raiya didn't know how to flip the seat forward so she could squeeze into the back seat. With a put-upon roll of the eyes, Becca climbed out and did the job for Raiya.

Settled into the back seat, Raiya tried to get comfortable. But the bench's other occupant, Louise, made it clear she didn't want to talk to Raiya. She, at least, wasn't pretending.

Raiya did her best to shake it off. She could easily be overthinking. Her mom said Raiya did that sometimes. Her strange abilities often steered her the right way, but not always. Maybe she'd get the hang of it someday, maybe not. Perhaps she'd even wake up one day to find she was no longer experiencing any of it or that there was nothing odd about herself after all, that she'd been wrong all along. Could be she was wrong this time.

Becca's excitement was contagious as she howled along with a song by The Beatles blasting over the radio. As the car pulled away, Raiya had no choice but to let the night play out, whatever that entailed.

For now, she'd simply tell her brain to be quiet.

"ARE YOU A WITCH?"

The mumbled question from Louise seemed to come out of the blue, the tone and the unexpected nature of the query leaving Raiya wondering whether she'd misheard.

"Pardon me?"

Louise leaned nearer, her face heavily shadowed in the darkened back seat. "Are you a witch? Everyone says you are."

Raiya's grandmother on her father's side never said anything nice about witches, quoting from the Bible on the few occasions when Raiya's skills had come up. No one raised it anymore, not in front of Grandma Everton.

Raiya had never truly considered this. Witches were Halloween lore—black cats and cauldrons and broomsticks. They weren't real.

Raiya faked a smile. She liked Louise less and less. "No."

"Everyone says it."

Raiya shrugged. "Can't help what people say about me."

And she couldn't. Why bother trying? Sticks and stones and all that.

Except sometimes words hurt. And sometimes they led to something beyond words.

Such as setting Raiya's thoughts to spinning again. She still didn't understand why she'd been asked along, but she was beginning to worry.

THEY WEREN'T HEADED for town. Raiya's family had arrived only recently, but her photographer mother loved to explore backroads on the weekends. Raiya often went along for the ride. To her knowledge, there were three routes into Holy Oak from this direction. Cary was taking none of them.

Raiya's worry rose several notches. She wasn't exactly shy, but she also wasn't comfortable in groups of people she didn't know well. Despite that, it seemed time to speak up.

"Where are we going?" she asked.

"Holy Oak," Cary said.

"This isn't the way to town."

Cary twisted slightly to leer at Raiya over the seat. The Rolling Stones lips-and-tongue logo on the sleeve of his jean jacket seemed to mock her. "Not that Holy Oak. The real one."

"What's that mean?"

"You'll see," he said, turning back.

Becca's laugh came without its usual twinkle. To Raiya, it sounded bad. She stopped short of lingering on the first word which had come to mind.

Evil.

THE TOWN LIGHTS appeared in the distance, then vanished as Cary's car dropped over a large hill on a lonely country road. It wasn't paved or gravelled, but the lane had been driven over so many times, the dirt was pounded smooth.

Raiya studied the road as the headlights illuminated it, watching as trees sprouted up ahead. A heavy, black wall of trees. As Cary passed beyond their border, Raiya peered out at them. Old growth, at least for this area. Trees with stories and lives, many of them large, knotted and gnarled. Many, for that matter, dead.

Sometimes it was as though nature spoke to Raiya. These trees were whispering a message, urgent and menacing.

Turn around. Leave. Now.

The serpent was fully awake, twisting and turning as though seeking escape through Raiya's ear canal. This was wrong. They shouldn't be here.

"Why are we here?" she demanded.

No answer. She tried again. "Why are we here?"

"Everyone says you're a witch," Louise said. "Thought you might want to prove it."

"What's that mean?"

Again, no answer.

Raiya had never felt so trapped, crammed into the small back seat of a car with three people who increasingly felt like enemies, a foreign and ominous wood closing in around them. She couldn't get out of the car without their say-so, and even if she did, where would she go? The only thing worse than being here with these people was being in this place without them.

It felt … wrong. No, not just wrong. There was that word again.

Evil.

Enough was enough. This wasn't just mean anymore. It was dangerous. "You need to tell me why we're here!"

And then Cary stopped.

THEY STILL HADN'T ANSWERED her question. Now hiking down a crude and narrow footpath, the group wound deeper and deeper into the dark woods.

They'd been walking ten, maybe twenty minutes. Raiya had thought multiple times of making a run for it. Always she was stopped by the reality that to run was to be alone. And to be alone was to become a sitting duck.

For what? That was the part bothering her now. Because she'd realized shortly after emerging from the car that the trees hadn't been threatening her.

They were warning her.

"There it is," Cary said, his flashlight playing across the thick trunk of an ancient tree. The wood was knotted, its countless branches twisted and gnarled. Overhead, one large branch in particular jutted straight out like an arm extended to point out a threat. Something about the tree gave Raiya the willies.

Becca pressed nearer to Cary, threading an arm through his. "This place freaks me out."

"Don't worry, baby. I'll protect you."

Raiya might have imagined it, but it struck her Cary leaned slightly on the word "you." As in, he might not protect anyone else.

What were these people planning?

"Please," Raiya said. "You have to tell me. What are we doing here?"

Becca turned enough to catch Raiya full in the face with the beam from her flashlight. She giggled unpleasantly before pivoting away. "There's a legend connected with this place. Didn't you ever hear about it? We thought for sure *you* must have." Leaning again on that word.

"I'm new here," Raiya said. "I don't know anything about Holy Oak."

"Should we tell her?" Becca asked, her tone the sound of a smug wink.

Raiya wasn't a violent person, but she was beginning to want very badly to slap someone. She held her tongue, waiting the others out. Little good it would do to beg.

Louise heaved a sigh. "Tell her already. God, you're so annoying sometimes, Becks."

Another giggle from Becca. "Okay, so this legend. Everyone knows it around here. You know the story about the Headless Horseman, right?"

That legend Raiya was familiar with. "Yeah."

"We've got our own," Becca said. "We call him Headless Henry."

"No one knows for sure who he is," Cary chipped in. "He's been seen in these woods for as far back as people's memories stretch. My parents remember stories about him. My grandparents before that. Word is he was a soldier, a member of the cavalry. He fought in the Battle of Holy Oak, leaving behind a wife and baby."

Becca cut in quickly, as though dissatisfied with her boyfriend's rendition. "I heard his wife died in childbirth."

Louise snorted. "No one even knows his real name for sure. How would anyone know anything about his family history?"

"Shut up, Louise," Becca snapped. "Anyway, it's not known how it happened exactly. They say that during battle, Henry ran off toward the woods here. Was he chasing someone? Being chased? No one knows. All anyone *does* know is what they found afterward."

"The buzzards," Cary said. "Tell her about the buzzards."

Becca elbowed him. "Cary, stop. That's gross."

"True, though, right?"

"How would you even know?" Louise asked through a sigh.

"Shut up, Louise," Becca said. Then to Raiya, "When Henry failed to return from battle, a search was mounted. That's when they saw vultures circling the woods, right up above our heads."

Raiya shivered. The air was crisp, and her jacket had proved a little too light for the weather, but she couldn't blame that for the tremble running up her spine.

"They followed the birds," Cary said. "And they found him, lying alongside this very tree. Only they didn't find *all* of him."

Becca chirped in quickly. "All of him but the most important part. His head."

"How'd they know it was him if there was no head?" Louise asked. "They wouldn't have even had fingerprint stuff back then."

"He had a photo of his family or something probably," Becca snapped. "Oh my God, quit it."

Cary took over again. "He was starting to rot already. The smell was unreal. They didn't want to take him back like that, so they just buried him where they found him."

"It doesn't end there," Becca added. "They never did find his head, and no one ever found out what really happened to him. Not long after they buried him, though, townspeople started to report strange happenings in and around the woods: a headless man, wandering the woods at night."

"No one stuck around for a good look," Cary said. "For sure no one tried to talk to him. Then one day, a man from just outside town didn't come home. He'd gone off to cut firewood in the woods here. No one knows what happened to him, except for one thing. When they found him, he was missing his head."

"Since then, two more people have gone missing in these woods," Becca said. "No one ever found out where they were or what happened to them. It's said they, too, were taken by Headless Henry and that to this day, they wander these dark woods, trapped here with the very ghost who murdered them. Without their heads, they can't find their way out. And until Headless Henry finds his, he'll continue to hunt those who trespass here. Who knows when the next head will roll or whose it will be? Maybe it will be yours, Raiya."

Suddenly, Becca, Cary and Louise spun toward Raiya, wild, hideous grins on their faces.

"Come and get it, Henry!" Cary hollered.

Then all three of them darted off, hooting and shrieking with laughter. Their shared flashlight beams bounced away into the darkness.

RAIYA SHUDDERED, rubbing her arms as she wandered aimlessly through the woods. It was chilly, but not so she'd freeze to death. That was perhaps the only positive about her current predicament.

She wasn't certain what time the others had left her, but it had to be getting close to an hour.

Raiya sniffled back tears as she made her way blindly through the woods, only the moonlight to guide her. She'd been crying on and off, terrified and betrayed. She hadn't heard a vehicle engine, so she hoped that meant the others were waiting for her to emerge. But then, she didn't hear their voices either. Whether they were still here somewhere or not, she had no way of knowing. Either way, it wasn't helpful to her. If they hadn't ditched her, it was likely only because they were waiting to leap out and terrify her.

Group of horrible, teenage bullies or a headless killer—Raiya wasn't sure whose company she'd prefer right now.

The crackle of dried leaves drew her to an immediate halt. Her ears perked up, her sixth sense along with them. Was that one of the other kids? A wild animal? Headless Henry?

She waited, breath held, pulse pounding a frantic rhythm in her ears. Damn her fear. She'd never hear anything above the pumping blood.

Another crack, a small branch underfoot. Raiya spun. The noise had definitely come from the opposite direction.

Her schoolmates. Had to be. They were encircling her, ready to spring their malicious trap.

"Becca?" The name croaked from Raiya's dry throat, forcing her to try again. "Becca? Louise?"

No response. Only a whistle of wind through the uppermost branches of the bared trees.

"This isn't funny, you guys."

Still nothing.

Raiya lowered her face into a hand, wiping away a tear as it slipped down her cheek. She squeezed her lids shut, willing away a fresh swell of emotion. She wouldn't let them see her cry. That would only make things worse. She'd dealt with bullies before. Give them an inch, they'd take a mile. That was what her grandma used to tell her, and about that, at least, her Grandma Everton was absolutely right.

Raiya lifted her head, blinking away the last of the tears.

Oh God. What was that?

Something dark—a shadow?—stood in the gap between two trees ahead. Raiya couldn't make it out, but she didn't think it had been there before. Everything was dark, late as it was, but the filtered moonlight had at least dissolved enough of the darkness she could find her way now that her eyes had adjusted. This, though, was pitch black, hovering ahead of her, large and imposing.

And decisively human-shaped.

"Cary?" she whispered.

It didn't respond, didn't move. Raiya blinked and squinted, peering harder into the darkness. She thought she should try to tap into her sixth sense to try to get a read of this, but for some reason, she was afraid to. It felt … unholy.

Evil.

And then it moved.

Raiya gasped and took a rapid step backward. She tripped on something, landed hard on her butt. Her eyes squeezed shut with the impact, but she opened them immediately after.

Gone. Not just in sight, but in mind. She couldn't feel it anymore.

Where was it? How could it have gone so quickly?

A scream cut the night. Raiya leapt to her feet.

The sound had been distant but loud, and there was no mistaking the source. Becca.

Another scream. Becca again.

That wasn't fake. It was the sound of mortal terror.

This time, when Raiya called Becca's name, her tone carried fear for someone other than herself. Raiya wasn't perfect, but among her gifts was an uncanny level of empathy. As angry as she could be at others, it never translated into hate—as deserved as it occasionally might be.

More screams shook the woods. They were moving now, not caught in one place. Becca was running.

From what?

Urgency gripped Raiya as she raced through the woods as fast as her feet and the moonlight would safely take her. She tripped several times or knocked into trees, undoubtedly leaving scrapes and bruises on her hands, legs and arms. She barely felt them, all her senses tuned now to whatever danger lurked in these woods.

A few minutes into her run, she paused, struggling to catch her breath before calling Becca's name once again. Another shriek reached Raiya's ears, but it was farther now rather than nearer. Becca was either running farther away, or Raiya was going in the wrong direction.

Stop, she told herself. *Stop. Calm down. You'll make all the wrong choices if you're not thinking straight.*

She forced another ragged breath into oxygen-starved lungs. Another one, longer and deeper this time.

Relax. Just relax. Think.

Think. Right. That would help. Her imagination was already

working overtime, picturing out whatever that dark thing had been, wondering what Becca was freaking out about. Thinking too much was exactly the wrong move as far as Raiya was concerned.

Keep moving. One foot in front of the other. Keep moving and you'll find your way out of here. Walk to town, get some help.

She'd be in trouble with her parents. She had no choice. If anything bad happened to her schoolmates and she had done nothing to help, she'd not only be hated by absolutely everyone, she'd hate herself as well. These kids might be lousy people, but she refused to become one of them.

She kept moving, eyes wide as she sought out any clues as to the right direction to travel. Fumbling over rocks and fallen trees, scraping up against rough bark and sharp branches, Raiya kept making her way forward.

She could no longer hear Becca. Nor Cary or Louise for that matter, but she'd heard neither of them to begin with. Louise tended to be quiet as a rule, but Cary surely should be chortling up a storm if this were the result of some horrid practical joke.

But the woods were silent. Dead silent.

Until they weren't.

As Raiya crashed through a web of whiplike branches, she caught the sound of sobbing just ahead. Raiya pressed two more branches aside, ducked around a big tree trunk and stepped into a small clearing.

There, hunched and rocking back and forth on the ground, face buried in her blood-soaked hands, was Louise. Next to her lay Cary, identifiable by the Rolling Stones patch on his jean jacket.

Louise didn't look up. And Raiya soon found reason to ignore Louise altogether.

Cary might be recognizable by his jacket, but only his jacket. Because as Raiya drew nearer, she realized a terrifying truth.

Cary's head … wasn't.

It was gone.

"Headless Henry," Louise moaned between sobs. "Headless Henry got him."

Louise's eyes snapped to Raiya's. If Raiya had been entertaining even a shred of suspicion that this was some elaborate joke, Louise's expression wiped it all away.

"Don't let him get me, Raiya," Louise begged. "Please. Don't let him get me."

CHAPTER 2

Present day

Sullivan "Sully" Gray massaged his temples as he stared at the page for the umpteenth time.

His fiancée, Sarah Leffler, had left him a handwritten list of potential wedding venues to call. They hadn't yet set a date, but Sarah wanted to get married next summer or fall. He thought that left him with plenty of time to organize things.

Boy, had he been wrong.

Sully had worked his way through half the list so far. Many were solidly booked up for all of next year. The ones which weren't looked as though they came at a premium or, in the case of a couple of them, were known to have ghost stories attached.

For anyone else, hauntings at classy hotels or businesses might not be a big deal, viewed either as highly unrealistic or oddly romantic.

In Sully's case, it meant work. A lot of work.

Sully saw ghosts. He had for as long as he could remember. Worse, the ghosts he saw were exclusively those who'd died due to some form of injustice—which, ninety-five times out of a hundred meant homicide. And homicide victims' ghosts were, ninety-five times out of a hundred, neither pleasant to look at nor deal with.

Unfortunately, two of the yet-available venues near the very top of Sarah's list were most definitely known to be haunted.

Sully loved Sarah more than life itself. She had learned a great deal about his abilities. She understood them. And he knew she'd accept it if he made his case as to why he didn't want a wedding at the Bell Park Hotel or the Brolly Lounge.

Sure, she'd be cool with it. She'd be a lot more cool if Sully had ready and equally attractive options.

Next on the list then. Sully pressed at the inner corners of his eyes, willing away a building tension headache. Then he returned to his task.

THE WHISPERING WINDS Resort was about halfway down Sarah's jotted paper—far enough Sully knew it wasn't near her first choice but enough removed from the bottom to give him some hope.

Having put in a quick call, he received even more reason for optimism. The events manager was temporarily occupied, but the facility's assistant manager assured him they had a fair few openings for weddings next autumn. Come on down, he said. Sully could have a tour, meet with the events manager to speak to details.

Good. Sully had spent enough time on the phone. A drive into the country seemed like a great idea.

And he wouldn't be going alone.

"YOU KNOW I had an awesome day off planned, right?" Dez Braddock complained as Sully slid into the passenger seat of Dez's SUV. "Why do I have to do this?"

Sully clipped on his seatbelt. "Because you're my best man."

"Yeah, like next year."

Sully lifted a brow as he eyed his older brother. "You know weddings take loads of planning, don't you? I mean, *you're* married."

Dez shrugged. "Eva and Mom planned nearly the whole thing. Anyway, it was kind of rushed, what with the baby on the way and all."

Sully frowned. "If you really don't want to do this, I won't make you."

Dez stared at him for a long moment. Finally, he growled. "I hate when you do that."

"Do what?"

"That pathetic thing you do that makes me feel sorry for you. It sucks."

Sully chuckled. Worked every time.

Sully had been adopted by the Braddock family at age seven. Since then, Dez had taken on the role of big brother with fervour. Rare was the occasion when Sully couldn't goad Dez into helping him out.

Dez pushed the stick into drive, shoulder-checked and pulled onto the street before continuing the conversation. "How fast are things booking up? I mean, it's like a year away."

"A year's not a lot, at least going by the bitch of a time I'm having locating a free venue."

Dez heaved a put-upon sigh. "Great. Maybe you can hire Eva and Mom as wedding planners."

Sully sank back into the seat. "Believe me, the thought's crossed my mind. If it weren't for all the work Sarah's putting in on her end, I might not feel guilty about offloading some of my own responsibilities."

"Yeah, I see your point," Dez said. "Gotta admit, bro, part of me was hoping you'd elope. I mean, not totally elope—just that you'd ditch the big crowd and go off somewhere with the rest of us in the immediate family. I hate all this rigamarole."

Sully seemed to recall Dez crying up a storm at his own wedding years back. Dez cried during tissue commercials and was a far bigger softie than he liked to let on. Sully kept the thought to himself. They were near enough to his and Sarah's apartment that he might find himself walking back should Dez eject him from the SUV.

Instead, Sully returned to the challenging task at hand. "I tried a few places in the city Sarah really wanted, but they're totally full. Whispering Winds Resort has some availability left." Sully gazed out his window at the passing street. "Anyway, I had enough phone time today. My ear was turning red. I needed to get out for a while."

Sully felt Dez's eyes and full attention on him without the need to look.

"What?" Sully muttered.

"You're not getting cold feet, are you?"

Sully shot him a stare. "Cold feet?"

Dez gave a light laugh. "You look like I slapped you."

"Weird question, is all."

"It's not though, is it? You're beginning the process of organizing your wedding. Things are getting real now."

Sully scraped his fingernails lightly over the window ledge. "We've been living together a while already. Things have been real for some time."

"Marriage is different though. You two are committed to each other, sure, but this takes things to another level. There's going to be a piece of paper with your names on it, a document tying you two together forever." Dez lightly drummed the wheel with his fingertips. "I've been there, bro. I remember the feeling. The anxiety almost killed me."

"You had a baby on the way," Sully reminded him. "That's what you were most nervous about. I remember."

"Sure, yeah. Having a kid is as big as it gets, commitment-wise. And hey, it's not that I ever wanted anyone except Eva. That's not the point either. Something about getting married, taking those vows in front of everyone—it hits you, full impact." All humour fell from his face. "I screwed up a lot in my life, Sull. You know that. Me and Eva, the whole marriage thing, it became one of the biggest deals I knew I couldn't allow myself to mess up. It made me think about it in a different way." He cast a glance at Sully. "Thought maybe you're going through some of the same."

There it was. Dez doing the whole big brother thing again. Inviting an open and honest conversation about a topic Sully hadn't even given voice to in his own private thoughts. Not recently, anyway.

Dez was right. Sully was growing increasingly anxious. Not about committing to Sarah—not entirely at any rate. This wasn't about her. It was about him. It always was.

Which made him feel like even more of a jerk. Why did everything always have to revolve around him and his weird paranormal life? What he'd give for one day of normal.

"I can't help thinking what I'll be dragging her into," Sully said. He'd uttered the words quietly while knowing Dez would hear him —not just the words but the full meaning behind them.

"You mean her getting married to a great guy who loves her more than anything?"

Sully eyed him. "You know what I meant."

"We've been through this. Hell, you've been through this with *her*. Why are we back here again?"

Sully brushed at a dust spot on the dashboard in front of him. "Guess it's like you said. It's another level of commitment. Getting serious, thinking about things in a different way."

"She said yes, you know. She's thought this through. And she's had loads of time to reconsider. And don't forget, she's marrying *you*, Sull, not your psychic thing."

"If you're with me, you're stuck with my psychic thing all the same. It's a two-for-one deal. No one knows that better than you do."

"Sure do. Which makes me totally the right person to say this to you: anyone would be happy getting stuck with your psychic thing if it means having you in their life."

A wave of emotion washed over Sully. Dez had a way of saying things.

Sully cleared his throat before speaking but didn't quite manage to squelch the frog. "You already got the best man job, D. You don't need to pad your application."

Dez laughed. "Hell, all the ghost hunts I've been dragged along with you on, I've been padding that damn application most of my life."

NEITHER OF THEM had ever been out to Whispering Winds Resort, though they'd both heard of it. The place was a major draw during the summer months, boasting a beautiful hotel, a web of nature trails, a river valley fit for a postcard and a nine-hole golf course Sully guessed was thoroughly booked throughout the spring and summer months. Plus it was near a decent-sized town which offered access to all the usual amenities.

All selling features he could use to persuade Sarah.

"It's kind of far," Dez noted mid-way through their drive.

"Yeah, I think that's why it wasn't near the top of Sarah's list," Sully said. "It'll be a tad inconvenient for wedding guests."

Dez shrugged. "Suits me. Fewer guests means less money. Anyway, you'll still have the ones who really count."

"I mean, Whispering Winds has the hotel and everything," Sully said. "As long as we can book enough rooms so people can spend the night, I don't see it being that much of a problem, right?"

"Right. Hey, for my part, I'd love to stay there. I haven't had a chance to go golfing for a few years. Make sure to book me some tee time, and I'll be sold."

The highway took a curve, dropping into a tree-filled valley. At the base snaked a narrow river, one the landscape suggested was once much, much larger. A sign ahead pointed the way to a campground in one direction, the town of Holy Oak in the other.

Dez dipped his chin, eyes dropping toward his fuel gauge. "I didn't fill up before leaving, and I'm getting low. Maybe I should pull into Holy Oak to get some gas."

Sully checked his map app. "Good plan. This is the last town before the resort, and I'm not sure they have a gas station at or nearer to Whispering Winds. It's pretty isolated all through this area. If we're going to do any hiking out here, I'd rather it be the nature trail kind rather than accidental."

Dez took the next turn. "How far?"

"Close. Less than five minutes up the road, I'd say."

Dez nodded once, then fell silent. His brow furrowed, and he scratched at his jaw.

"Something wrong?" Sully asked. He craned his neck to check the fuel gauge himself, finding it read a notch or two below the quarter mark. Plenty of gas to reach the town safely, so that couldn't be the problem.

"Something familiar about the name Holy Oak," Dez said. "Can't think what, but it's not good."

Sully quirked his lips. "If you can't think what it is, how do you know it's not good?"

Dez flashed him a glare. "I know, okay? Instinct or whatever."

For a non-psychic, Dez's instincts tended to be pretty solid. "Want me to look it up?"

Dez trained slightly widened eyes on Sully. "Not a chance. It seems to me there's some sort of ghost story attached to the place. I definitely don't want to know about it. Restrict any searches to finding the gas station for me, all right?"

Sully laughed. There was the other very obvious trait about Dez: his fear of ghosts. Years of working together on paranormal cases had somewhat dulled Dez's terror, but it had never rid him of it. If anything, Dez had come by far too much firsthand knowledge that ghosts could indeed harm the living.

Knowledge Sully himself would have as soon foregone.

So Sully had no problem with Dez's request, limiting his Holy Oak search to gas station directions—a straightforward-enough task given one such station was located on the main road into town and barely inside town limits.

"Happy?" Sully asked as Dez pulled up to a pump. "You don't

even have to drive much into the town itself. Whatever might be here, you won't have to deal with it."

"A miracle if I ever saw one," Dez grumped before stepping from the vehicle to greet the attendant.

Predictably, the young attendant's eyes grew wide as Dez unfolded his six-foot-six, muscular frame from the driver's seat. Sully shook his head with a smile before casting his eye around the place.

Not much to see of the town from here, but what Sully could make out told him this place had been here for quite some time. A spire rose in the distance, the sort which could only belong to a church built well over a century ago. All around it as far as the eye could see stood a mature growth of trees—oak, elm, poplar and evergreens, Sully thought based on his limited experience with tree identification—and in between these poked sloped roofs and brick chimneys. Aside from the church, the only tall building in immediate view was a long structure of perhaps three or four storeys in height. Likely an old hotel, maybe a hospital.

Too many smaller-sized towns had died away in this area, but from what Sully could see, Holy Oak was not only clinging to life—it was thriving. The gas station boasted new pumps and an exterior which had clearly undergone a facelift in recent years. Even the attendant was smartly dressed in a crisp uniform shirt.

Across the road, an outdoor recreation store held pricy-looking RVs and camper trailers while signage pointed the way toward a variety of downtown attractions for tourists to check out. One other sign, larger than even that one, featured a sweeping golf green with a happy family half-in and half-out of a golf cart as the father prepared to tee off. The sign read, "Good times await you at Whispering Winds Resort."

It wasn't to his surroundings that Sully's attention held though. With Dez having gone inside to pay—and more than likely to get some snacks for the road—Sully peered out over the parking lot to the other vehicles. One seemed familiar.

Or, rather, the person stepping from inside it.

Sully was out of the SUV as soon as he recognized Raiya Everton. Years back, she'd been instrumental in his getting a handle on his abilities, and she'd helped him through some rocky situations. As far as he was concerned, he owed her his life.

He paused after a couple of steps. She hadn't yet noticed him, giving him a moment to observe her. She was usually one of the most chill people. Today, she radiated tension.

Her body rigid and her face taut, she turned in his approximate direction. Then jumped, her mouth popping open slightly, as she recognized him. He worked a smile onto his face, relieved when she responded with an answering grin.

Raiya met him with a hug. "Sully! How are you?"

Her hands trembled as they rubbed Sully's back, and he pulled back to meet her eye. "I'm good. You can't say the same though, can you?"

She gave a dry laugh. "Doesn't take a psychic to see that now, does it?"

"Are you okay?"

For a moment, she appeared to be searching for the right response. "Something's come up. Something I've been struggling to get my head around. Seeing you here now, I wonder … do you have a few minutes to talk?"

Yes, Sully owed Raiya a lot. A few minutes' conversation was the least he could do.

"Sure," he said. "But Dez is inside. Mind if he tags along?"

Raiya's lips formed a humourless smile. "I remember your brother well. Hate to say it, but this isn't the sort of problem he's going to want to hear about."

Which could only mean one thing.

Ghosts.

CHAPTER 3

LEAVING Dez out of the loop wasn't an option. Nor was ignoring the problem of a friend.

"I have to tour a possible wedding venue," Sully told Raiya before Dez returned.

"Whispering Winds Resort?"

"How'd you guess?"

"I lived in Holy Oak for a little while," Raiya said. "I've kept tabs from time to time. I'm familiar with the area. I think they have a restaurant or a coffee shop on site. I could meet you there."

"Sounds good to me, as long as you've got a little time to wait. I don't think I'll be long checking the place out."

Raiya chuckled. "Don't underestimate the time required to plan weddings. I've never been married, but I've been in enough wedding parties to know these things. Don't worry, I can occupy myself until you're ready to meet me."

Sully checked over his shoulder to see if Dez was on his way. Not yet. Returning his attention to Raiya, he asked the obvious question. "This problem you want to talk about—just to confirm, it's ghost-related, right?"

"Afraid so."

"A not-very-nice one?"

"Not nice at all."

Great. "One I'll be able to see?"

"I'd expect so," Raiya said. "Not many people are known to behead themselves."

Sully grimaced. Oh boy, Dez was going to be some upset. "Okay, got it. You can fill us in on the details in a bit."

Raiya nodded. She began to pivot back toward her car but paused before returning her gaze to Sully. Grasping his arm lightly, she gave him an apologetic smile. "I'm sorry."

"For what?"

"For involving you. I hadn't intended this. But I also firmly believe in signs, and you being here now is very much a sign."

It was a sign, Sully thought. A sign Dez was going to kick his ass. "It's all right. I get it. Talk soon, okay?"

This time, Raiya did leave him. By the time she slid back into her car, Dez was on his way out, arms laden with junk food and two bottles of soda. "Was that Raiya I saw you talking to?"

"Yep."

"Do I want to know?"

"Nope."

Dez growled. "Ah hell."

Sully relieved Dez of some of his burden before leading the way back to the SUV. "She needs help with something, and I couldn't say no."

"Help with what? Please tell me she wants us to top off her windshield wiper fluid."

"Sorry, man."

Dez uttered a long groan. "Please, no. Not ghosts."

"I don't know the details yet, okay? Maybe it's not such a big deal."

"When is anything with you not a big deal?" But Dez didn't ask anything more.

Just as well, because Sully didn't want to tell him anything more—especially not as it pertained to a beheading.

Whispering Winds Resort was stunning. Set within a lush forest with a sprawling hotel backing onto the first hole of a golf course, this was a wedding photographer's dream—at least as long as they didn't get photobombed by a decapitated spirit.

Sully spotted Raiya's car in the lot, but she wasn't with it.

"Maybe we can run away before she notices us," Dez joked.

"Dez."

"I know, I know. Just kidding."

Sully gave him a light smack as Dez pulled into a spot and parked. Stepping out, Sully shut his eyes and drew in a deep breath. The scent of the place was awesome, taking him back to camping and fishing trips with their dad when he and Dez were kids. Whispering Winds and Holy Oak were far enough north of Kimotan Rapids to put them inside what locals termed "the tree line," where the remainders of prairie and valley gave way to the forest-heavy northern areas. Though there was plenty of oak and poplar, much of the woods consisted of pine and fir, providing a scent Sully had always loved.

He exhaled through a happy sigh. Ghost job or not, being here was amazing, putting him sizeably closer to making an argument for this being the spot where he and Sarah should get married.

"Glad you're enjoying yourself," Dez grumbled.

Sully cracked open an eye to inspect Dez's grumpy face. "Hey, you were the one talking about how great it would be to get in a round or two out here."

"That was before I knew my game was likely to be observed by a dead person."

Sully shook his head but otherwise laughed off Dez's latest issue. No matter where he and Sarah chose to get married, the chances of it being ghost-free was low. Whether Sully could see them or not, few places weren't haunted in some way. Spirits, after all, were everywhere.

Speaking of …

Sully pulled up short as he was about to make his way inside. A withered-looking and extremely pale elderly man stood in their path, a freakish grin marring his features. Sully had only seen parts of one of the *Poltergeist* movies, but this guy definitely called to mind the scary reverend.

The man stared straight at Sully, his toothy grin never wavering. Undoubtedly, he wore full dentures, and the narrowness of his face made the grin appear even larger and more unnatural. Slowly, he lifted a bony hand, turned his palm up and twitched a finger at Sully.

Come here.

No way in hell.

"Good God," Dez whispered. "If that's not the creepiest guy I've ever seen. He's like The Beast from *Poltergeist*."

Sully released the breath he'd been holding. "You see him too?"

"Yeah. Wish I didn't." He cleared his throat. "On second thought, nope, I'm glad I do. It means he's not a ghost."

Sully wasn't sure which was worse. "Think he needs help?"

"We can ask inside," Dez suggested. "Come on."

With Dez plucking at his sleeve, Sully fell into step next to him. They attempted to give the old man a wide berth, but with rows of trees bordering the walkway toward the front entrance, there was only so far they could go to avoid him. As Sully tried to pass the elderly man, he found his arm caught up in a surprisingly strong grip, forcing him to a halt. Sully pivoted, his eyes forced to meet the man's wild stare.

"He'll find you," the man breathed, his voice a cross between a whisper and a wheeze. The eerie smile never left his face, adding an air of sadistic amusement to the threat. "He's coming."

Sully's other arm was back in Dez's grip. "Come on, let's go." Dez's voice, though loud and forceful, contained a slight tremble.

Having become the rope in a tug-of-war, Sully was quickly and happily yanked by Dez out of the old man's grip.

"That has got to be the creepiest old guy I've ever seen," Dez muttered.

"I'm more concerned about whoever it was he was talking about."

"I don't think I'm out to lunch in guessing he's got dementia," Dez replied. "He probably has no idea what he's talking about."

"Maybe," Sully said. But he wasn't about to bank on it, not the way the old man continued to stare at him even now.

Dez gave Sully's arm another light tug, forcing him onward. They made their way inside.

AN OLDER MAN in a black-and-white uniform and a name tag reading Parker waited behind the front desk with a welcoming grin —thankfully one far less creepy than that worn by the man they'd just left outside.

"Welcome to Whispering Winds," Parker boomed out as Sully and Dez approached. "How may I help you?"

Dez tweaked a thumb toward the front entrance. "First, maybe you can help the guy out there. There's an elderly man outside. He seems sort of, um—"

The startled expression on Parker's face—upraised brows and lips forming an O-shape—kept Dez from finishing the statement.

"Oh my," Parker said. "Wait here one moment, please."

With that, he dashed around the desk and out the door. A few moments later, he was back, escorting the old man back inside. Parker leaned near the old man's ear as they walked, whispering something to him. Sully couldn't make out what, but whatever it was, it seemed to calm the old man. Thankfully, the creepy grin was gone, and he was nodding numbly as he stumbled along.

"I'll be with you in just a moment," Parker told Sully and Dez as he passed.

"No rush," Sully replied.

Parker took the old man through the lobby, disappearing with him through a doorway marked private on the opposite side of the large front counter.

Parker was gone less than five minutes, and he seemed flustered when he returned to his spot behind the counter.

"I'm so sorry about all of that," he said. "I hope he didn't say anything to upset you."

"It's fine," Sully said. "Is everything okay?"

Parker gave a rapid nod. "Oh yes, all is well. Not to worry. Thank you for alerting me. He lives here, but his mind's been going, I'm afraid. Age-related dementia. He wanders sometimes. Someone's with him now, though, so it's fine." Parker took a deep breath, releasing it heavily. "So sorry. I don't mean to go on. How may I help you?"

Sully told him he'd talked to someone earlier about looking at the place for a wedding.

"Oh yes," Parker said. "That was me on the phone. Our events manager is here, but she's in a meeting at the moment. I'm the assistant manager here. I'll get a message to her that you're here. If you'd like to wait in the restaurant in the meantime, I can give you a coupon for a free drink."

Sully was about to say they didn't need a drink, but Dez snatched the coupons before Sully could open his mouth.

"Thanks," Dez said. "We'll hang out until she's ready to meet."

"Never turn down a freebie, do you?" Sully chided as the two of them made their way the short distance to the restaurant.

"Hey, it's the least they can do to earn your business."

Sully elbowed Dez in the gut. "More likely they want to keep your stomach quiet while we talk."

Dez gave him a shove.

The restaurant gave off a cozy and relaxed outdoorsy vibe, the walls constructed of wood and exposed stone with two large fireplaces warming the place. Most of the tables were empty, so it didn't take long for Sully to pick out Raiya drifting across the room with a takeout cup in hand. She stopped as she spotted them, pointing to a table with brows raised in question.

Sully nodded, and Raiya moved to a table nearer one of the fireplaces.

"I suppose getting this over with would be a blessing in disguise," Dez mumbled before approaching the counter and eyeing up the offerings inside a glass display case. Plenty of cakes, pies and muffins as well as sandwiches, wraps and quiche. No way was Dez leaving without picking up something to chew on.

True to form, Dez bought himself a slice of cheddar and mushroom quiche and two muffins to go with his free coffee. Sully settled for the coffee.

"You're making me look like a pig," Dez said as he carried his tray across the room.

"Correction," Sully said. "*You're* making you look like a pig."

"You're lucky my hands are full, Sull."

Sliding into seats across from Raiya, Sully and Dez set down the tray and slipped out of their jackets.

"I was about to go out for a walk when I saw you come in," Raiya said. "You have a few minutes now?"

"Just until the events manager can meet us," Sully said. "Is it all right to cut things short if she calls?"

"Of course. We can always finish up later. This problem of mine has been around a very long time already. Another few minutes won't make a difference."

With no immediate sign of the manager in question, and with Dez now tucking into his food, it seemed a good time to let Raiya get started.

"You might recall me telling you I spent most of my childhood in St. Stephen's. When I was in high school, my father got a new job. Well, to be frank, he was fired from his old one. He found a position for himself at the paper mill just outside of Holy Oak. It's closed since, but it was quite the going concern in its day. At any rate, a job was a job, and we were provided with a rental home outside of town. Thankfully, we didn't stay long."

Raiya knitted her fingers together, peering down at them as she did. "I found Holy Oak quite different from St. Stephen's." She lifted her chin to meet Sully's eye. "You'll appreciate better than nearly anyone how difficult it can be for those like us to mix in with new people. I wasn't simply the new girl at school; I was the weird girl as well. Within days of our arriving, I was being called a witch. My younger sister was, in large part, responsible. In an effort to fit in, she told people about me. About the things I saw and felt."

Sully felt for Raiya. Having been put through the wringer himself as the strange new kid in school, he understood. But for Dez, school would have been unbearable.

"You might recall I don't see spirits the same way you do," Raiya continued. "For the most part, I sense them. Strongly. Like our friend, Marc Echoles, I'm what you'd call an empath. I feel energy around me—energy belonging to the living, the dead and the world in general. Over time, I've learned to tap into it, to use it to strengthen my gift and, by extension, my own being and my Wiccan practice. But it was a long process, and it was nothing short of a nightmare during my teenage years, back when I was all hormonal and struggling to control my abilities at the same time."

She wrapped her fingers around her cup and raised it to her lips for a slow, careful sip. Sully noticed her hands shook slightly, but Raiya managed to control it as she returned the cup to the table.

"There was a night," she said. "One night, and everything changed. It was the very worst thing I've ever been through. I've lived many years since, and I've grown in every crucial way. Yet that night has never left me. Every time I manage to convince myself I've moved past it, something happens to draw me back."

"Back to Holy Oak, you mean?" Sully asked.

"I meant I've been drawn back in thought and spirit. I've never physically been back. Not once. I couldn't bear it." She heaved a sigh. "There's a legend about this place. Perhaps you're familiar with it."

Sully shook his head. "I make a point of avoiding paranormal legends like the plague. I get enough of the real thing."

"Oh, this is real," Raiya said. "I've experienced it."

Sully felt Dez shudder, his arm brushing against his. "Oh, man. I think I know where you're going with this," Dez said. "I couldn't remember at first, but it's Headless Henry, right? That's the legend you're referring to."

Raiya gave a humourless smile. "The very one."

Dez's eyes were on Sully. Sully knew it without looking. He also knew exactly what Dez was thinking.

Get us the hell out of here, Sully. Now.

Sully offered him an apologetic hint of a smile. No choice. "What's the legend?" Sully asked Raiya.

"You had to ask," Dez grumbled.

Raiya turned the cup in her hands, grasping it as though warming her fingers. "It dates back a long time. Some say the first sightings occurred in the eighteen hundreds, around the time Holy Oak was first settled. No one truly knows the identity of this ghost, but one story runs that he was a soldier. According to that particular legend, he fled and was tracked down by either a ranking officer or an enemy combatant and killed—beheaded to be precise. Another story is that he was killed during a feud between families over a piece of land. Yet a third story claims the ghost lost his head during a vehicle rollover sometime mid-last-century."

"So despite the fact no one knows the truth, the stories all have something in common," Sully said.

Dez spoke mid-chew. "Some dude lost his head."

"Sightings of this spirit have been reported for decades," Raiya said. "Sometimes it's said he's little more than a shadow. In others, people claim to see a full-body apparition. In all cases, though, the ghost is headless."

Sully peered into the contents of his mug. "Which suggests some truth to the whole thing."

"Skeptics will claim these witness reports are either made up or are psychosomatic—that is, people see what they expect to see. Where a ghostly legend exists, you're always bound to find at least a few erroneous reports. That said, I can't get behind the skeptics on this one. You see, there's more to this story than simple ghost sightings. There have been deaths. Terrible ones." She ran a thumb over the ridge or her cup. "I was there for one of them."

Sully's shoulders slumped. "Oh, man, Raiya, I'm sorry."

"It happened a long time ago, but as you know, some traumas don't fade away. I've carried the memory of that night with me ever since. I believe it's why I've worked so hard to learn and control my psychic ability. I've always wondered whether I might have done something to stop it from happening if only I had been in control of my gifts back then."

Sully tilted his head as he eyed her. "What happened?"

"I was with some schoolmates. Not very nice people, it turned out. But they were kids. So was I. Kids do stupid things sometimes. It was Halloween, and they set up an elaborate and cruel prank, with me—the new, weird girl—as the target. They told me the story of Headless Henry before abandoning me in the woods in the middle of the night. I found them only because I heard screams. By the time I reached them, one of them—a boy named Cary Holdfast —was dead. Beheaded."

Dez shivered again. "Holy hell."

"That's awful," Sully said. "Are you saying a ghost did that?"

Raiya shook her head. "I don't know how it could have. As much harm as ghosts can create, I've never known one to be able to cause such a horrific level of physical damage to a human being. If a ghost was involved, it would more likely be a possession-type scenario."

"I take it they didn't find someone to pin it on," Dez said.

"They did—one of the girls who was in the group that night named Louise Penske. She was covered in Cary's blood and was completely out of it when I found her next to him. She was going on about Headless Henry having gotten Cary and was begging me not to let him get her too. She was in such a bad state, they had to sedate her and admit her to a psychiatric ward for a time. Perhaps it was the medication, maybe her mind erasing the worst of the memory, but she claimed later to recall nothing of how Cary died."

"Or maybe she really didn't know," Dez suggested.

Raiya paused for a sip of tea, then spoke over the rim while holding the cup. "Unfortunately for her, the police found an axe with Louise's fingerprints on it. A few people continued to blame it on the ghost, but most were far happier to pin it on a flesh-and-blood killer. Louise was ultimately committed to a psychiatric institution. While she never faced charges, you might argue her fate was worse, locked away as she was, deemed guilty without a trial to decide the case. I never did find out what happened to her after that. I suppose I never really wanted to know. Easier that way, avoiding reopening old wounds."

Dez shrugged. "Ach, who cares what happened to her? I mean, after what they put you through and all."

"But as I said, we were kids. No kid deserves such a fate, no matter how rotten they might act at the time. Anyway, I had a choice to make: become like them or work hard to be the opposite. I chose the latter path, and I've never regretted it. And the thing about that night is this: perhaps the authorities were right, and Louise did kill Cary. But something's always troubled me about that conclusion. You see, I did experience something that night besides bullying. I felt something in those woods—something wholly evil. It was so strong, I even saw it for a moment—a shadow of something human-shaped and headless. I'm not saying it directly killed Cary, but I firmly believe it played a role. How, I'm not so sure about."

Sully wasn't sure either. While he had experienced possession firsthand and knew the realities of it, he was reluctant to attribute this incident to possession without more information. The kind of power a ghost would have to yield to carry out such an act would be tremendous—even more tremendous if the ghost had committed the deed all on its own, no possession needed.

"You said you've never been back here," Dez said. "But you're here now. Why?"

Raiya frowned. "Dreams. Nightmares, really. I've had them before, of course, countless times. But all of those previous ones, they were based in memory. I knew upon waking they'd simply been the result of my brain attempting to cope with trauma. Lately, that's changed. The dreams now—they're not of the past. They're of the future."

She reached over, grasping Sully's hand. "The ghost is going to kill again. And I need to stop it from happening."

CHAPTER 4

DEZ DIDN'T LIKE THIS. He didn't like this one bit.

Leave it to Sully to turn wedding planning into a job involving a headless spook with a penchant for murder.

For his part, Dez held onto a fragment of hope that Raiya was wrong about this ghost—whoever or whatever it was—planning on going on another head-lopping run. The larger part of Dez's brain told him his hope was futile. Raiya possessed a strong psychic ability, one no amount of skepticism could refute. Dez was no skeptic, so if Raiya said something was going to occur, then it was going to occur.

Still, it made sense to ask. "Not that I doubt you for a second, but what makes you so sure this is about to happen again?" Dez asked her.

"My dreams have been horrific," she said. "While the events from that night are always with me in some way, I've successfully compartmentalized them for the most part. That I'm suddenly being overrun by such intense nightmares, such blatantly dark feelings, tells me something big is coming."

"Have you seen anything specific?" Sully asked. "Anything that might help us to decide how best to act on this?"

"You're wondering if I can tell you who, when and where. I

can't. I'm sorry. I wish I had the ability to provide such a level of detail, but often, my gift doesn't work like that."

"I understand," Sully said. "These things aren't easy to control—as you've taught me."

Dez didn't understand. Some things he would never understand. Why give people psychic abilities and not the capacity to fully use them? Sully had to be the strongest psychic Dez had ever met—and he'd met more than his share—but even Sully got bowled over like a headpin at times.

Somebody upstairs had a sick sense of humour.

"Was there something that brought you here specifically?" Sully asked.

"I'd hoped maybe I could tune into something more. As you know, placing yourself at the direct location of a haunting can give you clues you won't get elsewhere. The problem is, I suspect I'll need to place myself there at the right time as well. You see, this ghost is said to appear only once a year."

Dez stared at the remains of a muffin he'd been working on. He'd suddenly lost his appetite. "On Halloween," he said.

"You remember that part of the legend," Raiya observed.

"Who could forget?"

"The reason could be twofold. Either this man died on that date, or it's simply the easiest date for him to appear. The curtain between this world and the next is always thin, but it's the thinnest on Halloween. Not only does this mean spirits can more easily communicate or interact on this date, I believe they're more powerful in general. He might be incapable of interfering with the living the rest of the year, but those barriers drop on Halloween."

Dez gave his plate a push forward, farther away from himself. His appetite had *really* bailed on him. "Great."

Raiya gave him a sympathetic smile before returning her gaze to Sully. "All this said, I decided it was best to spend a couple of days in the area to try to get to the root of this. I expect I'll also need to plan to be in the woods on Halloween night."

Which, Dez knew, meant Sully would be in the woods on

Halloween night. Which, in turn, meant Dez would be in the woods on Halloween night, because no way he was letting his brother face down a decapitated killer ghost without backup.

"Where are you staying?" Sully asked.

Raiya swept an arm to the side. "This seems like a good option."

"No offence, but you don't strike me as a Whispering Winds Resort sort of person. You seem more likely to look for a quirky bed and breakfast."

Dez understood Sully's point. Raiya was an unusual person who expressed it through her personal style. She struck Dez very much as a once-hippie who'd never fully left it behind, rarely cutting or styling her wild hair and opting for floaty over functional when it came to her clothing. Today she was wearing a long, billowing yellow dress, a wide-brimmed felt hat and a heavy sweater with multiple snags. Dez could guess at where the snags originated given the number of cats Raiya owned.

"Oh, believe me, you're totally right," Raiya said. "Thing is, though, I have my reasons for choosing Whispering Winds. First, Cary's death happened somewhere very close by. That makes this place an ideal staging ground while I try to home in on the exact spot. Second, there's someone here I need to speak with."

Dez took a stab at it. "The other girl who was there that night?"

Raiya nodded. "Becca Symes. She works here."

Dez refrained from commenting, but he found himself wondering what Becca did here. Given she went to school with Raiya, she had to be around seventy years of age. Dez hoped when he turned seventy, he wouldn't have to put in any more hours of paid employment.

If Lachlan Fields ever let Dez retire. As stubborn as the man was, Dez thought it just possible Lachlan would outlive all of them.

Perhaps Raiya noted Dez's unasked question, because she quickly added, "I did some checking online. She's the owner and general manager here. She and her father started this place years back, and she's not the retiring type." Raiya snorted and leaned forward as if to impart a secret. "She's what you might call a Type-A personality. Very ambitious and very driven. I can't imagine too many people living up to her standards. I think it's quite probable she never found anyone good enough to take over from her."

Dez finished a sip of coffee before asking the next obvious question. "Why do you want to talk to her? I mean, is there anything specific?"

"Cary is the last person to have died in those woods. While I was there that night, I wasn't present when it actually happened. I heard Becca scream. I think it's possible she saw something. Something she never reported."

"Her friend was accused of killing Cary," Dez said. "If Becca had anything useful to share, why wouldn't she have come forward?"

"I can only guess. But as I said, she's always been very driven, very much committed to her own path in life. Louise suffered a breakdown and was branded as both mentally unsound and a murderer. If Becca were to come forward, alleging a ghost killed her boyfriend—well, you can imagine the fallout among certain segments of society. More than likely, she'd have been called a liar or crazy. She couldn't have stayed in this community afterward. Certainly, she and her father would have struggled to secure the investment capital needed to purchase, construct and open this place."

"That would make her pretty cold," Sully said.

"I won't go so far as to brand her a sociopath, but yes, there was a very cold side to Becca—as I discovered firsthand."

Dez frowned. One more question had formed in his brain. "Cold enough maybe to kill Cary and allow her friend to take the rap? I mean, you'd need a motive of course, but domestic violence isn't exactly uncommon, even among high school students." He shrugged. "Granted, I haven't heard of many cases in which a teenage girl beheads her boyfriend, but anything's possible, I suppose."

Raiya peered at him as though she hadn't entertained this idea before. "It's a thought, certainly."

"You mentioned Louise was covered in blood," Sully said. "What about Becca?"

Raiya frowned. "Good question. She wasn't found at the scene. She said she ran all the way home. Long way to go, yes, but the way she was screaming that night, I'd imagine her adrenaline was pumping like crazy. Terror can sure give you wings. At any rate, she wasn't ever considered a suspect as far as I'm aware. Whether she had blood on her or not, I don't know, but I suppose it stands to reason she might have, even as a witness."

Dez tilted his head. "Or she might have used the time and opportunity to conceal evidence."

Raiya pressed her lips together as though the thought were settling. "True enough. Well, one other truth: whether it was Louise or Becca or someone else behind the killing, it leaves us with another very significant problem. I don't believe the one who killed Cary acted alone. I know what I felt in the woods that night. It was evil. And I fully believe it had a significant hand in what happened to Cary."

Blessedly, the conversation ended there for the moment. Raiya straightened in her chair, her eyes shifting in a way that suggested someone was approaching. Dez pivoted to see for himself and noticed an elegant older lady making her way toward their table.

"I'm so very sorry," she said, extending a well-manicured hand as she drew near. "My events manager is still indisposed. I don't wish to keep you waiting any longer."

Dez noted she'd directed the comments at him. No doubt she'd taken him for the groom-to-be.

He stood alongside Sully and took the woman's hand. "I'm Dez Braddock. This is my brother, Sully Gray. He's the one getting married next year."

"Oh, forgive me."

"Don't worry," Sully said as he shook her hand. "Dez does look more the marrying type."

The lady's gaze darted to Dez's left hand. "So much so, you're already married. Again, my apologies for the mix-up. It's been a day."

Dez gave her a taut smile. It was about to get more complicated.

"Becca?" Raiya said as she rose to her feet.

The woman's mascara-rimmed eyes shifted to Raiya. "It's *Re*becca, not Becca."

Then her eyes narrowed as though taking a better look at Raiya. Rebecca blinked heavily, her brows lowering slightly as though she were combing through memory, attempting to attach a name to the face.

"It's been a long time," Raiya said. "I'm not sure if you'll remember me. My name's Raiya Everton. We went to school together for a short time."

Rebecca blinked again, twice. Then she turned a nasty shade of white. Her left hand shook badly as it fumbled for the nearest chair back, and Dez worried she was about to collapse.

"Sully," he said, but his brother was already on it, pulling out a chair for Rebecca. She sat solidly, all but falling into the seat.

"My God," she whispered. "My God."

Raiya's lips quirked. "I guess this means you remember me."

CHAPTER 5

Dez handed Rebecca a glass of cold water he'd gotten from the concerned-looking employee behind the till. Rebecca grasped it with a trembling hand and took a long drink, then pressed the glass to her forehead.

"Forgive me," she said. "I don't know what came over me."

Memory, Dez thought. Or maybe guilt or fear. Dez thought a case could be made for all of the above.

"Are you all right?" Dez asked.

"I will be." Rebecca's eyes found Raiya's. "What are you doing here?"

"Let's hold off until you're back to your right self. There's time."

Rebecca plonked the glass onto the table, splashing a little water over the rim. "I'd like to know now." She glanced around. The room was nearly empty, but it would seem not empty enough. "We can talk in my office. Follow me."

If the eyes were the windows to the soul, people's offices weren't far behind. If so, Rebecca Symes was everything Raiya had described.

A luxurious and ornate desk sprawled across the centre of the room, circled by a trio of plush, white chairs. Huge windows made up most of one wall, overlooking the golf green and the lush forest bordering it. Floor-to-ceiling shelves took up the entire wall behind the desk, housing a variety of leather-bound books—the sort Dez suspected were rarely, if ever, cracked open—along with pricy-looking knickknacks and landscape photographs. The opposite wall was adorned by a large fireplace with a luxurious marble mantle and a pricy set of pokers.

But pride of place belonged to a grouping of awards and plaques. Without counting, Dez estimated at least a dozen. Still more were mounted on the wall.

Rebecca had worked hard at her business, and she wanted the world to know it. More than that, she wished to look the part of the successful businesswoman, her decor and personal style the sort which would fit right in with some of the wealthiest business-people in Kimotan Rapids. Dez was far from an expert in such things, but he'd take a stab at it and guess that Rebecca had gone in for botox treatments or whatever else people spent money on to hold on to a youthful appearance. Dez's mom sometimes bemoaned her sagging jawline and the lines on her face; Rebecca, though a couple of decades older than Mara Braddock, had little sagging skin or an abundance of lines. Had Dez not known her to be the same age as Raiya, he might have put Rebecca's age in the late fifties.

Rebecca waved her visitors into the chairs before taking the one on her side of the desk. That left one person standing, and Dez opted to be that person. He was more intimidating this way, and given Rebecca's past treatment of a person Dez considered a friend, he didn't mind presenting the more menacing side of himself.

He felt Rebecca's gaze following him as he walked the space, making a show of reading the business licence and Rebecca's diploma in business management.

"This place is nice," Dez said.

"Thank you." That was it, no further comment from Rebecca in reply. Also no offer to track down an extra chair. Rebecca wanted this meeting over as quickly as possible.

"What are you doing here, Raiya?" she asked.

Raiya crossed her ankles and folded her hands in her lap. "I wanted to check the place out. It's been so many years since I've been here. I thought, what with Halloween around the corner and the way the town decorates the place, it would be as good a time as any."

Decorations. Dez hadn't considered this before. The gas station had been adorned in decor with stick-up skulls in the windows and plastic jack-'o-lanterns outside the door. While they hadn't driven far into the town itself, Dez had observed light posts festooned with orange leafy garlands and banners showing images of ghosts and ghouls. One sign on the way in had pointed visitors toward a festival being held on Halloween night in Hayfield Park.

Halloween was a big thing around here, but Rebecca wasn't on board. Who could blame her? After all, she'd encountered the worst side of the paranormal universe and probably had the psychological scars to prove it.

Rebecca's stare was piercing as she studied Raiya. She might not share Raiya's psychic gifts, but it was as though she saw straight through her all the same. "I don't think that's the whole truth, now, is it?"

A challenge, not a question. One thing about successful business-people: almost to a one, they'd gotten to be damned good at reading others.

"No," Raiya said. "I suppose it isn't. Becca—"

"Rebecca," she cut in. "I haven't gone by Becca since ..." She paused for a moment as though the initial answer was not the one she wanted to give. "Since high school."

"I'm sorry," Raiya said. "I forgot."

"Yes, well, I'm very busy so—"

"I know." Raiya drew in a long, deep breath, releasing it slowly. "There's no easy way to say it. There were things said about me in high school. Stories. Rumours."

"The witch nonsense?"

Raiya gave a slow nod. "The witch nonsense." She paired an exaggerated shrug with a sheepish grin. "Not such nonsense, after all."

Rebecca's perfectly shaped brows lifted. "Oh? And you came here to tell me that?"

"That and ... other things. You see, I've been having some strange dreams. Unpleasant ones. The thing that happened to us in these woods, I believe it's about to happen again."

Rebecca turned her head a few inches, allowing her to cast Raiya a side-eye. "Come again?"

"I need to know what you remember about that night."

Rebecca shot to her feet. "I think it best you leave now."

Raiya stood too. "Please, Rebecca. I wouldn't dredge this up if it weren't important. I can't let this rest. I know something's coming, and I need to try to stop it. You understand the danger better than anyone."

"The danger? You mean Louise Penske? She's gone. Dead for all I know. She's certainly not prowling the woods, axe in hand, looking to repeat what she did back then. There is no danger, Raiya. Not anymore."

"You can't know that."

Rebecca folded her arms. "In all these years, nothing's happened to anyone else. Why now?"

"I don't know. I only know what I've been shown. I have to find out for sure, and if I'm right, I have to try to stop it. You must see that."

Rebecca fired a glance at Dez and Sully in turn. "And these two? They're not really here for a tour of our facility, are they?"

"We are, actually," Sully spoke up. "We met Raiya here totally by accident. We're friends. We said we'd help her."

Rebecca turned her glower from Sully to Raiya. "I take it you're quite settled on this, then."

"I am."

"And you're planning on staying in the area?"

Raiya nodded. "I live in Kimotan Rapids. It's too far to drive back and forth every day."

For a long moment, Rebecca said nothing more. Finally, she heaved a frustrated sigh. "Fine. In that case, I'll see to it you're booked into a room. There's only one other major hotel in the immediate area, and what with the festival in full swing, it's full. I'd imagine the smaller accommodations are full too."

"But you're not?" Dez asked.

Rebecca glared at him. "Nearly. We're not right in town, and we're pricier. Most tourists opt for something cheaper and more central."

She leaned forward, palms coming to rest on her desk as she once more fixed Raiya in a purposeful stare. "I do have other guests, Raiya. I don't want them upset, do you understand? You can stay, but I don't want anyone catching wind that you're here to search out proof of silly stories."

Dez straightened and narrowed his eyes at Rebecca. "You call what happened silly?"

The heat left her eyes as they fixed on Dez. She cleared her throat. "Of course, I didn't mean … I was referring only to the ghost stories." She returned her glare to Raiya. "I'm not prepared to dredge up such a painful past, but I'll say this much: no ghost killed Cary, if that's what you're suggesting. The person responsible is long gone, and even if she weren't, she's not likely to kill again, is she? We're seventy years old, Raiya. We aren't kids anymore with out-of-control emotions and bad judgment. Whatever happened back then isn't going to be repeated."

Hopefully, she was right. Dez had learned long ago the dangers of banking on hope.

He was about to ask the next question when Sully beat him to it. "Any chance you have more than one room?"

Rebecca clenched her jaw, speaking through it. "One room or two?"

Dez spoke up quickly. "One room. Two beds—if you've got it."

He sensed rather than observed Sully's amusement. Hell, yes, if

Dez was going to be stuck at a hotel near the site of a violent haunting, he wanted to stick as close as possible to Sully.

Rebecca made a beeline for the door, moving at a pace which suggested she fully intended to avoid further conversation. With no choice but to follow, Dez did so—albeit slow enough to allow for a quick and quiet remark to Sully and Raiya.

"Does it seem weird to you that she suggested we stay here?" he asked. "I mean, I don't get the impression she'd much care if we exhausted ourselves driving back and forth."

Raiya stared at Rebecca's back as she neared the lobby at the end of the hall. "I can think of only one legitimate reason she'd allow us to stay. She wants to keep an eye on us."

CHAPTER 6

DEZ SCANNED the room he was to share with Sully.

Under ordinary circumstances—such as Sully and Sarah's wedding—this would be the perfect space to spend a couple of days. The room boasted two comfortable queen-sized beds, a huge TV, a small kitchenette and a huge, luxurious bathroom. The suite appeared to have been renovated within the past couple of years, suggesting the resort did well for itself.

"I wonder why they're not totally booked up already for next year's wedding season," Dez wondered aloud as he peered out the window. Yep, even the view was amazing, the window overlooking the golf course and the bordering forest. In the distance stood a large body of water, the sun reflecting off its surface. Idyllic—if it weren't for the immediate area's massive creep factor, of course.

"Yeah, it's nice," Sully agreed.

"Nice? It's amazing. I just wish it didn't come with a nearby resident ghost."

Sully spoke through a smirk. "Which might explain why it's not totally booked up for next year."

Dez stepped away from the window and faced Sully. "Yeah, I could see that. Did you notice where Raiya's room is?"

"Just down the hall a couple of doors." Sully checked his watch.

"Given this turn of events, I guess we'll need to stock up on a few things in town. Too far to drive home. Right?"

Dez frowned. Sully was right, of course, but he wished he weren't. A big part of Dez wanted to spend a couple of hours in the sanctity of his own home before setting out on another of Sully's misadventures. "I hate trying to buy new clothes in random places," he told Sully. "Good luck finding anything to fit."

"Look at it this way," Sully replied. "Doing a little shopping in town will give us a chance to chat with some locals. If Rebecca won't share anything with us, maybe we can find someone else who will."

Dez rolled his eyes. "Right. I'm sure loads will be happy to talk about Headless Henry. Problem will be finding someone whose stories are actually helpful."

"One place to start might be the police station. They'll have records of the original incident—if we can persuade them to share."

"Might be a job for Lachlan," Dez told him. "Much as I hate to say this, we'd have better luck checking newspaper archives. No way anyone who was around back then will still be working for the police. Heck, a good few won't even be alive anymore."

Sully nodded. "Good point. Let's stop off to grab some stuff for our stay and see if Raiya needs anything while we're at it. After that, we'll see if the town has a newspaper that'll let us scan their back copies."

Dez hated newspaper archives research, a job which tended to come up often enough in private investigations. Compared to traipsing through haunted woods, however, sifting through microfiche or dusty paper was a cakewalk.

First, though, he needed to call Eva and let her know he and Sully had landed in the middle of another unexpected investigation.

He'd just pulled out his cellphone when Sully's eyes, turned toward the window, narrowed. He pressed past Dez, approached the window and peered out, parting the drapes a bit farther as he did.

Dez didn't like the expression on Sully's face. It meant only one thing.

Dez had to ask anyway. "Sully?"

Sully now stood so close to the window, his breath was creating a small circle of condensation. "I thought I saw ..."

"What?" Dez demanded.

Sully straightened as he backed away from the window. "I can't be sure. It came and went too fast, and it was at the edge of the trees on the right-hand side there, partially in shadow."

This didn't help much. "Best guess, then. You obviously thought you saw something."

Sully faced him. "A shadow—or very near to one. It was the shape of it that drew my attention."

Again, Dez felt forced to ask. "What shape?"

Sully cast a glance over his shoulder, toward the window. His response did nothing to help Dez. "It looked like a man without a head."

Dez was thrilled to get away from Whispering Winds, even for a short while. The problem would be going back, and they'd have to do it eventually. For now, though, they had things to do in town.

Raiya, bless her, came up with a plan which made Dez feel slightly better about the next couple of hours. The town did, in fact, have a newspaper, and a long-running one at that. Raiya was happy to go there and do the research while Dez and Sully grabbed what they needed.

"Did I mention how much I appreciate that woman?" Dez said to Sully once he'd dropped Raiya off outside the newspaper office.

Sully chuckled. "Except for all the spooky stuff she can do, right?"

"Hey, her spooky stuff has kept us upright more than once," Dez corrected. "I've come to appreciate that part too."

The newspaper was located on the long Main Street, inside a

large, two-storey brick building that appeared to date back to the early half of the twentieth century. As they drove the length of the wide street, Dez got his first good glimpse of Holy Oak.

As communities went in this part of the world, Holy Oak was old, and it wore its history on its sleeve. While plenty enough structures were newer, others had clearly been here for much of the town's life and were carefully maintained.

Near the centre of town, Main Street opened up onto a large green space—Hayfield Park according to a wrought-iron sign posted atop the large entry gate. Inside, beyond the wrought-iron fence and the tall border of trees, Halloween decorations could be glimpsed.

For that matter, Halloween decorations were everywhere Dez looked. If Holy Oak maintained its history in its structures and green spaces, it took a heavy measure of pride in its eerie past as well. Not only were windows, light posts, doorways and trees festooned with ghosts, ghouls and monsters; Headless Henry had been given pride of place in many spots.

"Does this seem weird to you?" Dez asked Sully as he steered past the recessed doorway of a hardware store in which stood a life-sized, black-attired mannequin with no head.

"What seems weird?"

Dez cast him a glance to see if he was serious. Sully wasn't smiling.

"Really?" Dez asked. "All this Headless Henry junk?"

"It's a local legend. Sleepy Hollow probably does the same thing."

Dez frowned. "Okay, but does Sleepy Hollow's past include actual cases of decapitated citizens? All I'm saying is it's weird they'd celebrate it."

Sully shrugged, his own eyes drifting toward a bank window painted with a Headless Henry image. "I get your point. But I guess, to be fair, the last decapitation-related death we know of happened more than fifty years ago. It could be most people who actually knew Cary Holdfast either moved away or died themselves. And it was blamed on a living person, not a dead one. And don't forget the other big thing: the Headless Henry legend is a boon to Holy Oak. Lots of small towns have died out or are in the process of it. This one is booming, and I'd imagine a lot of that is because of the story."

Sully pointed at the edges of the street out the windshield. "I mean, have you seen many empty parking spots? And look at all the people on the sidewalks. I think it's safe to say loads of these people are visitors, here for the Halloween festival. That's all thanks to Headless Henry. If you were trying to keep a small community afloat, you'd want to pull out all the stops—even the ones that might seem distasteful to some."

Dez shrugged. "I guess so, yeah. Still, I don't like it. It seems kinds of demented."

This time, Sully did smile. "Trust you to say it." He held up a palm before Dez could protest. "And hey, D, for my part, I agree with you. If Headless Henry does exist—and if Raiya says he does, I believe her—then he's nothing to celebrate. If anything, he's going to be hell to deal with."

Dez grimaced. "That's the part that worries me the most."

DEZ WAS no slave to fashion, but he preferred the items in his own closet over the options in Holy Oak's men's store. Dez had been inside Cal's Closet less than five minutes when he'd made up his mind that Cal should have kept the contents of his closet to himself. Not only was there precious little even close to his size, the items that were larger were the kind Dez preferred to leave on the rack.

Sully managed to find himself a pair of jeans and a long-sleeved T-shirt. Dez settled for a short-sleeved T-shirt, a button-down he'd need to leave unbuttoned and a pair of cargo pants Eva would make him give to charity as soon as she saw them. Luckily, the store also carried underwear and socks, so they picked up a few of those as well.

An older man stood behind the counter, ready to ring them

through. He wore a beaming smile and had the sort of eyes Dez would describe as twinkly. "Find what you were looking for?"

"Not exactly," Dez said. He pointed an index finger at his own frame by way of explanation. "Bit hard to find stuff that fits."

The twinkle dulled a little. "Oh, I can imagine. So sorry. Perhaps the consignment store on the twelve block has something. We've had a taller man or two in town over the years. If they donated anything, it might be there."

Dez wasn't desperate enough to warrant more clothes shopping. "Thanks. What we could do with are some men's toiletries. My brother and I didn't come prepared, unfortunately."

The man winked. "Didn't expect such a great many activities as part of the Halloween festival, hmm?"

Dez debated going along with it to avoid sharing more than he wished. As he considered the man's age—he appeared to be somewhere in his sixties—Dez reconsidered. If he was a local, this guy would have been in town long enough to have a solid grasp not only of the Headless Henry legend but maybe also a little about Cary Holdfast's death.

"We're here for something else, actually," Dez said. "My brother, Sully, and I are private investigators from Kimotan Rapids. We rolled into town on personal reasons and found ourselves in the middle of something we're trying to wrap our heads around. Looks like we're stuck here for a couple of days."

The man leaned forward, brows raised, pausing in his effort to open a bag for their purchases. "Not to be nosy, but could I ask what you're looking into?"

"It's a bit strange maybe, but we ran into a friend who asked us to help her check into something to do with the Headless Henry legend."

The brows lifted higher. "Around here, those are magic words."

"The town's really into the whole ghost story thing, huh?"

The man chuckled. "Suppose you could say that. It brings in visitors, and visitors bring in money. But for that money, we'd probably be just like every other small town in our immediate area—

dead or dying. We've got more abandoned towns around here than you can shake a stick at. The ones still here, you hear on the news year after year how this one lost their school or that one lost their post office. Barely a store operating in any of them. Lots come here now for their groceries or hardware or clothing. Preferable for many than going into the city. So yes, I guess we do have a certain fondness for ol' Henry."

"What about the incident that happened in the seventies?" Sully asked.

The twinkle vanished. "What do you mean?"

Oh boy, Dez thought. He hadn't wanted to have to spell it out. "We're familiar with the death of a local boy back then. We understand it bore similarities to the legend."

The man frowned. "Only in certain details. Unless Headless Henry was a disturbed teenage girl, I fail to see what the two have in common."

"Louise Penske?" Sully asked.

The man's gaze snapped to Sully's face. "I'd prefer not to discuss it."

Something in the man's expression, in the way he straightened and tensed, in the change inside his otherwise-bright eyes, had Dez suspecting this was more than a local businessperson working to avoid painting the town in an unflattering light.

"You knew him," Dez said.

The man fixed Dez with a long, discerning stare. Sizing him up, determining how much to say or whether to say anything more at all. When the man finally blinked, exhaled and allowed his shoulders to release, Dez knew he'd made up his mind to share something more.

"I did know him," the man said. "Cary Holdfast. My name is Cal Holdfast. Cary was my big brother."

CHAPTER 7

When Sully had picked Holy Oak out of Sarah's list of potential wedding venues, he hadn't expected to find a ghost job waiting for him. And he certainly hadn't expected to find a homicide victim's brother manning the clothing store they'd located.

Raiya believed many events held meaning and that there was a grander purpose behind psychic abilities and the things that happened to those who possessed them. If so, Sully had ended up in Holy Oak and had wandered into this store for a reason.

More and more, it was becoming clear he'd be here for the long haul.

"I'm sorry," Sully told Cal. "We didn't know."

Cal studied him, sizing him up. A couple of seconds passed. Then his face formed the barest of smiles. "Yes, well, you wouldn't have reason to. Most around here know the story, but some of the younger folks don't know who I am from Adam. They know about what happened to Cary, of course—everyone talks about it—but many don't remember his full name anymore." He exhaled heavily. "I'd imagine it won't be long before, one day, Cary's death becomes just another legend—one few recall the actual details of. It'll be embellished, elements will be added or removed. It'll become the stuff of campfire stories and ghost story vlogs. It'll be like Cary was never a real person, like he never had people who loved him and cried over him."

Sully held his eye. "You'll remember though. Others from town will remember. One day, we all become ancient history. Only a handful of people are remembered more or less as they should be. But no, it's not right for violent deaths to be treated as entertainment. It's not fair to those left behind. It's not fair either to those who've died."

"You sound as though you've given this some thought."

Boy, hadn't he? "I suppose you could say it's my business to think about these things."

"Because you're a PI? I always thought private investigators were busier with cheating spouses or insurance fraud, those sorts of things."

Dez chuckled. "Normal PIs, yeah. Sully and I aren't what you'd call normal."

Sully's turn to laugh. "He's not kidding."

He'd been of two minds whether to tell Cal anything more about what he did. After all, he had no indication Cary Holdfast was hanging around, haunting the town or the woods where he'd been killed.

That changed abruptly when Cal next spoke. "Normal. I can't say I fit the bill either. I've given up counting the number of times I've seen Cary since his death."

Sully swallowed back his surprise. He hadn't seen any sign of Cary as of yet, nor could he sense him. And rare was the occasion when a stranger offered up the sort of information Cal just had—at least someone who hadn't first sought out Sully's psychic services.

"Where have you seen him?" Sully asked.

Cal waved a hand in the air in front of his face. "Ach, forget I said anything. I sound like a nut."

Sully gave him a smile. "Not even close." Time to offer up some truth of his own. "Thing is, I see ghosts too. It's what I do. Lots of people seek us out because of it. Dez and I have helped plenty of clients with ghost problems. I think we end up working as many jobs with a paranormal element as we do regular ones."

Cal's thick, grey brows lifted as Sully spoke. Now he turned to Dez. "Do you see ghosts too?"

Dez snorted. "Nope. And thank God for that, is all I can say."

"You've seen a couple," Sully reminded him. Then to Cal, "I've got heightened psychic abilities, but all people are capable of having psychic experiences. It's built into everyone. It's just that I've been overloaded with it, you could say."

Cal canted his head as he eyed Sully. "And do you see him now?"

Sully shook his head. "He's not here. Truth be told, I haven't seen any sign of him so far. I can't feel him around either."

Cal gave a curt nod. "That's about right. All the times I've seen him, it's not been around here. Not in town either." He turned, his eyes casting vaguely to the right as if seeing something in his mind's eye. "He's in those woods near town. The woods where he died."

Cal faced Sully again. "I used to go there a lot. Trying to make sense of things, I guess." His lips tightened into a flat line as he winced slightly. "Something more to it though. Sounds macabre, but I spent a lot of time searching those woods, wanting to put him back together. You see, no one ever found his head."

Sully's turn to wince. "That's awful."

"Tell me about it. It's become part of the sideshow for the ghost hunters these days. People always refer to that bit when they tell the story. Guess it sounds more horrible, stating the fact there's a head rolling around those woods somewhere." He leaned forward again, nearer Sully. "I've done lots of reading about ghosts over my lifetime, and I've heard it said that some hauntings are attributed to a body not being whole at the time of burial."

Sully had heard that too. He'd never personally witnessed such a case. "I've dealt with more homicide cases than I want to think about. Lots of times, victims are in a bad state. Sometimes they're missing parts. I can't say any of them were sticking around because they needed to be reunited with a body part. More often than not, they needed justice or they had to make things right with someone they loved. Sometimes they're being held there by some other paranormal force. Maybe Cary's there because of something like that."

Cal shrugged. "Maybe. Guess I'll never know."

"You don't go back there anymore?" Dez asked.

A head shake. "Nope. Gave up on the head thing after a few years. After a while, I figured if I hadn't found it by then, I never would. Hell, if the police and their sniffer dogs hadn't found it, why would I? Then I got to thinking I probably wouldn't *want* to find it. God knows what that would have done to my own head, seeing something like that. As for the ghost, I was scared to death the first couple of times. Eventually, I plucked up the courage to try to talk to him, but he'd vanish before I could get a question in. A few seconds here and there, that's all I got. Sometimes just a corner of the eye sort of thing. So if you're going to ask if I tried getting him to lead me to his head, nope, I didn't get the chance. Honestly, I can't say I would've had the guts to follow him anyway."

"You're sure it was Cary, right?" Dez asked. "It wasn't … you know."

"Headless Henry?" Cal supplied. "No, I saw enough to know it was Cary. I recognized his jacket. He had this denim thing with the Rolling Stones logo sewn on—you know, the lips and tongue one." His mouth twitched into a sad smile. "He had ambitions with that jacket, wanted to get patches for all the groups he liked, couple'a sports teams too. I think many times about that, about all the other things he never got to finish. Lots of years passed since then, but I still feel it sometimes, the injustice of it all."

Sully glanced at Dez, then back at Cal. "Listen, we were planning on going out to the woods. Like we said, a friend's asked us to check into the whole Headless Henry thing for her, so we'll be there anyway. I'll look for Cary while I'm there, see what I can see. If I find him, I'll do my best to talk to him. With luck, I can find him and get him to cross over."

Cal straightened. "You can do that?"

Sully nodded. "It's part of what I do, yeah."

"If you find him, then could you wait for me before you send him anywhere? I'd very much like to talk to him one last time if possible. If not, well ..."

He appeared so downtrodden at the idea, Sully quickly came back with, "Absolutely, I'll do my best to connect you two before I try to send him across. Okay?"

Cal nodded. "Okay. Thank you."

Dez cleared his throat. "Sorry to bring it up, but I've gotta ask. How much do you know about the night Cary was killed?"

Cal's mouth worked as though chewing on the inside of his mouth. "A fair bit. Now, granted, I was just a boy when it happened. Cary was sixteen. I was five years younger. My parents did their best to shield me from the worst of it, but you can imagine how people talked afterward. It's a relatively small town. Someone dies, even of natural causes, it's the talk of coffee row for days. A murder, now, that'll preoccupy people for years or longer. Add in the legend and the sheer brutality of what happened to Cary, and you've got decades of chatter to contend with."

He frowned. "Now, I suppose the issue is that rumours got folded into the truth, so it's hard to say anymore what's real and what isn't. There wasn't a trial; the girl was never charged. So that means nothing ever came out about it in court. As for my parents, they went to their graves never talking about it with anyone. Too painful. So yeah, I know some, but I'm quite certain I don't know it all."

Sully debated whether to mention the other detail—that Cary had been bullying the school's unusual new girl when he died. He decided against it.

For now. The way these things tended to go, the truth rarely stayed buried for long.

CHAPTER 8

HAVING OBTAINED contact info for Cal, Sully and Dez made a quick pass through a nearby drugstore for necessary toiletries. After that, they left to pick up Raiya at the newspaper office.

She was waiting outside by the time they pulled up, nothing about her appearance suggesting her search had been a rousing success.

Sully asked the obvious question anyway as Raiya slid into the back seat. "Find out much?"

"Not a whole lot more than we already knew, to be honest," she said. "I've made copies of the relevant articles. Let's go grab a bite to eat somewhere, and I'll fill you in."

THE RESTAURANT RAIYA most remembered from her youth was long gone. A quick consult of the internet revealed three sit-down eating places in town, but as they drove past, all had lineups of would-be diners waiting outside the doors.

"Halloween festival," Raiya noted, her tone one of minor frustration. "Let's try the park. I'm not normally a hot dog gal, but I spied a cart as we drove past earlier."

Sully eyed Dez. Yes, he was three short steps from salivating. If anyone loved a hot dog cart, it was Dez.

Finding a parking spot near the park was another challenge. The revellers were out in force, enjoying the decorations and festivities. Hayfield Park was Headless Henry Central, unless one counted the woods where he was actually purported to roam. Dez lucked into a parking spot a short walk from the park, Sully having spotted someone backing out.

"Good eye, Sull," Dez muttered as he nosed in. The spot was a bit tight, but beggars couldn't be choosers.

Sully noted Dez had to peel his fingers from the steering wheel. Already saddled with a horrifically creepy ghost job, Dez was now stuck too with navigating a super-busy town with next to no parking—far from his idea of a good time.

Stepping from the vehicle, they were instantly assailed by a classic Halloween song being piped over someone's loudspeaker. As they made the brief walk to the park, the sound grew louder as did the chatter of human voices. Sully knew they'd find a busy site before they'd even crossed the park's boundaries.

Headless Henry was everywhere—on signs, on booths, even frosted onto cookies and cakes for sale at one stand. A line of games included one offering festival-goers a chance at a prize for pinning a head on Henry. If people were genuinely terrified of meeting a grisly end at the spook's hand, Sully couldn't tell as he wandered the park's gravel paths.

"These people have no idea," Raiya said. "None at all."

Sully leaned in, although he still needed to raise his voice to be heard above the din. "Makes you wonder what they'd think if they knew we were planning on confronting their favourite ghost."

Raiya nodded but said nothing more as they reached the food area. Not just a hot dog stand awaited them but a variety of food trucks. Thank goodness for that, Sully thought as he wove his way over to one serving souvlaki. He could tolerate hot dogs, but they weren't his go-to. Meanwhile, Raiya gravitated to one advertising vegetarian meals.

They met up again next to a large grouping of tables. Everything was full, though, so Raiya guided them farther through the park, toward a thick stand of trees. A pathway led them to a quieter area next to a small pond. Several benches bordered it, and thankfully, one was empty.

Dez, who had the longest legs by far, made a beeline for it and sat with his two large hot dogs in hand, scooting over for Sully and Raiya. It was a tight fit for all three but, again, beggars and choosers.

They sat quietly a few minutes, allowing them to tuck into their food. Once they'd finished and were sipping at their respective drinks, Dez opened the necessary conversation.

"Sully and I had an interesting encounter," he said, then proceeded to tell Raiya about their meeting with Cal Holdfast.

Raiya raised her brows. "Oh my. I don't recall knowing Cary had a brother. Poor Cal. It must have been so hard for him, growing up with such a horrible tragedy."

"Speaking from experience, I know," Dez said.

Having lost his younger brother, Aiden, to murder as a child, Dez was keenly aware of the realities Cal would have contended with. Sully noted Dez hadn't shared his personal story with Cal today. Perhaps the time for sharing would come, but it was a hard thing for Dez to talk about—not the sort of topic to automatically bring up to a stranger. Regardless, if Cal had questions about the men who'd been in his store, a quick internet search would tell him all he needed to know.

Having listened to Dez and Sully with clear interest, Raiya stared down at her cup, her expression thoughtful. "All this talk about Henry, I'd lost sight of the possibility Cary might be out there too. If he is—if there's a chance of reuniting him briefly with his brother—we need to do that."

"We will," Sully said. "It's what I do."

She squeezed his hand.

"What about you?" Dez asked her. "What did you find out at the newspaper office?"

Raiya slumped back against the slatted bench seat and heaved a sigh. "Not much, unfortunately—at least, not much more than I already knew. As you can imagine looking around this park, there are plenty of stories in the local paper about the Headless Henry legend. It seems to be an annual Halloween staple that someone writes an article touching on it. But as far back as I went, I could find nothing to reveal how the legend began. If Henry was a real person before he became a ghost, it's not in any edition I could find."

She toyed with her straw as she continued. "I was able to find stories as far back as the nineteen-twenties, so we can trace the legend to at least that period. Possibly, of course, it dates to well before that, but it either hadn't yet become public knowledge or no one wished to write about it. What I can tell you is I found nothing in the newspaper archives to suggest the ghost was directly blamed for any deaths in or around Holy Oak."

Sully nodded as he stared at his drink cup. "How about indirectly?"

"That I couldn't tell you. Certainly, nothing of the sort became official record via the paper. But I did find reference to four local decapitations over the town's history. If you ask me, it seems odd so many people suffered such an injury, particularly given the town's relatively small size."

Sully was struck by the same thing. "What happened in those cases?"

"Well, there was Cary as you know. He was the last. Prior to that, a young man was found decapitated following a car crash. That detail was included because, as with Cary, the head couldn't be found and officials thought it best to warn the public in case they should happen upon it. Earlier, a man hanged himself off the Old Toll Bridge. Apparently, the impact of the drop caused a decapitation, and again, the public was warned for similar reasons. And before that, back in the early twenties, there was a case involving a man who vanished inexplicably for several days. His body was found with no head."

"Let me guess," Dez said. "The head was never found in that case either."

"Give the man a prize," Raiya said with a wry smile. "So while none of these cases was attributed to the ghost, they share two significant traits. All took place within the borders of the same woods—granted, a large area but the same forest nonetheless. And there's the other obvious factor, of course. Beheadings are unusual enough to my knowledge, but add in the fact the heads weren't recovered—well, I'm certainly not one to go in for such blatant coincidence."

"You think Headless Henry was responsible for all of them?" Dez asked.

Raiya frowned and shrugged. "Who's to say for sure without additional information? But if I were a betting woman, I'd definitely know where to lay my money down."

Sully met Dez's eye. "Maybe we could see if Lachlan could work a source with the coroner's office. Even if police won't share, the coroner's office might—at least with the historic ones."

"We can ask," Dez said. "And you never know, maybe Lachlan even has his own file or two kicking around."

Lachlan Fields maintained a storage container on the outskirts of Kimotan Rapids—one in which he kept numerous files on all things he either found interesting or had personally investigated during his years as a police officer. Sully was doubtful as to the legality of Lachlan's possession of a great many of said items, but given those files had led Sully and Dez to solve more than one otherwise-unsolvable homicide case, the line between right and wrong was substantially blurred as far as Sully was concerned.

"We'll need some names," Sully told Raiya.

"I'll e-mail you the copies I took," she said. "I also did some checking into Cary's death. I have to admit, I never did read about it in the papers. I suppose I wanted to put it behind me. I had no desire to read about it or to learn more about it. It was too hard. Even now, sitting in the newspaper's library, I found myself in a very dark place as I read through them. While the nightmares were a terrible thing in and of themselves, reading those details in black and white was another punch to the gut for me."

Sully gave her a hint of a sympathetic smile. "I'm sorry."

"Thank you, but I'm doing all right—at least for now." She paused for a long sip from her cup before continuing. "So, getting back to what I found, there was a story immediately following the incident explaining Cary had been found dead under what was described as suspicious circumstances. Few details were provided, other than that an unnamed teenage girl was taken into custody and was being questioned. We, of course, know that to be Louise Penske. Due to the nature of the death, there were daily stories for a time, though most centred on Cary's family's response, details about the funeral and the impact of such a shocking tragedy on the community at large. It wasn't until a few days after the incident that the other story came out, that the head hadn't been found despite an exhaustive search."

Dez leaned forward as he eyed Raiya. "Did the paper say anything more about Louise?"

Raiya nodded. "It did. For a time, all articles simply said police had no additional information about suspects or charges. Finally, about a month after the death, police released information that no one would be charged. While they released no further information themselves, a reporter talked to Cary's parents, who revealed they were told the girl involved—they, at that time, identified her publicly—wasn't being charged due to her mental condition. Apparently, a psychiatrist had completed an assessment and had found her incapable of forming the necessary intent to commit murder. The assessment determined Louise was in a state of psychosis at the time and was hallucinating. She claimed to have no memory of the event, save one: she described a tall, shadowy man wielding an axe—a man she said had no head."

Dez stated the obvious. "Headless Henry."

Raiya gave another nod. "She claimed she fought him briefly, which I suppose might explain how her prints ended up on the axe police found. Well, you can imagine how her story went over. As much as the community relies on the legend for a large portion of its annual tourism—something else I read, by the way—no one was eager to lay the blame for a violent death at the hands of a ghost. So people blamed Louise, even though police were later forced to add they didn't have sufficient evidence to lay charges, even if she'd been in a fit mental state. Without any direct witnesses to the murder, there was a degree of uncertainty as to the chain of events."

Sully scratched his jaw. "What about Rebecca? They questioned her too."

"Yes, just as they questioned me. But as far as I can tell judging by the article's wording regarding lack of witnesses, Rebecca had nothing helpful to share. Without asking, I'd imagine she probably said she merely happened upon the scene after it happened, just as I did."

"Only you happened upon it afterward because they'd ditched you," Dez said. "Rebecca was with them."

Raiya tilted her head. "True. Another question to ask her, if we can persuade her to talk about it."

"How about Louise?" Sully asked. "Did you find anything more about her?"

"Afraid not," Raiya said. "There was a story about her grandmother's house being vandalized—incidentally, the reason police released information about insufficient evidence against Louise. But there was nothing more I could find about Louise in the papers. It's as though she simply disappeared. For all I can tell, it's as some people have surmised, and she wound up permanently in an institution somewhere or died."

Sully chewed lightly at the inside of his lower lip as he considered this. "As far as I'm aware, there's only one institution in the immediate area."

Just as Dez hated bringing up Aiden's death, Sully loathed the topic of Lockwood Psychiatric Hospital. At one time, he'd been forced into so-called care there—"care" that entailed psychological and medical torture at the hands of its then-chief psychiatrist. While the place was under proper management now, Sully's memories were no less horror-filled.

Dez, his head shaking slowly side to side, had clearly sensed the turn of Sully's thoughts. "No, Sull. Don't even say it."

"A phone call," Sully told him. "That's it. Just to see if they'll tell us if Louise is or was a patient there. I don't know, maybe they won't tell us anything, but we need to try. One phone call is no big deal, right?"

Dez groaned. "Since when is anything involving Lockwood no big deal for us?"

CHAPTER 9

It wasn't a big deal, as it turned out. While Sully wasn't put through to the chief psychiatrist's office, the person who answered the phone said Lockwood had no patient by the name of Louise Penske. While she couldn't say whether such a patient had ever been in their care, Sully thought it likely Louise must have been once. There was no other psychiatric centre in the area, and as far as he knew, there hadn't been for a long, long time.

"She might have been a patient in the past but was long gone by the time the current crop of staff came along," Dez said. "I remember from my policing days, full mental health assessments usually took around thirty days. Those were for court purposes, mind you, and from what we've learned, Louise didn't end up before the court, so I have no idea what sort of time she'd have spent in care. But if there was even a thought she might have had involvement in Cary's death, she would most certainly have been checked out in great detail."

"And treated," Raiya added. "I saw her that night. She was shell-shocked. And if it's true she couldn't remember anything about the event afterward, it might be suggestive of a larger mental health problem."

"Not necessarily," Sully said. "Shock and trauma can be enough to mess with people's ability to remember details. Plenty of people suffer a form of amnesia after going through a horrific event."

"True," Raiya said. "But Dissociative Identity Disorder or a psychotic breakdown might create a similar symptom."

"I suppose so," Sully said. "For that matter, so can spirit possession."

Dez growled. "Ah hell, I was hoping you wouldn't go there."

"Well, regardless, we know for sure now that Louise isn't a patient at Lockwood," Sully said. "Saves us the trip we didn't want to take."

Dez tried for another sip from his straw but ended up finding noisy proof his drink was down to its last dregs. He gave up and met Sully's eye. "Still be good to track her down though. You never know—even if she didn't remember details at the time, something might have come back to her."

Sully nodded. "We'll do some digging. Hopefully, something will turn up."

SMILING faces and laughter were everywhere within the park and the town's busy downtown core. That Halloween was this place's bread and butter was clear enough to Sully as they made their way back to the SUV.

Again, Sully found himself questioning what type of response they'd have from town residents should they discover a trio of visitors had gone to battle with Holy Oak's chief spook and had—should he find Headless Henry in time for his Halloween haunt—banished him to whatever awaited him in the great hereafter. Maybe it wouldn't matter. Legends, after all, had a life all their own.

Not Sully's concern either way. All he was concerned with was stopping Henry from hurting anyone else.

With little more to be gained in town for now, they returned to Whispering Winds.

By the time they arrived back, the parking lot—all but empty when they left—was crammed with vehicles. The scene inside was much the same, the lobby brimming with people toting suitcases and young children, harried desk agents booking people in, existing guests weaving a path through the hubbub as they made their way outside or to the restaurant. Sully was grateful he, Dez and Raiya had arrived when they did. Hard to say how many more would find rooms here.

"I know it's pricy," one woman said to another lady in front of her in line. "But this is the only place near Holy Oak that might be available. Everywhere in town is booked up."

"Always are this time of year," came the reply. "I would have booked early as usual, only I hadn't expected to be here this year. Change of plans, so I thought I'd make the trip after all. If you haven't been before, the festival is amazing. Definitely check out Madame Olga, the tarot card reader. She's spot on every time I've gone."

Sully repeated the name to himself as he stepped around the line and followed Dez to the hall leading to their room. Madame Olga. Sully didn't typically put much stock in show psychics, but he'd met a few who were, as the one woman had said, spot on. If he had the time and inclination, maybe he'd pop into her tent and see for himself.

Raiya reached her room door before they did, and they saw her off for the evening.

"I need a shower, some reading time and a good sleep in that order," she told them. "I'm played right out."

"Me too," Dez said. "And I don't have the excuse of being—"

Raiya held up an index finger while giving him a playful warning smile. "Be careful how you finish that statement."

Dez chuckled. "I wasn't going to make an age comment, all right? I was going to say I'm not a psychic. You guys get hammered with a lot more than I do. I'm fully aware."

Raiya patted his arm and finished with a gentle squeeze. "Good answer." She next met Sully's eye. "I don't know how things will play out over the next couple of nights, but if you should see or experience anything, please let me know. I'll do the same."

"We will," Sully said. "Have a good sleep."

"You too. Although in my case, I'm not banking on it—not if the nightmares I've been having return to haunt me."

"Wake us if you need anything."

Raiya gave him a grateful grin. "Highly appreciated."

Keycarding herself into her room, Raiya gave them a little farewell wave before disappearing inside and shutting the door. Having seen her safely back, Sully and Dez continued down the hall toward their own room.

"I'll never understand how people find this stuff fun," Dez grumbled as he used their keycard to access their room.

"Ghost stuff, you mean?"

"Anything paranormal."

Sully tailed Dez inside and dropped his bags onto the bed farthest from the door. As a rule, Dez liked to claim the one nearest the air conditioner, so Sully left that one for him. Too cool, Sully thought, to put the machine on, but Dez's views on what constituted cold differed from Sully's.

"Maybe you wouldn't feel the same about the paranormal if I didn't do what I do," Sully told him. "It could be you'd find it fun too."

Dez gave his head an exaggerated head shake. "Not a chance. I was scared of ghosts even before you came along."

True enough. Sully dropped it.

Dez pulled a few items out of his shopping bags: all-in-one shampoo and conditioner, a disposable razor, a travel-sized shaving cream and a fresh set of boxers. "I'm gonna grab a shower. Need the bathroom for a few minutes?"

Sully shook his head. "I'm good, thanks. Have at it."

Dez promptly vanished behind the bathroom door, leaving Sully to sort through his own purchases. Having pulled out what he'd need for a shower, he located the TV remote and sat on the end of his bed as he scrolled through the selections on the screen.

Unsurprisingly, there were plenty of Halloween specials on offer. He skipped the scary ones—Dez hated those with a passion, and Sully disliked them with only slightly less vehemence—before settling on a classic cartoon he remembered from his childhood.

He had watched a few minutes of it before it dawned on him. This was a cartoon version of *The Legend of Sleepy Hollow*. The Headless Horseman.

Sully clicked it off.

He found himself gravitating toward the window, intending to see whether anyone was beginning a round of golf at this hour. He suspected not, and he was proven right. The green leading to the first hole was empty.

No. Not quite empty. There. Standing alongside the green, partially concealed by a thick stand of trees. A man. Or rather, the shadow of a man.

Sully narrowed his eyes, trying to see better. As was the case earlier today, it didn't help. Sully could make out no details of any importance. All he knew for certain was the figure appeared tall and strongly built. It was too dark to tell what the figure was wearing, and a tree branch blocked his view of the area where the head and face should be.

Though he couldn't see properly, Sully was pretty sure what he'd find should the branch move aside. No normal living person should be lingering in that spot, standing still at the green's edge with nothing to look at and no one to talk to. Then there was the fact this was the same exact spot Sully had seen the headless spectre earlier today. While the added light and a slight breeze had afforded him a better look at the space where a head should be and wasn't, the similarities between the two figures told Sully this had to be the same spectre.

His first inclination was to head out there, see if he could get closer. Such a move, though, would lead to a blow-up from Dez, and anyway, Sully had stopped being stupid about such things thanks to one too many run-ins with dark spirits. No, he'd wait for Dez. Then he'd go take a look.

Dez appeared so relaxed when he stepped out of the steamy bathroom, Sully hated to shatter his good mood.

Dez sensed it before Sully had so much as opened his mouth. "God, what?"

Sully offered a pathetic grin. "Sorry."

"No. No way. *Now*?"

"Sun's setting. Maybe this is when it's most active. Wouldn't surprise me given the stories."

Dez gave up towelling his ginger hair dry, allowing the towel to droop toward the floor. "Same ghost as earlier today?"

Sully nodded. "Yeah. Same spot too."

Dez dropped his head and rubbed hard at the back of his neck. "Bloody hell. Of course it is." He raised his head and heaved a sigh. "Okay, let's go. But let's get Raiya first, all right? If we have to track a violent, headless ghost, two psychics are better than one."

CHAPTER 10

Raiya didn't answer the door when Sully and Dez arrived there a few minutes later. Risking funny looks should anyone emerge from their rooms, Sully pressed an ear to the door, trying to gauge what Raiya was doing. The sound of running water gave him his answer.

"Shower's running," Sully said for Dez's benefit.

Dez grunted. "Figures. Should we wait?"

Sully gave it a moment's thought before shaking his head. "Ghosts don't tend to stick around for long, at least not in a way I'll be able to see. If we don't try to find this guy now, we might not get another chance—not easily, anyway."

"I was afraid you were going to say that."

Sully settled for sending Raiya a text message, letting her know they were checking out a sighting. He did the best he could at describing the location. Then he and Dez made for the exit.

The golf course was closed for the day, but the grounds appeared to be open to those wanting to explore the area on foot. Sully led the way to the tree line along which he'd observed the shadowy figure, eyes and senses peeled for anything out of place. Whatever he'd seen, it was gone. Yet as they drew nearer the approximate spot, a chill came over him, causing the hair on his arms and the back of his neck to stand on end.

Dez had long since become an expert at reading the finer details of Sully's expressions and body language. "You see something?"

Sully scanned the area for one more long moment. "No. But I feel something."

Dez grimaced. "Which actually could be worse. I prefer it when you can see whatever nasty thing is coming at us."

"You have a point."

Dez balled and un-balled his hands. Tension rather than cold. Sully was good at reading Dez too.

"What is it you're feeling, exactly?" Dez asked.

"I don't know yet. It's not a good feeling. As to whether it's coming from Headless Henry or Cary Holdfast, I can't say. We'll need to get closer for me to figure it out."

Dez growled low in his throat. "Closer. Great."

Sully managed a light chuckle, hoping the attempt at levity would calm himself as much as Dez. He hadn't been exaggerating. This was far from a good feeling. The fact he could see the ghost told him it was a homicide; that alone explained to a large extent the dark sensations crawling over him. Maybe the bad feelings could be put down entirely to the violence connected with Cary's death. Maybe it was something else. Something darker.

Sully moved slowly along the perimeter of the woods, focusing on what he was sensing. He took a few more steps, stopping when the creepy feelings reached a crescendo.

Here. This was definitely the spot. Nothing stood here now—at least not in a form he could see. But it was close. Very close.

"What now?" Dez asked, voice near a whisper.

He wouldn't like the response. "Now we go in."

"Into the woods?"

Sully spared him a glance before training his gaze on the darkness settling rapidly beneath and between the trees. "Where else?"

Dez managed a wry chuckle. "Anywhere else."

"No choice, Dez. We need to take a look. If this is Cary, he needs our help."

"And if it isn't? What then?"

Dez wouldn't like the answer to that one either. If they were dealing with a spirit strong enough to either influence someone to behead a person or, worse, decapitate a person on its own, Sully's first instinct would be to get the hell out and not look back. He'd dealt with enough violent spirits to have learned what a nightmare they could be. And as bad as the situation could get for Sully, sometimes they went after Dez. For Sully, it didn't get much worse than that.

Yeah, if Sully became certain he was directly facing Headless Henry, he'd run for it and pull Dez with him. They'd come back later with Raiya. Power in numbers—at least when those numbers included two strong psychics.

"Let's take it slow," Sully advised. "Follow my lead. If I tell you to, you run. Okay?"

"Run. That I can totally do."

Sully didn't bother voicing the other obvious issue: no matter how fast they ran, ghosts were always faster.

THE SUN HAD BEEN close to setting on the golf course green. Here in the depths of the surrounding woods, night had already come fast and hard.

They'd made sure to both use their phones' map apps to drop joint pins on their initial location. Getting lost in thick, unfamiliar woods in the dark was a near certainty, as was the drain spirits often created when close to electrical or battery-powered devices. With two phones recording their location, the chances were better at least one of them would work when they needed to find their way out—possibly in a hurry.

They hadn't thought to stop off for the flashlight Dez kept in his SUV, and already Sully regretted it. While Dez had lately begun eyeing up some new, extra-bright flashlights—Sully intended to get one of those for Dez's next birthday—the one currently enclosed in the hatch of the SUV was at least brighter than those on their cellphones.

For now, they'd make do with what they had as they powered on their cellphone flashlight apps. Far from perfect but way better than relying on what moonlight filtered through the bared treetops.

The woods closed in the farther they went, the spaces between trees increasingly narrowing and the undergrowth snatching at their clothing. Except for the rustle of branches in the light breeze, the woods were silent as though not a single creature dared to encroach within.

Well, none except Sully and Dez.

Despite the fresh air and the moonlight poking through overhead, Sully felt claustrophobic, like he were instead crawling through a deep, dark cave. And the entire time, he was plagued by the feeling of being watched.

No, not just watched.

Hunted.

"Sully?" came Dez's quiet voice from directly behind.

"Not seeing anything yet." Sully kept the rest to himself for now. Dez was already as alert and cautious as he could possibly be. No sense adding more terror to his existing fears. Sully would alert him if and when the threat became less vague and more imminent.

A few more minutes in, Sully drew to a halt.

Dez bumped against his back. "What is it?"

"Shh. Listening."

"You can't hear ghosts."

"The other listening. The psychic kind."

Dez piped down. Sully focused, pushing out with his consciousness, feeling the energy of the world around him. Sometimes when he was in an old forest and took a moment to tune in, a sense of peace and calm rushed over him. Trees, after all, had an energy and a spirit all their own.

These trees did too, only it wasn't peace and calm flowing from them. It was tension. A bowstring ready to snap.

Sully had lived in both low-crime and high-crime neighbourhoods. The latter often radiated rage, grief and fear—at least to those with the empathy to feel for it. In their own way, forests did the same; haunted woods had a way of letting you know it. Like the Forks in Kimotan Rapids, these woods had seen terrible things, and they'd been poisoned by it.

Sully pictured a teenaged Raiya, abandoned by her classmates on a dark, cold Halloween night in these woods. He imagined her pushing past branches and tripping over roots and rocks, desperately seeking a path out. A scary enough predicament for any kid, but add in the fact she could feel energy as Sully did—it only made his stomach sicker over the whole thing. He knew how terrified he would have been in her shoes at that point in his life. That she'd endured the horrors of that night and had still grown into such an awesome person struck Sully as nothing short of a miracle.

He pushed forward, reaching back to tap Dez on the arm to let him know they were moving again. He couldn't pinpoint any specific spirit—not yet—but he was increasingly certain he'd find one in time. The bigger question was what he'd do once that happened.

Farther and farther into the woods they went, ducking tree branches, tripping on foliage and uneven ground. At times, the sensation of spirit activity was strong, at others it dulled. Always, Sully tried to redirect himself to where it felt strongest, but more than once, he sensed it was on the move.

Sully decided he should warn Dez. "It feels like it's trying to lead us somewhere."

"Where?" Dez's tone was, as Sully predicted, one of alarm.

Sully rolled his eyes though Dez wouldn't see. "How would I know that, dummy?"

"Hey, you're the psychic."

"Not that kind of psychic. Anyway, the bigger question I have right now isn't where. It's why."

Dez grunted. "Yeah, that's kind of an important question, all right. How sure are we about wanting to finding out?"

Sully bent to avoid a branch. "Not sure at all. But here we are."

Another few minutes passed in silence, the two of them focused on their surroundings while Sully divided his attention to watch out for additional ghostly evidence. He wondered if his eyes were playing tricks on him when, more than once, a shadow flickered in the corner of his vision only to vanish when he turned to check head-on.

He was anxious. Not quite scared but getting close. Anxiety and fear weren't good, providing fuel to a dangerous fire.

Sully checked his phone. Close to two-thirds charged when they left, it was nearer now to one-third.

Proof those skirting shadows were more than tricks of the light.

He drew up short, felt Dez again collide with his back.

"What now?" Dez whispered urgently.

Sully shook his head. "Don't know. It's like something's messing with us."

"You mean *him*?"

Dez wasn't going to say the name Headless Henry out loud. Sully didn't blame him.

"I'm not getting anything quite that dark. Not at the moment. I mean, something's around that could well be him, but what I'm seeing and sensing now could be Cary. He died pranking someone. Maybe he's pranking us."

Dez snorted, keeping his voice low as he replied. "The guy literally lost his head doing it. I don't think he'd look at it in a joking manner."

"He's not looking at anything in any manner," Sully deadpanned. "He's got no head."

Dez was silent a moment. "Sully? Was that a joke?"

"A bad one."

"You're telling me. You usually leave the rotten humour to me."

Sully cast a quick look over his shoulder at Dez, intending an answer. His response died on his lips, and he froze.

There, behind Dez. There was no mistaking what he was seeing.

A headless figure of a man standing just behind Dez's right shoulder, right arm raised as though to deliver a blow.

"Dez, move!" Sully yelled, whipping around and shoving at Dez's arm to knock him aside.

Sully could control spirit, but he needed a couple of seconds to focus. He didn't have them.

His sole thought protecting Dez, Sully acted instinctively, hurling himself toward the spirit as if launching himself into a physical brawl. Stupid and futile, yes, but desperation led to many a stupid and futile move.

Or not so futile after all. The ghost vanished just as Sully reached it.

"What the hell?" he muttered.

Dez grabbed his arm. "What's going on?"

"Wish I knew." Sully spun in place, his cellphone flashlight tracking his wide-eyed stare. He saw nothing. More importantly, he felt nothing.

Whatever had just come at them was gone.

The crunch of leaves had him wheeling in place all over again.

Dez had yet to let go of him. "What was that?"

Sully shook his head but said nothing. He had no idea. All he knew was if it were a ghost, he shouldn't have heard it.

Dez stepped closer, his voice an urgent whisper. "Maybe it's an animal."

"A deer maybe."

Dez's flashlight scanned the area. "There are bears and wolves up here too, you know."

Bears and wolves. Sully wasn't sure which he'd prefer: large animals with claws and teeth or a powerful, murderous ghost. He was still considering it when another crackle—nearer this time—told them whatever this was, it was getting closer.

"Ghost?" Dez asked. "Yes or no?"

Sully concentrated. The blanket of spiritual darkness all around them lingered as heavily as before, but this time, Sully couldn't pinpoint it. Whatever haunted these woods, it was no longer drilling down on them.

"Not a ghost," Sully said. "Not this time."

Dez shifted, positioning himself partially in front of Sully. "Then this one's mine."

"Ours," Sully corrected, muscling up next to Dez. "You're a big guy, D, but plenty of bears are bigger. If we can't outrun whatever it is, we'll fight it."

They got ready, putting themselves into sparring position. Sully quickly cued up a particularly loud rock song on his music app and ensured the volume was cranked to full. He'd heard of cases in which loud music had been enough to startle animals away.

He was about to press play when Dez's flashlight caught something moving ahead, coinciding with further crunching and cracking. Finally, Sully could make out what this was. Definitely not an animal.

It was the old man from Whispering Winds Resort.

He moved as though in a trance, his eyes unfocused, his jaw slack. He wore only light pyjamas and, Sully noted with concern, no shoes.

"Oh good lord," Dez groaned.

Dez rushed forward, toward the man. "Sir? Sir, are you all right?"

The old man's head turned slowly toward them. For a moment, Sully wasn't sure Dez's question had registered. Hell, he wasn't certain the man even saw them.

Dez tried again. "Sir?"

The man blinked. His eyes at last seemed to focus. "Quiet! Quiet, goddamn you! He'll hear!"

"Who?" Dez asked. Sully was pretty sure he regretted asking the question as soon as it was out of his mouth.

Especially when the answer came—not so much in words, but in a gesture. The man lifted a long, bony finger, trembling a little as he pointed.

"Him," he said.

Sully followed the finger.

And found a tall, dark figure hovering in the trees ahead. A tall, dark, *headless* figure.

This wasn't Cary. And, while radiating fury and hate and power, he was moving.

Toward them.

"Dez," Sully said. "Grab the old man and run. *Now*!"

Dez did as told, moving fast as he grabbed for the elderly man and hauled him up onto his back. Then he was running, crashing through the undergrowth as he went. Sully started to follow, making it a few paces before a jolt of panic rippled inexplicably through him.

He wasn't going to make it. He knew it in an instant.

One instant before something heavy collided with his head.

CHAPTER 11

DEZ PICKED up the old man piggyback-style, hoping the guy wouldn't take exception and start fighting him. At the moment, all any of them seemed to want was to get as far away from the headless ghost as soon as was humanly possible.

Dez hadn't seen anything himself. He hadn't needed to. Between the old man's frightened words and Sully's desperate command, Dez knew exactly what he was dealing with.

He had no idea where he was running. He could set down the man to check the stored coordinates on his phone, but he couldn't spare the time or the distraction. That would need to be up to Sully.

"Sully, check your pin!" Dez puffed out as he ducked to clear a big branch his wobbling phone flashlight had illuminated.

No response.

Dez came to an abrupt stop and wheeled in place. Setting the man down for a moment, he played the beam from his flashlight over the area, searching for his brother.

He wasn't there.

"Sully!" Dez yelled. "Answer me!"

Nothing.

Shit.

Dez called out again for Sully but stopped when wiry fingers gripped his arm.

"Shut up," the old man snapped. "You want him to find us?"

"I need to find my brother."

"There's nothing to find. He's already dead."

Logic told Dez this guy couldn't possibly know something like that. Fear had Dez worrying the old man was right. Either way, he needed to go back for Sully. He couldn't leave him out here like this.

"We need to go back," Dez said, as much to himself as the old man.

Silence from the man had Dez flicking his gaze back to him. The man blinked, shook his head, blinked again. Finally, he pivoted to stare up at Dez.

"Where am I?"

Oh boy. "In the woods."

"Why did you bring me here?"

Dez turned to more fully face him. The man seemed to be getting upset, whatever was going on inside his brain having taken him in a whole new mental direction. Dez was tempted to ignore the questions, but the search for Sully would only be harder if Dez had an unwilling charge to tow around.

"I didn't take you anywhere," Dez said. "I found you. I'm going to take you home again, but first I need to find my brother."

"Home."

"Yeah, home. Follow me."

Taking the old man carefully by the arm for safety's sake, Dez attempted to retrace his steps. But the woods were dark, and he'd noted no features remarkable enough to help him determine his former path.

"Sully?" he yelled into the darkness. "Sully, say something!"

The old man's grip tightened, then released. "I want to go home."

"Soon," Dez said. "I promise."

He pressed on, calling out every so often, wide eyes tracing the short path revealed by his flashlight. He rued not having set up his and Sully's phones so they could track each other's devices, making a mental note to do so once they'd located each other.

And yes, they'd locate each other. Dez would allow himself no thoughts to the contrary. He would find Sully. Anything else was unfathomable.

With the old man gently in tow, Dez pressed on through the woods. His pounding heart drowned out most other sounds, and the pressing darkness kept him all but blind. Every step he took, he was painfully aware of the possibility Headless Henry could be standing right behind him. Every sound became a footstep, every shadow concealed a spirit.

Dez was losing it, his fear of the ghost compounded by his dread over Sully. It didn't help he was lugging along a man who apparently had some form of dementia. Then again, the old man had been aware of Henry before; maybe he'd become so again and alert Dez before heads rolled.

If one hadn't rolled already. Why the hell wasn't Sully answering him?

Another crunch sounded from somewhere behind Dez. Then another and another.

Dez wheeled, pressing the old man back in order to shield him from this potential new threat.

Footsteps. Unquestionably footsteps. Ghost? Human? Deer? Bear? Whatever it was, this was something substantial. Definitely no squirrel.

Dez held his phone in one hand, shining his light, while holding the man behind himself with the other.

"Who's there?" Dez called out. If this was a person, hopefully they'd answer. If an animal, Dez hoped his shout would be enough to make it rethink coming this way.

If a head-hunting ghost … well, that didn't bear thinking about.

"Dez? Is that you?"

Dez straightened, a relieved breath whooshing from his lungs. "Raiya?"

More movement sounded ahead until, seconds later, the beam

from a flashlight poked between a particularly thick stand of trees and shrubs.

"I see your flashlight," she said. "My, these woods are thicker than I remember."

"Be careful," Dez responded. "Watch your step."

A minute or so later, Raiya's face blinked into view ahead. Her hair was still wet from her shower, and though pulled back into a knot, it had accumulated a dusting of flakes of dead leaves and a small twig or two. Her expression—focused eyes, pinched lips and a clenched jaw—showed a mix of determination and anxiety. Dez could only imagine he looked much the same to her.

"Where's Sully?" she asked.

Dez peered uselessly behind himself into the dark. "I don't know. We found this guy"—indicating the man sheltering behind him—"in the woods a ways back. He said something about the ghost, and next thing, Sully's telling me to run. I ran. Now I wish I hadn't. Sully's back there somewhere, and he's not answering me."

Raiya reached for Dez's arm and gave it a squeeze. "Don't worry. He'll be okay."

"I wish I had your confidence. If he's not answering, something's wrong."

"Your brother is the strongest psychic I've ever met, and he's a strong person in general. Not only that, but if he was no longer with us on the earthly plane, I'd know it. His death would cause a ripple among psychics who know him—a ripple that, for those like myself, would swell to a tidal wave. When I say he's all right, I'm not trying to make you feel better. I know it in my soul."

Something inside Dez released. Again, his breath left his lungs in a great puff of relief. That said, he wouldn't be fully satisfied until Sully was back with him.

"Can you find him?" Dez asked.

Raiya nodded. "Absolutely, I can. He's a beacon. Given a bit of time, he'll lead me right to him."

"Okay, let's go."

"I want to go home." The old man, more insistent this time. Dez was so stressed he could have bitten the poor guy's head off, but Raiya, placing a calming hand on Dez's chest, stopped him in his tracks.

"You should see him back to the resort," Raiya said. "He'll be missed by now. Leave Sully to me."

Dez shook his head. "No. I can't ditch him out here, not with everything that's happening."

Raiya smiled. "If only I'd known someone like you when I was young." She gently wound her fingers into the material of Dez's jacket, just enough to give him a light shake. "You can trust me with your brother. I won't fail him."

Dez eyed her, debating whether to go along with her plan. In the end, he knew she was right. He couldn't keep this frail, frightened man out here any longer, and he certainly wouldn't abandon him. Anyway, if there was a need to do battle with a nasty ghost, two psychics beat one psychic and one non-psychic any day.

"Can you get out of the woods okay?" Raiya asked him.

"Yeah. You?"

She tapped the side of her head. "This will get me out. Not to worry. I'll just walk in the opposite direction of the nastiness. It'll get me back."

Dez frowned once more into the darkness behind him. "I thought we figured out Headless Henry only comes out on Halloween."

Raiya shrugged. "That's the legend. Maybe it's usually true. Then again, I'd venture to say Henry didn't often have multiple psychics prowling the woods looking for him. Could be he's feeding on Sully's energy."

Which, Dez knew, was not a good thing. "What if he feeds on yours too? Won't that make this worse?"

Raiya's lips turned down at the corners. "Huh. Good question." She gave another shrug. "Can't be helped. Still better to have both Sully and me against this beast. If it comes to a fight, we're stronger together."

Dez forced a grim smile. "That's usually my line."

She patted his chest. "Tonight, it's mine. Go."

Dez took her hand, squeezing her fingers. "Call me as soon as you have him."

"Promise," she said.

And with that, she stepped away, leaving Dez standing with the old man. For a long moment, Dez watched Raiya's light bobbing away. Only when it disappeared into the trees did Dez return his attention to his unhappy companion.

Fighting every urge he had to turn back and join the search for Sully, Dez started moving toward the pin on his phone screen, gently maneuvering the man alongside him.

"Come on," Dez told him. "I'll take you home."

CHAPTER 12

THE SENSATION of movement hit Sully first.

Walking. No, stumbling. He was stumbling through the forest, his eyes half-open, only half-seeing.

It was dark, cold. His face hurt as though it had met with a few sharp branches before awareness had returned.

He squinted into the darkness, struggling to see anything ahead or around him. The moon was high overhead, its light remarkably strong.

Weird. Earlier, the moon was only at a quarter or so. Now it was full or nearly so.

What the hell?

His brain still fuzzy, Sully lowered his gaze and gave his head a light shake. It hurt, but not too badly. He blinked, checked his surroundings again. Brighter than before, definitely. Maybe his eyes were getting adjusted. It would be easier, of course, with some added light.

His cellphone flashlight. Why wasn't he using it?

Because he wasn't holding it, he realized. Peering down at his hands, he noted they were empty.

His hands. These weren't his hands.

Sully's heart thudded solidly against his ribs as he studied the large, rough hands in front of him, a few sizeable scars marring the flesh of two fingers and one palm.

He checked his clothing next. Dark pants stained with mud, a thick shirt and a heavy, oversized coat. Definitely not the jeans and jacket he'd had on before. Worse, the body beneath wasn't his own long, lean form. This body was heavy with muscle and sinew.

A rush of panic seized Sully. What the hell was going on? Who was this? More than that, how'd he become ensnared in what had to be a paranormal vision?

One thing was for sure: he hadn't consented to this, hadn't so much as seen it coming. He'd taken a blow to the head. Now he was trapped inside another man's memory.

And that man wasn't a good person. Not even close.

The man was prowling the woods, searching. Endlessly searching.

All Hallows Eve. This was *his* night, his best chance at accomplishing his goal. He'd become legend, and legend had become his fuel, feeding his need by bringing him more foolhardy souls. Like any hunt, it wasn't often he managed to locate prey, even less often he succeeded in taking it. When he did though …

The thought thrilled him, gave him new energy as he passed between and through the trees, silent as the grave.

If nothing came to him soon, he'd return to the tree, feed himself on its energy. Then, if need be, he'd go farther afield, as far as these woods stretched.

THE SCENE CHANGED. Same night, Sully suspected, based on the size and position of the moon. But the location was different. He knew it because for the first time, he stood facing a feature that was nothing short of remarkable.

A huge, twisted tree. Sully was no expert at tree identification. Yet he knew without being told this was an old bur oak, dead or nearly there after growing here for several hundred years.

It had seen things. Terrible things. Worse, it had played a role in those things.

It had helped to end his life, this man whose thoughts played out in his head.

He stepped up to it, his calloused fingers ghosting over its bark. He felt nothing physical; he was no longer capable of such things. What he felt was something more.

Power. Energy. Electricity.

Yes, the tree was dead, at least in the botanical sense. In another way, the tree breathed energy. It had been imbued with it, and even without the roots and leaves to feed it, this tree sucked in energy and released it to those with the ability to feed.

Ability like that possessed by this man. No, this spirit.

He wasn't alive. Not anymore. He was alive in the same way the tree was, drawing on the energy of other people, other things—a parasite of sorts.

A parasite needing to be fed. Tonight.

It had been years. Too many years since he'd last taken a human life. It was time. Any longer and both he and the tree he was connected to would fade, then vanish.

Vanish the way his head had.

He reached up, touched at his shoulders. Shifted his hands to feel the gruesome, raw opening of his neck—the place where his head should be and wasn't.

This endless night, this hopeless existence—once he'd thought it could be ended once he found his head. Then he'd hoped he could rest once he replaced what he'd lost by taking it from another.

Now though, he'd learned otherwise. There was no peace, no end to this blackness. A long, unnatural life stretched before him, a waking hell in which he ruled as the sole devil.

And so he walked. Walked and hunted and, whenever possible, killed. Soaking in energy and trading in fear.

If he couldn't rest in peace, neither would others.

A sound of weeping. A girl.

Not his usual prey. He preferred to take men. They were bigger, stronger. They made him feel closer to vengeance. He had never taken a female's life, and he wasn't eager to now.

But if this was all he had in front of him this night—well, a meal was a meal.

He found her nearby, a teenage girl with wild hair and wild eyes. He watched her a moment, hovering there, questioning how best to do this, whether he could make do another year without claiming a life.

Her head pivoted. Shiny, tear-rimmed eyes locked onto him.

She saw. By God, she *saw* him. Not the way others sometimes did, when he willed it and concentrated his energy to make it happen. She saw him without his intending it.

He moved toward her. She backed away, tripped, fell over. Terrified and sprawled on the forest floor, she was an easy mark.

Yet something about her—she was powerful in a way she didn't seem to grasp. Powerful enough to perhaps justify his claiming her life? Maybe. Maybe not.

A sound in the distance. A crunch of leaves underfoot.

That wasn't a female. He sensed it as much as heard it. A male.

A thrill rippled through him as he flashed away, toward the sound and the energy he'd find there.

Toward the kill he needed to survive.

"Sully! Sully, look at me! Focus!"

More movement, this time shaking rather than walking.

He blinked. Blinked again. Where he'd seen trees and a wild-looking young girl, he saw now an older lady. Same hair, only grey. Same face, only creased with age. Same eyes, only holding more concern and less fear.

He knew her.

"Let him go," she snarled. "Release him."

Her voice was commanding, holding a threat she seemed confident of making good on.

She reached for his throat. He took a step back, but she was there, following. She seized at something—a cord hanging around his neck. She drew something out, held it in her hand and muttered something he couldn't quite make out. When she pressed it suddenly to his forehead, it felt like fire.

He cried out, fell to his knees. She didn't let up, holding it there while continuing to mutter. An incantation of some sort. Yes, she was powerful. Only now, she knew it. And she'd learned to control it.

This wasn't safe. Not with both of them to contend with.

He fled.

Sully crumpled forward, managing to catch himself with his hands against the cool, damp earth. Raiya released the small, wooden cross she'd pressed to his head moments ago, the one Sully had been gifted years back to better protect him from dark spirits.

"It's been a while since I last blessed it," Raiya said. "You've faced a lot of evil since then. The poor thing is overwrought. Once we get back to Kimotan Rapids, come by, and I'll re-bless it."

Sully lowered his forehead to the ground. The dirt and leaves he found there were wonderfully cool, easing the painful tension behind and above his eyes.

Raiya's hand, only slightly less cold, settled on the back of his neck and provided additional relief. "Are you all right?"

Sully gave a half-hearted nod against the ground.

"I'll need you to do better than that," Raiya said.

"I'm fine," he got out. "Thanks to you." He snapped his head up, a thought leaping into his brain. "Dez? Did you see Dez?"

Raiya held up a palm in a calming gesture. "He's all right, don't worry. I sent him back to the resort with the old fellow. He wasn't eager to go, believe me, but I suspected on this occasion, it would be me you'd need more. Turned out I was right. Speaking of Dez, I promised him a phone call once I found you."

Sully nodded, then returned his head to the soothing ground. "Do it. He'll be back in here otherwise, looking for us."

"Borrow your phone? I don't have mine with me."

Sully patted himself down, hoping he hadn't dropped his cellphone. But no, thank goodness, there it was in his jacket pocket. He unlocked it, then handed it to Raiya, allowing her to call while he focused on settling down.

Even though the phone wasn't set to speaker mode, Sully instantly heard his own name barked by Dez.

"No, it's me," Raiya replied. "I'm with Sully. He's okay."

Dez's voice returned, though Sully didn't catch what he said.

"He took a blow to the head," Raiya told Dez. "I don't think he's got a concussion, at least from what I can tell. I believe it was rather a means to stun and overpower him. He was being possessed when I located him."

"What?" Dez exclaimed. That Sully had easily heard.

"Don't worry. I dealt with it. The spirit possessing him decided moving on was a good idea. Even so, I think it's best Sully and I return to the resort immediately."

Another indecipherable rumbling from Dez.

"Watch for us," Raiya said. "But don't enter the woods, you hear me? Whatever and whoever this is, he's strong. Strong enough to possess Sully. And if he can do that, I fear there's little he can't do."

Raiya pulled the phone away, checking the screen before returning to the conversation. "Speaking of leaving, I'd better disconnect. The battery's draining fast, and I think we'll need this phone to get out of here."

They disconnected a moment later. Raiya helped Sully to his feet and returned his phone to him. She was right—the battery was nearly drained.

Sully tapped into his map app, grateful to see the pin he'd dropped earlier was still there.

"Let's go," Sully said. "We've got a bit of ground to cover, and we'll need to do it before the phone goes dead."

"I can probably get us out," Raiya said. "But your technology will definitely make it easier and quicker. Lead the way."

SULLY EASILY PICKED out Dez's hulking form on the golf green when he and Raiya finally pushed through the last of the woods. Dez made it clear he'd seen them too when he started sprinting toward them.

Reaching them just as they passed beneath one of the overhead lights on the green, Dez grabbed Sully in a hug before pulling back and maintaining a hold on his shoulders. "Sull, you okay?"

Sully nodded as he reached up to pinch at the inner corners of his eyes. His headache hadn't quite gone away, though the cool night air had helped. Now free of the woods, the tension had lessened more still. Even so, he wanted nothing more than to down a painkiller and go to bed.

"Let's just go back to the room, okay?" Sully asked.

Dez wasn't there yet, his hands now on the sides of Sully's head. Dez turned him gently as if to get a better look. "You're bleeding."

"That's what made me think he must have taken a blow," Raiya said. "He doesn't seem to be slurring his words or not making sense though, so I don't suspect a significant head injury."

Dez peered hard into Sully's eyes for a long moment. Checking his pupils for size and focus, Sully realized.

"I'm fine," Sully told him.

"I'll judge that for myself once we get back to the room." Dez got an arm around Sully and pulled him into step next to him. "What's this about possession?"

"I don't know how it happened exactly," Sully said. "Like Raiya told you on the phone, I took a blow of some sort. Next thing I know, I'm walking through the woods. Only it wasn't me. I mean, it was me, but when I looked at myself, I saw someone else. Someone else's hands, body and clothing. And I had someone else's thoughts in my head drowning out my own."

"Whose?" Dez asked.

Sully glanced up at him. "No idea. I didn't catch a name. I did get one thing though that might be kind of important when it comes to identifying him."

"Which is?"

Sully frowned. "The lack of head."

Dez grimaced. "Oh hell."

Sully turned to meet Raiya's eye. "One other thing: there's a tree. I got the impression it's really important to him. They're connected somehow, maybe even feed off each other."

"The Holy Oak," she said. "The one the town's named for. Has to be."

"We need to find it," Sully said.

Dez grasped his arm, towing him along. "Not tonight though. Finding a tree connected to an evil spirit seems like the kind of thing we should do by daylight."

CHAPTER 13

Dez kept his eye on Sully all the way back to the hotel. Raiya was confident the possession was over, and Dez had no reason to doubt her, but it was clear the experience had taken a lot out of Sully. The only thing Dez would allow for the rest of the night was sleep.

He was rarely so thrilled to see a hotel as he was this night, his shoulders and jaw releasing as he finally reached the building's interior. With warmth washing over him from the heater inside the rear entrance, it made Dez even more eager to crawl into bed and stay there until well into the morning.

The halls and the lobby were empty of all but a handful of staff, and the restaurant was closed. Thankfully, there was no sign of the old man, and Dez hoped someone was keeping a close eye on him. If he was prone to wander off, it was a wonder he hadn't yet had his head lopped off by the maniacal spirit they'd encountered tonight.

Dez nodded to the girl behind the front desk as he passed by with Sully and Raiya. The girl had been working there earlier when Dez arrived back with the old man. She'd been helpful, immediately making a phone call that had Parker dashing into the lobby from the employees-only area and taking charge of him. Where they'd gone after that, Dez didn't know and didn't care, as long as everyone stayed in for the night.

For now, all he cared about was keeping himself, Sully and Raiya in for the rest of the night, and he made a beeline for the rooms, plucking at Sully's sleeve to keep him moving. They had said little to each other since those first moments after Dez had reunited with Sully; Dez suspected the others, like him, were too tired and too drained for conversation. Or maybe it was the sort of topic best left for the light of day. Suited Dez fine.

While Raiya fished for her keycard next to her door, Sully broke the silence. "Thanks for coming, Raiya. You really saved my ass."

She patted his chest. "Not a problem, my friend. Get some rest. I need some too, big time."

She shifted her hand, plucking at the wooden cross around Sully's neck. "Listen, I know I don't have all of my Wiccan accoutrements with me, but I can do a little something to cleanse this for you, at least a little. Once we're back home, I'll make sure to get you by to do a proper cleansing. First thing, drop it off with me, and I'll see what I can do with the smaller crystals I carry with me. Sound good?"

"Sounds good," Sully said. "Thanks again, Raiya."

"Yeah," Dez said. "A massive thank you from me as well. I feel like you picked up the ball I dropped."

Sully wheeled on him. "You didn't drop anything."

"Other than you."

"We'll talk about this later," Sully muttered. "Good night, Raiya. Hope you have a good sleep."

"You too. Fill me in tomorrow, all right? I don't think I can handle more tonight."

With that, Raiya keycarded herself into her room, leaving Dez and Sully to continue the few doors to their own.

They'd just gotten inside, Dez having closed and locked the door behind them, when he found himself ensnared in a heated glare from Sully.

"You didn't drop the ball," Sully snapped at him. "You hear me? You did exactly what I needed you to do."

"I did exactly what I least needed *me* to do," Dez returned. "I lost you. Hell, I nearly lost you permanently. You were there, then you weren't. It's my job to make sure that doesn't happen."

Sully grabbed him by the front of the jacket. "It's your job to trust me to do mine. We couldn't leave that old guy out there, and you know it. Between all of us, I'm the one best able to handle paranormal threats."

He released Dez before continuing. "If anyone dropped the ball, it was me. I don't know if I let my guard down, or if this ghost was just too quick or too strong in that moment. Either way, I didn't see it coming. And if I didn't, how the hell would you?"

"Still …," Dez said. He didn't add to it. There was no arguing with Sully, not when he had a valid point. Even so, Dez remained sick about how the night had played out. He wouldn't allow a repeat—old man or no old man to get to safety. Need be, Dez would carry three people all the way back, as long as one of them was Sully.

"No arguments," Sully warned him. "I mean it. You didn't ditch me. You're not capable of it."

"Whatever," Dez said. "I'm too tired to do battle with you over this. I should take a better look at your head. After that, we'd better hit the hay."

"Let me grab a shower first," Sully said. "I've got bits of leaves and junk all through my hair." As if to prove it, Sully pulled out the elastic and ruffled out his hair. Dez watched as flakes of dried foliage and bits of twigs rained to the ground.

"Housekeeping's going to be pissed," Dez said.

"Not as pissed as I am," Sully said. "One thing I cannot tolerate is being possessed against my will."

Dez hadn't planned on discussing this tonight, but since the topic had come up anyway, and his anxiety was nearly back to where it had been earlier, this seemed as good a time as any. "You said you were someone else. Any clues as to who?"

"I didn't catch any names, and I couldn't make out much by way of distinguishing features. All I can say for sure is he was Caucasian, and he was well-built. And he had rough, scarred hands—the sort which suggest he did a lot of physical labour. Granted, I had the impression he lived quite some time ago—probably well over a century—so lots of people used to have to cut their own firewood or do other heavily physical things to run their homes. But this man gave me the impression of someone who did work along those lines, not just that he did it to maintain his home or whatever."

Dez crossed his arms. "Anything else?"

Sully visibly shivered. "Yeah, but you probably don't want to hear it."

"No, I don't, but wanting to and needing to are different things."

Sully leaned up against the room's dresser, bringing up a hand to rub at his head where his hair was caked lightly with blood. Dez took this as his cue, stepping in and using the bright light by the door to better inspect the injury.

"Talk," he told Sully as he carefully parted his hair to search for the wound.

Sully grunted in pain but did as asked. "He didn't show me anything from his life. I saw him only while he was already dead. He's searching for victims—like, all the time. I mean, I do believe what Raiya said—that this ghost is powerful mainly at Halloween—but it doesn't mean he doesn't get ready for it. Maybe he's dormant the rest of the year, or he's too weak to act, but by the time Halloween rolls around, he's ready to roll."

"As are heads," Dez deadpanned.

"The tree though," Sully said. "The one I told you he's connected to—the Holy Oak—I really think it holds the key to this somehow. He draws energy from it. And it's weird, because I also got the impression he died there."

"At the tree?"

Sully nodded. "I don't know how, but yeah."

Dez found the site of the injury. Caked with blood, but nothing was coming from it now. Head wounds always bled a lot. It was a good sign this one had quit bleeding. Even better that Sully was showing no signs of a concussion or other serious head injury.

Stepping back, Dez crossed his arms. "You'll live."

"Thanks, Doc."

"So back to the other major topic. Headless Henry—it had to be a murder that ended him, right? If it weren't, you wouldn't be able to see him."

"Murder's one kind of unjustifiable homicide," Sully said. "I've seen executed people on occasion too, remember?"

Dez raised a brow. "You think it was a hanging tree?"

"Big, old oaks like that used to be used for those purposes from time to time. Tell you what: if that tree played host to violent deaths —legal executions or otherwise—I can totally see how it might have become poisoned with that energy over time. That type of energy doesn't often leave buildings. Why would it leave something living, like a tree?"

This was a new one. All the years Dez had listened to his mother talk to her plants, he hadn't considered the possibility they were actually listening. Sully had a point though: if buildings and people could be haunted, why not trees?

"Someone around here must know where to find this tree," Dez said. "Tomorrow morning, we'll ask around, see if we can get some directions."

"Sure," Sully said. "First, though, I want to find out more about it. Forewarned is forearmed."

CHAPTER 14

Dez was exhausted when he crawled into bed, but it mattered little when it came to getting a good night's sleep.

He spent much of the night tossing and turning, alternating between fitful sleep and staring at the ceiling. The few times he did fall deeper into sleep, he was startled awake by horrendous nightmares.

In them, he was fighting through an endless, dark wood. Somewhere, Sully was screaming for help, and no matter how far and how fast he ran, he couldn't find him. At other moments, it was as though he were wading through rivers of molasses, rendering him incapable of moving at anything faster than a crawl.

What relief Dez had felt upon waking to see Sully in the next bed vanished when he thought about what difficulties lay ahead. Raiya had found Sully this time; what if they weren't so fortunate the next?

Dez finally managed to settle into a better sleep around four or five—he wasn't sure exactly when rest had finally come for him—but it didn't make up for what he'd lost. When he again opened his eyes, muted daylight spilled through the window, and Sully was tiptoeing around, making efforts to quietly close the drapes.

"It's okay," Dez grumbled. "I'm awake."

"Did I wake you up?"

"No, anxiety did."

Sully gave up on the curtains and dropped heavily onto the edge of his bed, facing Dez. "I woke up a few times. You seemed as though you weren't having a good night either."

Dez passed a palm over his face. "Putting it mildly. Between the insomnia and the nightmares, I got maybe a couple of hours uninterrupted."

"Yeah," Sully said. "Me too." He gave Dez a smile. "Hey, I'll bet I know something that'll make you feel better."

"Surprise me."

"Breakfast? I hear they do a pretty great buffet in the restaurant."

Dez felt the first small burst of enthusiasm, his stomach uttering a grumble as though providing agreement.

Sully made it clear the sound hadn't gotten past him. "I'll take that as a yes."

"Let's go now," Dez said. "In case they run out of the good stuff before we get there. We'll shower and shave once we're back."

A LIGHT DRIZZLE dotted the windows as Dez sat across from Sully with his plate. Dez's, as usual, was a mountain next to Sully's molehill, but neither of them commented on it as they ate.

Raiya hadn't joined them. She'd appeared weary as well upon answering her door and said she planned on getting another hour or two of sleep before so much as attempting to face the day. She did, however, take Sully's wooden amulet, telling them she'd work on cleansing it that morning. She'd text later once she'd finished.

In the restaurant, Dez scanned the faces around him a few times, but mostly he focused on his food. Sully was right—the buffet was fantastic, offering everything from healthy fruits and whole-grain cereals to the stuff Dez preferred: bacon, sausages, scrambled eggs and thick, syrup-coated pancakes and waffles. Dez had managed to take a little bit of everything and was contemplating returning for seconds when movement headed their way cut into his plans.

"Oh, good lord," Dez muttered. "It's Rebecca."

Sully checked over his shoulder. "She doesn't look happy."

"Wonder what we did now?" Dez said.

They didn't have long to guess at it before Rebecca reached them. "Once you're finished eating, could you please come and see me? I'll be in my office. Parker's working the desk. He'll show you back."

With that, she was gone.

Dez lifted an eyebrow at Sully. "What do you think that was about?"

Sully frowned down at his leftover scrambled eggs. "No idea, but I'm not sure I want to find out."

NOT MUCH CHOICE. Dez debated ignoring Rebecca's pointed request and heading into town with Sully instead, but that would have left Raiya to deal with Rebecca. That didn't seem fair, so upon paying for breakfast, Dez and Sully headed to the front desk where, as Rebecca had told them, Parker was waiting.

"Oh yes," he said. "She did mention she wished to speak with you. I'll let you back."

Showing them through into the employees' area, Parker pointed them needlessly toward the office.

"We've been there once before," Dez told him. "We'll find it."

"End of the hall," Parker told them nonetheless before heading back through the door and toward the front desk.

Sully's lips flapped as he exhaled in frustration. "I don't want to do this. After last night, I don't want to deal with her issues. We've got our own."

"Tell me about it," Dez said. "Let's just get this over with. Afterward, we'll head into town and see if we can find out more about this oak tree. Maybe Cal Holdfast can help. He's spent lots of time in those woods."

"Good plan," Sully said. "Although maybe we could check first with Parker. If he's native to Holy Oak, he'd probably have some idea where to find it—especially since he works so close to the woods. Besides, he seems friendly."

Dez considered this a moment before thinking better of it. "Sure, but if Rebecca's got issues with the whole thing, I don't want to put one of her staff members in a difficult position."

"True," Sully said. "Cal it is, then."

For now, though, there was Rebecca to speak with. Neither Dez nor Sully moved at a particularly fast pace as they approached the office. Dez wasn't eager for a tongue-lashing if it turned out they weren't supposed to be walking the grounds after hours. Given Dez had escorted the old man back last night, their late night activities were undeniable.

Rebecca was waiting, seated rigidly behind her desk, her lean, blazer-clad arms folded atop the surface.

"Thank you for coming," she said. "I hope you enjoyed your breakfast."

"It was great," Dez said. "Thanks."

Rebecca reached into a top drawer and retrieved something which she pushed across the desk toward them. "These are vouchers for tomorrow's breakfast buffet should you still be staying with us. Consider it a thank you."

Dez eyed the vouchers, then Rebecca. She still wasn't smiling.

"I don't understand," Dez said. "Thank you for what?"

She frowned at them for a long moment. Finally, she waved them toward the chairs opposite hers. "Please, sit down. You had questions for me yesterday. I suppose it's only fair I answer a few."

Dez was tempted to ask why, although he also didn't want to look a gift horse in the mouth.

She solved the dilemma for him by providing the answer on her own. "The elderly man you brought back last night was my father."

That had Dez making for one of the chairs. Sully joined him a moment later.

"Your father?" Dez asked.

Rebecca's shoulders drooped. "He's been suffering from dementia for a few years now. I'm afraid it's getting worse. I've made him a home here where I can keep an eye on him, and I have an aide who attends a few hours each day to ensure he's taking his medication and is otherwise cared for when I can't be present. Some of my staff, particularly Parker, are a big help as well. But it's rapidly becoming an around-the-clock task. I'm afraid I'll need to make some tough decisions soon as to his future care. I thought being here, in the place he helped to establish years back, he'd feel at home and would perhaps even come back to himself a little. It hasn't happened. He wanders sometimes, often late at night. When he got out last night, I'd been asleep. I had no idea he was gone until Parker brought him in. He told me you found him and returned him. So I want to thank you for that."

"It's all right," Dez said. "Happy to help."

"What were you doing out in the woods?"

There was the question Dez had been hoping not to hear. "Uh, I don't think you'll want to get into it."

"Headless Henry," she said, eyes rolling ever so slightly as she uttered the words.

Dez nodded. "Afraid so."

"And? Did you find anything?"

Dez glanced at Sully. This question would be his to answer if any response was to be given.

Sully turned his gaze from Dez back to Rebecca. "Uh, yeah, actually. We did. Or at least *I* did."

Rebecca blinked twice heavily. Dez might have imagined it, but he thought he'd caught a flash of something resembling fear.

"I know you don't want to hear it," Sully said. "But there's something in those woods. Something evil. And your father knows it. He's aware of it."

Rebecca uttered a humourless laugh. "He's aware of precious little these days."

"I don't think that's true," Sully said. "He saw something last night, and he wasn't making it up. I saw the same thing. There's a ghost stalking those woods, and he's not a nice one. Your guests aren't safe, ma'am, and neither are you, your staff or your family. I'm going to do my best to end the threat, but I've got some work to do before I can pull it off." He nodded toward Dez. "We both do."

"It would help if you could tell us anything you know," Dez said. "It's a safe bet you're one of only a few people alive who've come that close to Headless Henry and lived to talk about it. What happened that night?"

Rebecca's posture went straight back to rigid. "There are some things I don't wish to revisit. The death of an old friend is one, as I'm sure you can appreciate."

"We can," Sully said. "And if this were strictly a matter of the past, we wouldn't encroach on your privacy. But it isn't only about the past. There's a genuine risk to people now and in the future if we don't do something about it."

Rebecca sat forward so rapidly, Dez jumped a little. "There's nothing to tell. As everyone is aware, the person who killed Cary Holdfast was arrested and managed to escape charges. She convinced everyone she was mentally unhinged, and as a result, a murder went unpunished. There's nothing more to say."

"You really believe that?" Sully asked. "You really believe there's nothing more going on? No ghosts in those woods?"

"If there is, I never saw anything."

"Raiya heard you screaming that night," Dez said. "You sure saw something."

Rebecca glared at him. "You helped my father last night. But what you saved him from was the risk of hypothermia or accident, not some non-existent spook. I don't believe in such things. My high school boyfriend died a terrible death many years ago. Whatever Raiya thinks she saw or heard, I can't speak to. All I can tell you is that I wasn't present when it happened. Logic and reason are sufficient to explain events. Louise Penske killed Cary Holdfast. The sooner you accept that and move on, the better for all of us."

She pointed at the vouchers. "Please, take them and redeem them in the morning. Once you have, I hope you'll consider a return to the city. Good day, gentlemen."

Rebecca had clearly signalled this conversation had reached its end. It seemed the same could be said for her gratitude.

"If you change your mind and decide you'd like our help, you know where to find us," Dez said.

With that, he stood and walked out of the room—but not before taking and pocketing the breakfast vouchers.

CHAPTER 15

SULLY AVOIDED conversation with Dez until they were back in their room. There, Sully was treated to the expected explosion.

"What the hell is the matter with her?" Dez snapped. "With her dad wandering around out there in the dark, you'd think she'd be a little more grateful we'd found him. Even if she doesn't believe the whole ghost thing, she could at least consider the possibility."

Sully pressed his lips together before replying. "The lady doth protest too much."

"Huh?"

Sully eyed him, head canted to the side. "Shakespeare."

"You're quoting Shakespeare now? Damn, you must have taken a harder blow to the head last night than I realized."

Sully plopped down on the edge of Dez's bed. "Sorry. I'm tired." As if to prove it, he lowered his head into his hands. The darkness that met him was welcome, a slight headache plucking at the area behind his eyes.

"You okay?"

Sully glanced up, finding Dez's appraising stare on him. "Fine. You?"

"Don't get cute. After last night, I've got good reason to ask."

Back to the shadowed relief of his palms. "I'm not possessed anymore, if that's what you're wondering."

Dez snorted. "I'm aware of that much. All these years with you, I've become unsettlingly familiar with what you're like while possessed."

Sully straightened, deciding he'd better at least go through the motions. Dez was anxious enough without the perceived need to watch hawk-like over Sully. "Okay then, I'm fine in every other way besides. Could have used more sleep is all."

Dez studied him a long moment before sitting next to him. "Yeah, me too. Man, I wish we were anyplace else right now."

Sully managed a smile. "I take it that means you'd like me to scratch this place off the list of potential wedding venues."

Dez's gaze snapped toward him. "Figured you would too."

Sully shrugged. "Maybe. Probably. I don't know. I mean, if I'm able to get whatever's out there to cross over, it won't be so bad here, right?"

A little growl escaped Dez. "Memory can be a powerful thing."

"True—which might go partway to explaining why Rebecca's not eager to share her memories with two strangers."

"Maybe. Can't help feeling there's more to it though."

"Me too, thus the Shakespeare quote. What happened to her was traumatic—whether or not she was present to witness anything. You know how hard it is to talk about stuff like that. And not everything gets easier with time. "

Dez leaned forward, head hanging. "I know all that. What I'm wondering is whether her reason for keeping mum might have to do with what Raiya told us. Rebecca's ambitious, and whatever else she might be, she seems to definitely be a good businessperson. If there's one thing around here that's good for business, it's Headless Henry. We get rid of their local legend, we drive away business—and Holy Oak ends up just like every other town around here. Dead."

Which left Sully with one more point to make. "Better the town dies than a human being."

Raiya had finished with Sully's amulet when they rapped on her door soon after. She handed it to Sully through the opened door, a slight smile on her face.

"I've done the best I can with what I have to work with," she said. "I'll do a more thorough job back in Kimotan Rapids, but this should hold you for now."

Sully slipped the cord around his neck and tucked the small cross beneath his shirt. As he felt it tap against his skin, he realized just how vulnerable he'd felt without it. Having it back was a comfort.

Raiya seemed as though she could do with some comfort herself. "You look drained," Sully told her.

This time, Raiya gave him a bigger grin. "Not much for compliments today, are you?"

"I didn't mean—"

She held up a palm. "I know what you meant. And your observation is accurate. I'm bushed. We're going to be up late tonight again, no doubt. I think I'd best try to stay ahead of the game by getting some shuteye during the day. Maybe you should do the same."

All Sully wanted, though, was to get out and see what else they might uncover. The more information they had going into tonight, the better for all of them.

"Dez and I will head out for a bit, do some nosing around," Sully said. "With luck, we'll get some answers before we meet up with Henry again. Plenty of times, it makes a load of difference, being able to poke at weak spots."

"I see your point. Would you like me to come along?"

"No," Dez said. "You rest. I think we both want you alert and fully operational when we head out again later."

The plan suited Raiya fine. Once she'd gone back into her room, Sully and Dez made their way down the hall toward the lobby.

"We should go back to see Cal," Dez suggested. "Even if we

can't persuade him to come out with us, maybe he could give us some decent directions."

"I'm hoping for the former," Sully said. "Directions to a tree in the middle of a big forest don't sound to me like they'd be all too helpful."

CAL, it turned out, wasn't in. In his place stood a man in his twenties who clearly wanted to be someplace other than a men's clothing store.

The guy proved useless in terms of locating Cal. Either he was telling the truth that he didn't know where his boss was, or he was a damned good liar. Either way, it was obvious he didn't care where Cal was or why two strangers were looking for him.

"Maybe try the park," the guy said. "Everyone's at the park." He rolled his eyes dramatically. "Everyone but me."

The young man didn't seem the sort to care about a Halloween festival. Sully suspected the guy's girlfriend was over there somewhere.

"We'll give him a call," Sully told the employee.

Dez shook his head. "No good. The number he gave me was for the store."

"What about a cell number?"

He and Dez both looked to the staffer, but he shook his head. "He doesn't have a cellphone. As for his home number, I'm not supposed to give it out."

Dez fished out a business card and slid it across the counter. "My cell number's on there. Please call him and ask him to contact me as soon as he can."

The young guy glanced at the card, then placed it next to the till. Sully wasn't convinced Cal would be getting a call anytime soon.

"It's important," Sully said. "Please."

"I'll let him know," the guy said.

Sully and Dez left the shop and walked the short distance down the block toward where they'd left the SUV.

"Seems a shame to leave a perfectly good parking spot," Dez said.

Sully checked the clock on his phone. "Close to lunchtime. We'll never get anything closer. Let's walk it. Given how much you're likely to stuff in your face once we get there, a walk would probably be a good idea."

He danced away as Dez took a swipe at him.

SULLY WOULDN'T HAVE THOUGHT it possible after yesterday's excursion, but the park was even busier today.

Lineups for the food vendors and games booths were each at least a dozen deep, and there wasn't a free bench or a table to be seen. The children's tent had to be packed given the sheer amount of racket coming from within, and a face painting booth had apparently been set up somewhere as evidenced by the colourful faces rushing around the festival site. Music was once again blaring, meaning countless voices were raised to be heard above it.

Given the choice, Sully would have turned tail and left the crazy behind. Unfortunately, they had someone to find, and since an internet check revealed Cal Holdfast wasn't listed, this was the most logical place to start.

"The guy at the shop wasn't kidding when he said everyone's at the park," Dez said. "Looks like not just the entire town is here, but everyone from every surrounding town besides."

An exaggeration, of course, but only just. "I don't like it either," Sully said. "Let's try to find Cal. Maybe we can convince him to join us someplace quieter."

"Sounds like a great idea to me," Dez said. He was already craning his neck, his gaze travelling the length and breadth of the viewable area of the park. Good thing he was on the job; no one in

Sully's view came close to rivalling Dez for height. If Dez couldn't see Cal, no way Sully would.

With Dez busy searching for their would-be search assistant, Sully turned his attention elsewhere. With all these people at the park—most, if not all, of whom shared a fascination with Headless Henry—there had to be someone with helpful knowledge of the legend and the woods he haunted.

"If we can't find Cal, maybe we can try touching base with a local conservation officer," Dez suggested. "If anyone's familiar with the wooded areas around town, it should be them."

"How about ghost tour companies?" Sully asked.

Dez shook his head without sparing Sully a glance. "Nope. I thought of that last night, actually. Did some online checks. There's a campfire ghost story night as part of the festival—tonight, as it happens—but no ghost walks or anything. Thank God for that too. I don't want to wake up tomorrow to find out some schmuck got his head lopped off because he opted to wander away from the group."

"In a way, I'm surprised," Sully said. "A ghost tour would have been quite the moneymaker for the town. Imagine how much they could charge to load people up on a bus and drive them out to see the haunted woods."

This time, Dez did meet his eye. "Ask yourself the next obvious question: who owns those woods?"

It took Sully only a few seconds. "Ah."

"Right. And no way Rebecca Symes would allow a bunch of ghost hunters to turn her precious resort into an amusement park. She might have the Headless Henry legend to thank for driving people to the area, but she's made it clear that while she's fine with profiting off it, she doesn't want any share in the marketing. And as you pointed out, who can blame her?"

Sully ducked around a giggling group of teenage girls before replying to Dez. "All right, so I guess that leaves us with our initial plan involving locating Cal or, if that fails, your Plan B of checking in with the conservation officers. I'll suggest a Plan C as well, where we ask about people who've lived around here their whole lives.

There has to be someone who explored those woods before Rebecca and her family shut things down."

"You're probably right," Dez said. "When we were kids, we loved playing in the trees. And even though you and I would have given haunted woods a wide berth, loads of kids would have flocked to places like that."

"Hard to say if they'd have known which tree was the right one," Sully said. "Probably more than one old oak in the woods."

"I have a feeling if and when we find the right one, you'll know."

Sully chuckled. "You sound like Mom after Chloe Kleiman dumped you in the tenth grade."

"Shut up," Dez said. "Mom was right."

Sully's humour vanished as Dez drew to an abrupt halt in the middle of a busy pathway. Dez's eyes were fixed on something, and his expression and posture were decidedly tense.

Sully tried to track his gaze, but being six inches shorter, he couldn't see whatever Dez did.

"What?" Sully demanded.

"A lady over there. She's staring at you."

Sully tried again. This time, a break in the crowd allowed him to spot what had Dez so nervous. It wasn't just any lady. The woman, standing in front of one of the festival tents, wore a long headscarf, large glasses with thick lenses, loads of makeup and a long, flowing robe.

Then Sully noted the large sign mounted above the tent flap. *Madame Olga: Clairvoyant.*

Sully's eyes locked with hers. A second later, she lifted her right hand and twitched a finger slowly in his direction.

Come here.

"She probably wants to scam you into a reading," Dez said. His tone, however, suggested he wasn't sold on that suggestion.

Sully broke eye contact with Olga to peer at Dez. "I don't know, man. There's something about her. I can't explain it, but I think we need to talk to her."

Dez hung his head. "Oh boy."

"Hey," Sully said. "You're the one who said something about two psychics being better than one. How much better would it be if we could make it three?"

Dez gave his head a shake. "Whatever, dude. Your call. Let's go see what she wants."

Sully returned his gaze to where Olga had been. She was gone.

Plucking at Dez's sleeve, Sully started toward Olga's tent.

CHAPTER 16

STILL NO SIGN of Madame Olga as Sully and Dez approached the tent. Sully would have questioned whether she was a ghost had Dez not noticed her first.

"She moves fast," Dez observed. Sully caught a note of nervousness in his voice. Not surprising. Dez had never been a fan of fairground psychics.

Sully wasn't entirely sold on many either. There were a few gems, but most, he'd found, were in it for the money and had no true ability to back their claims. Sully had wound up visiting several earlier in his life, back when he was trying to come to terms with his own gifts and was searching for guidance. He'd emerged with nothing but a sense of being more alone than ever in the things he saw and experienced. It wasn't until later on he'd started meeting true psychics and realized he wasn't the freak he'd considered himself during his youth.

He didn't know yet whether Madame Olga was the genuine article or not. Whatever she was or wasn't, he was about to find out.

Unlike the other vendors, no line of people stood outside Madame Olga's tent. The reason became clear as Sully and Dez drew near enough to spot a sign hanging on the closed front flap, proclaiming she would return in half an hour.

"There you go," Dez said. "Let's come back later."

"Please, come inside," came a low voice from the opposite side of the canvas.

Sully peered at Dez from below raised eyebrows and shrugged. Dez frowned.

As he stepped toward the tent, Sully spotted the flap lifting as an apparent invitation to enter. Behind it stood the figure of Madame Olga herself, cast substantially in shadow.

She stepped away as they ducked through the entrance. "This way, gentlemen."

Madame Olga turned before Sully could manage a good look at her. She had a slight stoop and she shuffled as she walked. Either she'd developed a problem with her bones or joints, or she was putting on one hell of an act.

The tent was dimmer than it should have been, even with the clouds and off-and-on drizzle outside. The reason became clear as Sully scanned the walls to find them covered completely in black drapery. Various occult symbols had been painted on the fabric, although pride of place went to a large chart listing Madame Olga's services and associated prices.

With Olga's back turned, Dez took the opportunity to point out the price attached to the full package: a one-hour reading involving tarot, palmistry and spirit guide communication.

Two-hundred and fifty dollars.

Dez jutted his chin toward the price. Sully read the turn of his thoughts easily enough.

Not a bad side gig should you ever want to rake in some extra cash, Sully.

Sully shook his head at him, then returned his attention to Madame Olga as she pushed through a gap between two heavy curtains. The tent had been divided into two sections: an antechamber of sorts and what was clearly her inner sanctum—the place where she did her readings.

Sully had half-expected a crystal ball. Thankfully, no such orb stood on the round table at the dim room's centre, but it was perhaps only because the table was already cluttered with other things. Three separate tarot decks, a handful of crystals and an ornate box took up much of the space on her side, leaving the other open presumably for the card layouts or whatever else she did.

Sully was surprised by one detail in particular: the reading space was quiet. Really quiet. Despite the flurry of activity outside, the sounds filtering through seemed muted and far-off. Whatever fabric she'd used inside seemed to be doing the trick, as did some quiet new age music that was coming from somewhere inside.

At last, Madame Olga turned, one arm sweeping dramatically toward two wooden chairs on Sully and Dez's side of the table. She waited until they were seated before lowering herself gingerly into a slightly plushier chair.

Madame Olga shifted a little, then folded her fingers atop the table. Her joints there showed no signs of the problems she seemed to be experiencing elsewhere, no knots or swollen areas that Sully could make out. Then again, she had so many big rings, it was hard to tell. Her fingers were topped with long, dark purple fingernails, the tips more pointed than rounded. Sully was pretty sure she could put out an eye if she wished to.

He felt her eyes on him and shifted his gaze from her hands to her face. Sure enough, eyes made smaller by the thickness of her lenses stared back at him. It was difficult to guess at her age, the dim lighting and the large amount of makeup she wore rendering it difficult, but Sully thought it likely she was over sixty.

"You're Sullivan Gray," she said.

Sully tried to keep his surprise hidden, but he didn't think he'd managed it. "Uh … yeah. How'd you know?"

"I saw you yesterday, here at the park. I hoped you'd be back."

Not exactly an answer.

Dez provided one of his own. "Sully was all over the news a little while back. You probably saw him there."

The small eyes flicked to Dez as if seeing him for the first time. "And you're Desmond Braddock."

If Dez was disquieted by the recognition, he wasn't showing it. "His brother, yeah."

She tilted her head as she regarded him. "You're protective of him."

Dez allowed his posture to provide his response as he crossed thick arms across his chest.

"That's good," she said. "Everyone should have someone to look out for them." Her eyes returned to Sully's. "Especially those who are different. Those like us." She leaned forward, her chair creaking beneath her as she did. "Those who have crossed true evil."

Sully stared back at her, transfixed. He still wasn't convinced she was on the level, but there was definitely something about her drawing him in. Psychic or not, she'd seen things, experienced them. And she carried that darkness with her.

Dez cleared his throat loudly, breaking the short-lived spell. "Evil? I hate to ask, but what are you talking about?"

"You're here with a purpose. Given the time of year, it doesn't take a particularly gifted psychic to make an accurate guess."

No sense beating around the bush. "Headless Henry," Sully said. "Honestly, it wasn't our intention to get mixed up in this whole thing when we came here. It kind of landed in our laps."

One long fingernail lifted into the air next to Madame Olga's head. "For a reason. You have a gift, and your gift led you here." Another shift, another creak. "Your brother is right. I'm a news junkie. I do recall you from the news. To be perfectly honest, I was rather obsessed with your story. I know you see the dead. Is there anything else you can do?"

"Well, he definitely can't juggle," Dez grumbled.

Sully gave him a light kick beneath the table. Dez was making it very clear he didn't like or trust Madame Olga, but his rudeness was uncharacteristic. The woman wasn't being unpleasant, after all.

Sully offered her an apologetic smile followed by an honest answer. "I do see the dead, although it's really only specific ones. Simply put, people who've died by homicide. I can sense other spirits, but I wasn't given the ability to see or communicate with them.

For some reason, I can't hear ghosts, but they can communicate with me by touch. I see the things they want me to see—and sometimes things they don't want me to. And I've learned to control spirits where necessary—sort of like a reverse possession."

The small eyes had grown larger with the explanation. "That's incredible. Truly incredible. Do you see anyone here now?"

Sully shook his head. "No. But I do get the sense we're not alone."

Madame Olga appeared curious. "Any idea who might be here with us?"

"No. As I mentioned, I really only see the ones who've died by homicide."

She nodded. "Fair enough. For what it's worth, I sense them too."

Great. That would thrill Dez to pieces.

Madame Olga readjusted herself again, causing another squeak of her chair. Sully debated suggesting she find herself a new seat before this one collapsed.

"I suppose a beheaded soul counts as a homicide," she said.

There it was. "Yes," Sully replied. "I'd imagine it does."

The small eyes narrowed. "And have you seen him?"

"Maybe. I'm not sure what I saw."

"You do know though. I can see it in you. You've seen him. And you have only to decide now what to do about it."

Sully's turn to search out a more comfortable position. "I figured out a long time ago the reason for my abilities is to help people. This spirit is threatening people, maybe even killing them. If I can stop it, I need to try."

Olga straightened as much as her back would allow, her eyes never leaving his. "Yes, you do," she said. "And I intend to help you do it."

This was unexpected. Unexpected and unwanted. As much as an added psychic might be of assistance, Madame Olga clearly wasn't in the best physical condition. The last place Sully wanted her was deep in haunted woods—especially if they needed to move fast.

And he certainly didn't want either himself or Dez bogged down having to carry her. Raiya was seventy, but she was in good shape. Sully wasn't concerned about her holding her own or being able to move fast if need be. The same likely couldn't be said about Madame Olga.

Sully searched for a good answer but came up empty. "Uhh …."

Dez did a little better. "No offence, ma'am, but Sully and I usually work alone."

"You're not alone. You were with a friend. A fellow psychic, if I'm not mistaken. Well, I can tell you something as strong as this spirit will require all the power you can muster. Yours alone won't be enough. You need my help."

Sully tried again. "Madame Olga—"

"Olga, please."

Sully corrected himself. "Olga, it isn't that we don't appreciate it. We do, really. But the woods are pretty rough, and—"

"I know. I've been there. Which is exactly why you need my help." Her eyes flicked from Sully to Dez and back again. "You're not merely searching for a spirit. You need to find the source of his power. The Holy Oak."

Sully couldn't resist exchanging a glance with Dez. "Yeah, actually. Are you saying you know where it is?"

"I do."

A thud as Sully's heart pumped against his ribs. "Can you tell us how to find it?"

"No, I can't." Olga's lips turned up into a smile. "But I can show you."

CHAPTER 17

Olga had to stay at the park until at least five—though she warned them she might need to put in a little additional time if she found herself with a long line of potential clients.

As far as Dez was concerned, the longer the line the better if it meant avoiding Olga entirely.

"What's wrong?" Sully asked him as they made their way from the tent, leaving Olga to a waiting trio of customers.

Dez had an answer at the ready. "I don't like her."

"I noticed. What's the problem?"

A shrug. "Don't know. Just don't like her."

Sully sighed. "Is that the best you can come up with?"

Dez stopped in place, forcing Sully to as well. "Look, you've got a killer sixth sense. Anyone who knows you has to agree with that. Well, in my own way, I've got one too. You read paranormal energy. I read people energy."

Sully scanned the ground. "I know that. I wasn't doubting you. Just asking."

Dez passed a hand over his face. "Look, I can't explain it yet. At this point, it's just a feeling I've got. I don't trust her. There's something off. When I figure out what, you'll be the first to know."

Sully lifted his head to meet Dez's eye. "So what do you want to do?"

Dez quirked up one side of his mouth. "Get into the SUV and drive us the hell back to KR."

Sully met the smile with his own. "Aside from that."

"Good question." Dez pivoted back toward the pathway and the busy festival, tugging at Sully's sleeve to get him moving next to him. "Right now, let's grab a snack. After that, we can have another look for Cal. If we can get him to show us how to find the tree this afternoon, we'll have a good excuse to avoid meeting with Olga later."

Sully laughed. "How'd I know food would factor into your plans somewhere?"

AN HOUR LATER, Dez was pleasantly full of food but otherwise unsatisfied. He'd had no problem locating a food cart with one of the best burgers he'd ever eaten; finding Cal was another story—one without a similarly satisfactory ending.

Cal hadn't responded to Dez and Sully's request to his employee to give them a call. Maybe he was ignoring them, but Dez thought it far more likely he simply hadn't checked in and the guy working the shop today hadn't bothered to contact him.

"Maybe we should swing by the shop again," Dez suggested as he and Sully headed for the park exit. "If the doofus working there today hasn't tried to reach Cal, we can light a fire under his ass."

"Something tells me you mean that literally," Sully said.

Dez ignored him. They had to pass close to the clothing store on the way back to the SUV anyway; seemed a shame to waste a perfectly good opportunity to stop in.

The same guy was working when Dez and Sully stopped back in, although it took a moment to find him. Busy as he was rehanging a pile of clothing near the fitting room, he barely cast them a glance.

"Haven't been able to reach him," the man said as he buttoned up a shirt.

"How long ago did you try?" Dez asked.

The guy shot him a glare. "I didn't check the clock, okay? It's been busy. Loads of people stop in during the Halloween festival, and as you can see, some of them aren't the neatest clientele in existence."

He seemed to think better of his snappish retort a second or two later—possibly because Dez's own glare was more dangerous.

"Look," the guy said. "I called him a few minutes after you left. I left him a message with your contact deets. Best I can do."

Dez supposed it was—at least barring providing them with an address. "Is it like him to not return a call?"

"It's his day off, dude. On my days off, I do my utmost to avoid answering calls from work."

Dez couldn't blame him. If he had the choice, Dez might ignore a full third of Lachlan's calls. "Okay, thanks for trying."

"Sorry for adding another thing to your day," Sully added. "But it's important—to Cal as well as us."

This time, the employee gave a conciliatory nod. "I'll try him again, all right? I'll text you guys either way."

Thanking him, Dez and Sully left the store.

"Maybe we should try Lachlan," Dez said. "He might be able to work a source and get us an address for Cal."

Sully stuffed his hands in his pockets. "Let's leave it for now, all right? If we need additional information later on, and we're getting nowhere on our own, we'll call him."

Dez saw the wisdom there. While they'd been entertaining the idea, the reality of calling Lachlan in on a job usually meant more than a little grumbling, and that always left Dez grumbling as a result.

"Maybe we can find someone else in or around town who can help us track him down," Dez said. "I'd suggest Rebecca, except I can imagine how well that'd go over."

"How about Parker at the front desk? I mean, that's assuming he's been in the area a long time, but if he has, he's of a similar age to Rebecca and Cal, right? He might be willing to point us in the right direction."

"Suits me fine," Dez said. "Anything that doesn't entail dealing with Rebecca or Olga sounds like a good idea to me."

TIME WAS TICKING. If they didn't locate Cal by the end of the afternoon, they'd be stuck using Olga for directions to the tree from hell.

Of course, finding Cal would become irrelevant if it turned out he didn't know where to find the tree, but Dez decided they'd cross that bridge if and when they needed to.

For now, they would focus on Parker, and thankfully, he was right where they hoped he'd be—behind the Whispering Winds Resort front desk. Doubly great was that he told them he had indeed lived in the area his whole life.

"Cal Holdfast?" Parker said upon Dez's asking about him. "Sure, I know him. I lived in town many years, and it's a small community. Why do you want to find him?"

One thing about small towns Dez hated as an investigator: residents were rarely willing to answer questions without asking some of their own. Many distrusted strangers, and few wanted to be the one to share inside information with one. Then there was the coffee-row crowd who were only willing to trade information if they gleaned a little of their own.

Parker didn't strike Dez as the coffee row sort, so he decided he was more likely the circle-the-wagons type. Dez could lie, but lies had a way of catching up—particularly during a fast-moving investigation. Better they share enough truth to keep them in Parker's good books should they need his help again.

"Sully and I stopped in at his clothing store earlier today," Dez told him. "We got to talking about his brother." Time to go for some sympathy. "I had a similar experience as a kid with losing my own brother. Sully and I wanted to check in on him, only the guy working at the store today can't reach him. Since you're from here, is there any chance you can locate him for us?"

"I can give him a call."

When Parker reached for a phone book, Dez halted him. "He's not listed. We tried that route already."

"Oh, of course. Plenty of people are unlisted these days. Heck, I do the same thing." He checked his watch. "Tell you what though. I'm due for a lunch break in a few minutes. I can make the drive into town and see if Cal's at home. You can hop in with me if you like."

Dez liked.

CHAPTER 18

Cal Holdfast lived in a large two-storey house on a leafy street filled with idyllic homes straight out of a magazine.

Dez was far from an architectural expert, but he knew quality when he saw it. Eva adored this style of house enough that they'd toured a few when they were searching for a family residence. All had been out of their price range, but Eva held out hope they'd get there one day.

"My wife would kill for a house like this," Dez told Parker as the three of them climbed out of his car.

"It's a lovely part of town," Parker said. "Not the absolute oldest standing residences in Holy Oak but not far from it. This property has housed the Holdfast family since its construction in the nineteen-thirties."

Dez studied the facade—big yellow door, a sweeping veranda and intricately carved trim along the eaves. Mostly though, his eyes scanned the large windows, locking onto each in a likely pointless search for something within them. "Cal grew up here then?"

"He did. His parents inherited it from Cal's grandfather. Cal, in turn, inherited it from his folks."

"So was Cary living here when he died?"

"Yes, that's right."

Dez's gaze switched to Sully, wondering what, if anything, he saw. Sully answered the unspoken question with a head shake at Dez. Nope. Nothing.

Dez held a relieved sigh in check.

With Parker in the lead, they made their way to the front door. En route, they passed by a long driveway at the end of which stood a single-car garage. Nothing was parked in the drive, although it was possible the garage was currently being used.

"He usually leaves his car out until wintertime," Parker said as though sensing the turn of Dez's thoughts."I don't think he's home, but let's check anyway."

Parker pressed a doorbell to the right of the entry, then stood back and watched the door expectantly. No one came. While Parker gave it a second attempt, Dez walked along the veranda until he stood in front of a big bay window. Risking the derision of nosy neighbours, Dez cupped his hands against the window and pressed his face between them, granting him a partial view inside. No sign of anyone from this vantage point.

Parker was having no luck either. Stepping back from the door, he met Dez's eye. "Probably not home. I'll check the backyard and the garage. Wait here."

With Parker on the move, Dez turned to Sully, whispering his question to avoid Parker's overhearing. "You getting anything?"

Another shake of the head. "Nothing—at least not the kind I can sense."

Which meant if Cary Holdfast had become earthbound after death, he hadn't made his way home.

"Guess that's a good thing in a way," Dez said. "Still, I'd love to find Cal."

"Me too," Sully said.

His tone got Dez's attention. "What's going on?"

Sully pinched at his lower lip for a moment. "I don't know. Just a feeling. Something's off."

A couple of minutes passed before Parker returned, shaking his head as he rounded the corner from the driveway.

"No one seems to be home," he said.

"Anywhere else we might try to find him?" Dez asked.

Parker stared up at the house. "Oh boy, I don't know. Right now, everyone always seems to be down at the park. Cal volunteers a lot on his days off. He mans people's booths for them sometimes at various events, when they need someone to pick up a shift here or there."

"We were just at the park," Sully said. "Unless we missed seeing something, he wasn't there."

Parker scratched his head. "Huh. Well, there's a puzzler. He's a bit of a homebody when he's not working. Could be he had some errands to run, I suppose."

"How about family?" Dez asked. "Wife? Kids? Grandkids? Someone must know where he is."

"He never married. No children or grandchildren."

"Neighbours?" Sully suggested. "Maybe someone saw him go out today."

"We could ask."

They did, although they left the asking to Parker. Far more likely residents of a small town would be more comfortable providing information to a fellow local.

In this regard, they were more successful. They had only to go next door to find their answer—or at least the start of one.

"He went out shortly before eleven," said the elderly lady who came to the door. "I recall the time because I was about to start watching my usual game show."

"He took his car?" Dez asked.

The lady peered at him through narrowed eyes. "Who are you?"

"My name's Dez Braddock, ma'am. My brother, Sully, and I met Cal yesterday and had promised to provide him with some information about something we discussed. We're from out of town, so we need to catch him before we leave again."

"I can see you're from out of town. I know everyone around here. Festival always brings in strangers." She didn't seem pleased about this fact. Dez suspected she'd be less pleased without the festival given its significant role in the town's continued financial success and therefore its survival.

Parker stepped in again, perhaps sensing this conversation wasn't headed in the right direction. "Sorry to be a pest, Doris, but I wonder if you happen to know where he was off to."

It said something for Parker's friendly demeanour that Doris responded with an amused smile rather than a snappish tone when she shook her finger and said, "Well, now, Parker, you must know I'm not Calvin's keeper. I can't rightly say where he's gone to."

"Fair enough, Doris, thank you. If you happen to see him, could you—"

"He was wearing his hiking boots, mind you. And he was carrying a shovel."

Dez glanced at Sully. Sully peered back, a question in his gaze.

Parker, to his continued credit, asked it for them. "A shovel?"

"Used to go out like that all the time years back. Can't say I've seen him do as such since …" She trailed off, but the darkening of her expression told Dez the reason for her unfinished statement was the presence of a specific memory rather than a search for the right one.

Dez took a chance and finished it for her. "Since his brother died?"

Doris's head snapped toward him. "What do you know of that?"

Parker offered a disarming chuckle. "Well, honestly, Doris, everyone knows about it—at least if they bother to do a scan of newspaper archives."

The lady wasn't done, however. Pointing a finger in the direction of Dez's midsection, she snapped, "It was a terrible time for the Holdfast family. A terrible time for the entire community. I don't agree with all this making light of it these days. Most around here are too young to have lived through those days. Not me though. I remember them. There was no joking about Headless Henry back then."

"Did people blame the ghost?" Sully asked.

"Of course not. The girl did it. Everyone knows that. But Cary

Holdfast's death was a tragedy whichever way you look at it. Nowadays, I hear there are ghost chasers traipsing through those woods at Halloween, treating Cary's death like a cheap form of entertainment. It's wrong, I tell you."

"I agree with you," Sully said. "And it's not why we're here. To be honest, I came to the area to look for a place to get married next year. We got to exploring the town, and we met Cal. My brother and I don't think there's anything entertaining about murder. We're just concerned about Cal, that's all."

Doris was silent a long moment as she fixed Sully with an appraising stare. "Yes, well … I suppose I can be a little bearish at times. Hard not to be when your hometown gets invaded every Halloween."

"I can appreciate that," Sully said. "Cal told us he used to go out in the woods years back to look for … uh, well, you know."

The wrinkling of Doris's nose told Dez she did know. "Yes."

"Does he ever talk to you about it?"

"He doesn't talk to anyone about it, as far as I know. I'm surprised he talked to you."

"Do you know much about the woods?" Dez asked. "Where he might have gone if he's got it in his head to start looking again?"

Doris canted her head. "You mentioned a wedding. I'd imagine you're taking a look at Whispering Winds."

"They are," Parker said. "It's how I got to know them. They're guests."

"Then they're already a step ahead in locating Cal. Whispering Winds Resort's property sits right on top of the spot where Cary died. If Cal's truly back on his hunt, you'll find him there."

CHAPTER 19

All roads, it seemed, led to Whispering Winds.

All but one. To Sully, it felt increasingly likely he'd shortly be back on the hunt for a spot to get married. No way he was coming back to this place once they'd put this job to bed.

"You know, I can't think why it didn't dawn on me before," Dez said once they arrived back in their room. "Probably because I've been freaked out this whole time about some head-lopping ghost stalking the woods just across the golf green."

Sully took a stab at it as he sat on the edge of his bed. "You're thinking about the fact Rebecca helped to build a resort at the approximate spot where her high school boyfriend was beheaded."

Dez lifted a brow before disappearing into the bathroom and shutting the door. "Did it just occur to you too?" he called from within.

"Well, we already knew that."

"Sure, we did. We just hadn't discussed how weird it is—especially since she's so determined to avoid talking about it."

Sully slumped forward, allowing his head to bow and his neck and upper back to feel the stretch. All the time they'd spent on their feet combined with a lack of sleep had left him feeling stiff and tired. He didn't have the time to be stiff or tired.

"Yeah, you're right," he called to Dez. "It does seem weird. Or maybe it isn't. She's money- and success-driven, remember? She'd have wanted the best location for her new business at the cheapest rate. I'll take an educated guess here and say property connected with a super-gruesome murder would come at a discount."

A flush, the sound of the sink running and Dez re-emerged, wrinkling his nose as he appeared. "Ugh, yeah. Add that to the legend surrounding Headless Henry, and you've got a situation where someone might pay a buyer to take it."

"These days, there would be a fair few people who'd line up to purchase something like this. Look how much the town relies on the legend to bring in tourists. Think how much a single business could rake in if it was located in a spot where they could offer ghost walks."

Dez uttered a dry laugh as he made for the TV stand and picked up the remote. "Right. I can totally imagine that tour group. At least some of the time, you'd come back with one less tourist."

Sully shrugged. "We don't know anything for sure. I mean, we know there's something dark in those woods, and I'm pretty sure it's nasty enough to be totally cool with taking lives. I'm just not sure how it goes about it."

Dez cast him a side-eye before dropping heavily onto his own bed and lifting the remote to click on the TV.

"Don't get comfortable," Sully warned him. "We should check in on Raiya. After that, we'll have to start thinking about meeting Olga. She said she'd come out after her shift."

Dez heaved a sigh and dropped his head dramatically into his hands. "Oh, good lord. I'd actually forgotten."

"We need to look for Cal," Sully said. "He's probably fine—or at least he will be as long as he heads home before dark. Either way, if we're in the woods anyway, we can watch for him."

"Make sure your phone's charged up before we go," Dez said. "With luck, Cal will see the note we left taped to his door and give one of us a call." He straightened and clicked off the television without so much as watching the guide. "Man, that's one phone call I'd love to get right now."

"Me too," Sully said.

He checked his phone screen. No missed calls, and his battery was still doing pretty well. Even so, it paid to be extra careful when it came to ghost energy and battery drainage, so he heeded Dez's advice and plugged in.

"Tell you what," Sully said. "Let's sneak in a quick nap. Part of me definitely wants to head out there now and start searching, but the logical part knows that's a bad plan. I'd rather I'm at full steam when it comes time to deal with this ghost."

Dez scooted backward and stretched out, clearly fine with this new plan. "*I'd* rather you're at full steam when it comes time to deal with this ghost. And speaking of, I'll need to eat before we head out."

Sully shook his head. "Of course, you will. That's you at full steam."

BY HIS ESTIMATION, Sully managed about an hour of rest—not a proper deep sleep, but after last night, anything was welcome.

Dez didn't appear to have fared much better when he levered himself off the bed.

"Eat?" was all he said.

Sully rolled his eyes. "Sure. Let's check with Raiya if she wants to join us though."

She did. Unfortunately, the Raiya who joined them in the restaurant was a far less vibrant one than the person Sully had come to know.

"Don't take this the wrong way," Sully said while they waited for their food. "But you don't look well."

"I don't even have a smart comeback for you," she said. "I don't feel particularly well. I'm drained."

"Maybe you should stay behind. Dez and I can check things out ourselves."

Dez pivoted toward Sully, brows lifting. "Oh, we can, can we?"

Sully ignored him, continuing to address Raiya. "If we need you, we can come back and get you."

She shook her head. "You will need me. Trust me, if I'm feeling the way I am, it's for a reason. The energy is so powerful around here, it's draining the life out of me. When it comes to a fight, you'll need my help. Little good I'll be sitting here while you're putting yourselves at risk."

Dez shifted a stare fully at Raiya. "What kind of risk, exactly?"

"You know the risk, my boy. The same kind others have suffered already."

The way Dez twisted his head left and right and pulled at his collar showed he'd most definitely gotten the point.

"We might have some other help on the way," Sully said. "There's a woman working at the festival who goes by Madame Olga. She called us over while we were at the park today looking for Cal. She said she can show us where to find this Holy Oak tree."

Raiya tilted her head as she peered at Sully. "Madame Olga?"

"She reads tarot and palms. Does some other stuff besides."

"And what was your impression of her?"

Dez snorted. "She's a crank."

Raiya eyed him. "You sound certain."

"I don't trust her, put it that way."

"Why?"

"It's a feeling, same as I told Sully. I can't explain it better than that."

Sully shrugged. "I don't know about her either, but I trust Dez's opinion. If he says something's off about her, I've got to go with it."

Raiya nodded. "So what you're telling me is she isn't actually likely to be of much help."

"She might not be a real gifted psychic or anything, but there's something about her. Some people give off a certain energy. Add that to the fact she works with stuff many view as occult, and it might be she's capable of attracting certain types of spirit energy."

Dez's head snapped toward him. "Hang on. You didn't say anything about this before. You want to use her as bait now?"

"Not bait. Not exactly. I do know one thing though: loads of people visiting for the festival are bound to want to crawl through the woods on a hunt for Henry. I'd rather find him myself before someone else does. I can't help thinking our chances are better with someone like Olga around. Even better when combined with people like me and Raiya. The more we can act like a beacon for this entity, the more likely others come out unharmed."

"And what about us? I'd like to come out unharmed too."

Sully patted Dez on the arm. "You will. I'll make sure of it."

"I've heard that promise before."

They stopped talking as their food arrived, focusing instead on eating and watching their fellow diners. In glancing over the crowd, Sully found himself wondering how many of them might wind up tonight somewhere within the woods, searching for a ghost they'd be luckier not to find. If Sully's own luck held, he wouldn't happen upon any of these people later tonight, headless or otherwise.

Wisps of cloud blew across the darkening sky as Sully, Dez and Raiya crossed the green toward the section of woods they'd entered last night. Sully had maintained last night's dropped pin on his map app, making it easier to start the search somewhere they'd already seen some action. This time, he'd seen no spectral person standing along the treed border. Yet there was an undeniable feeling upon entering the woods that they were being watched.

"We're not alone," Raiya whispered. "I can't pinpoint a location. It's as though it's all around us."

"Maybe that explains the problem I've been having in tracking this ghost. If he's figured out how to use energy from the forest itself, it'll make it hard to pin him down."

"Let's focus on searching for this tree," Raiya suggested. "It's more than likely a focal point in these woods. Could be it acts as an anchor for him as well."

Dez paused to clumsily withdraw his big flashlight from the inner pocket of his coat. Tonight he'd made sure to grab it out of the SUV. "Gotta admit," he said, "I'm kind of surprised Olga didn't show."

"She said she might end up working late," Sully reminded him. "I gave her my cell number. If she gets here later, she can give me a call."

Dez clicked the power button on his flashlight, got nothing and then clicked it again after slapping the side. A bright beam broke from the device's business end. "Man, this is like day and night compared to cellphone flashlights. Anyway, getting back to Olga, I kind of thought you'd have tried calling her to check in."

Sully toyed with his phone until he had his own, smaller flashlight beam to add to Dez's larger one. "Are you kidding? After everything you said, I kind of figured you'd throttle me if I tried." He redirected his gaze to meet Dez's eye. "Seriously, though, if you don't trust her, I've got no reason to either. I won't involve her if I don't have to."

Dez smiled. "Appreciate it, bro." He checked his own phone screen now, frowning as he did. "Damn. I really hoped Cal would have called one of us by now. I don't know, man. I'm getting a really, really bad feeling."

Sully nodded. "Hate to say it, but so am I."

Raiya sighed. "And I hate to say it, but I've got to add my agreement to yours. Something's very off in these woods—even more so than last night. It feels … stronger. Like it's fed."

Dez played his beam from the forest edge into the shadowy depths within. "Fed?"

Raiya poked a finger into his tricep. "Don't make me spell it out for you, Desmond."

Dez blinked at her. "Oh God. Don't say it. Cal?"

"I don't know. Maybe it's only that it's nearer to Halloween so this entity's strength is growing. But somehow, I don't think that's totally it. There's something more to this. The energy's changed, like something's been added to what was already here. I don't know how to explain it better than that."

Sully scanned what he could see of the darkening woods, watching for human-shaped shadows or unusual lights that would indicate the presence of a ghost. So far, he saw nothing, but that didn't mean something wasn't here.

"Hold on," he said. "If your read is right, and Headless Henry's taken another life, won't that mean he'll be dormant for another year? We'll have missed our chance."

"Let's hope we haven't," Raiya said. "For everyone's sake."

CHAPTER 20

THE SENSE of a presence rose in Sully from a whisper to a shriek the farther they pressed into the woods. Periodically, he or Raiya would utter a warning, but so far, nothing had resulted besides the continued feeling of being observed.

Stalked.

Sully hated every minute.

Unsurprisingly, Dez finally had enough and leaned in, whispering to Sully, "Do you have any idea yet where this guy is?"

Sully didn't need to ask to know Dez was referring not to Cal but to Headless Henry.

Raiya proved she'd overheard when she answered for Sully. "He's everywhere. It's as though this energy is completely interwoven with these woods."

"That can't be good," Dez muttered.

It wasn't. Because it meant not only that they couldn't pinpoint the ghost, but it had the unending ability to pinpoint theirs.

"If that's definitely the case, I don't know how I'll be able to control it," Sully said. "I have to be able to find the outer edges of spirit energy to do what I do. If this ghost has infected the entire woods, I can't do it."

"Not unless it centres its energy and manifests in that moment,"

Raiya said. "We've seen it happen. I think it'll need to do so in order to harm someone."

"And if it already did, then what? What if we're too late?"

It was Dez who provided a potential answer. "Maybe we don't need to wait it out. We've tangled with ghosts plenty of times who draw power from specific places, people or things. So if we can't battle the ghost directly, we locate the source of its power and destroy that instead."

Raiya spoke through a smile. "The Holy Oak."

Sully answered her grin with his own. "You offering up lumberjack services, Dez?"

"Hey, I would have been fine with it had we done what I wanted in the first place and come back in here during the day. Instead, here we are again at sunset, tripping over roots and trying not to get our heads cut off."

A flash of movement ahead had Sully tensing and gripping Dez's arm to warn him. He didn't bother saying anything to Raiya; without asking, he knew she'd seen or sensed it too.

"Heads up," she said.

A shadow darted left to right, too fast and silent to track. This was no animal, and it most definitely wasn't human either. At least not a living one.

More rapid movement, right to left now. This time, though, Sully saw something beyond the shadow. He saw colour.

Blue. Denim blue.

"I don't think this is Henry," he said.

Raiya provided the conclusion. "Cary."

The spirit rushed toward them so fast, Sully flinched, his abrupt movement drawing a sharp intake of breath from Dez.

Not just denim now. Sully saw red. The Rolling Stones logo. And blood. A lot of blood.

He didn't wait for the ghost to still. No point when he wasn't. Already, Cary Holdfast was on the move again, backward now.

"Cary," Sully said. "We're here to help. We're trying to find Cal. Can you show us where he is?"

Right to left. Left to right. Back and forth. Never for a second did Cary's ghost stop jerking around like a pinball.

"Sully?" Dez said.

"He's really unsettled," Sully said. "I don't think I'll get him to stop long enough to talk to me."

"Question: how does a ghost with no head actually talk?"

Yes, that was a question, all right. A good one. Maybe that was why Cary was whipping around all over the place, kind of like a chicken after being butchered. Sully, however, suspected the answer was something else.

Again, Raiya voiced Sully's thoughts. "He's terrified. I feel it. There's an incredible amount of fear in the air."

"Do you see him?" Sully asked.

She shook her head. "No, but I can pinpoint the energy nonetheless. It feels significantly different from the other energy."

It certainly did. As angry as Sully wanted to be at Cary for being such a jerk to Raiya all those years back, all of that faded the more he watched the ghost darting around, terror radiating from his core. More than fifty years had passed since the night Cary was killed. If he'd existed like this all that time, he'd more than paid for his awful behaviour.

"Cary, please," Sully said. "If you can hear me—"

"He's got no ears either, Sull," Dez cut in.

Sully tried again. "If you know I'm here, I need you to stop for a second, okay? I'm trying to find your brother. Can you help me?"

This was, of course, dependent on whether Cary had noticed Cal in here and if he even recognized him all these years later. Cal had been a kid the last time Cary had seen him; modern-day Cal would appear nothing like the boy he'd once been.

Sully had crossed over a lot of ghosts though, plenty of cold cases among them. To a one, they'd always recognized their living family members, even many years later. Some things transcended time and space. Love was one.

Perhaps this, then, explained Cary's sudden pause between two large trees just ahead. Sully was unable to communicate with him like this, but he knew without being told.

Cary knew about Cal. More than that, he was horrifically upset about him. In that moment, Sully got the answer he didn't want.

Cal Holdfast was dead.

"Damn," Sully said. Then to Cary, "We need to find him. Please. Show us where he is, and I'll make sure you're both safe from now on."

He had no way of knowing clearly whether Cary had heard him. Usually, Sully could tell by looking at a ghost's face what impact his words had taken. With Cary, he had no such means of knowing. In any case, Cary didn't react as Sully hoped, back to racing back and forth.

Raiya must have sensed it, stepping to Sully's side and placing a hand on his back. "Let me try."

Her gaze directed in Cary's general direction, she lifted her voice as she addressed him. "Cary, I'm not sure if you remember me. My name is Raiya Everton. Many years ago, we visited these woods together. We were with two other girls: Becca and Louise."

Yes, he remembered. Sully knew Cary remembered because he stopped again, hovering there about twenty feet away, his form squared toward Raiya.

"He's listening," Sully told Raiya.

She gave a tight nod and continued, her tone calming and confident as she spoke to the ghost. "You believed then I was a witch. It was some time before I reached the point of admitting it to others, but as it happens, you were right about me. I can do things. And the young man with me here—Sullivan—he's the strongest psychic I've ever met. When he says he can help, he's not lying. He truly can protect you and your brother. You need to give him a chance."

The ghost drifted closer, arms limp at his sides. Still listening, which was great. More than that, it seemed as though he wanted to make something known himself.

Ordinarily, Sully might have asked him to communicate through touch. Not tonight though, not with Headless Henry out there somewhere. Even if he had already made a kill, the sort of energy bouncing around the woods told Sully the spirit was no less a threat. If anything, it felt stronger. Emboldened.

No time to communicate with Cary or Cal. No way Sully could risk being taken under by a spirit, losing himself to a vision. It would put him out of commission for at least a minute or two—plenty of time for Henry to find them. Sully would need to remain fully alert, fully present.

Sully read Cary's energy, sensed the turn of his thoughts without the need for communication.

"He's sorry," Sully told Raiya. "Obviously, he's upset about what happened to him, but I think he's had plenty of time to consider his actions that night, and he regrets them."

"I know," Raiya said. "I can feel it too." Then, to Cary, "It's okay. You were a kid. It was wrong, but kids do wrong things sometimes. Know that I came to terms with who I am and have used it for good. It was a horrible night for all of us, but in the end, you're the one who suffered the most for it. I'm sorry about that. You didn't deserve any of this. And for what it's worth, I forgive you."

Something akin to a wave of relief washed over Sully as Cary took in Raiya's words and her accompanying forgiveness. Any other time and place, this would be the moment Sully would open a doorway and usher Cary through.

Not now though. Not until they found Cal.

"Help us find your brother," Sully said. "I'll protect you both until I can get you out of here and to a safe place. Permanently."

Cary, it seemed, needed no further sales pitch. He darted away, pausing in the trees ahead long enough to convince Sully he was attempting to lead them.

"Come on," Sully told Dez and Raiya. "He wants us to follow him."

They did, rushing off through the trees, Dez's flashlight beam guiding them. Sully caught Raiya's hand and held on, determined to avoid outpacing and accidentally losing her. He didn't have to worry about Dez so much; between long legs and fear, Dez would be the one to catch up to.

Cary was fast, the sort of fast only those in the spirit world were capable of. Once in a while, as they got briefly snagged up in thicker stands of trees, they lost sight of him. But always he'd find his way back to them, waiting again until they had nearly caught up.

Sully couldn't help but think how fifty years ago Cary had done everything in his power to leave Raiya alone in the dark. Now here he was, relying on her presence to escape his own dark fate. The spirit realm came with a sense of justice all its own.

Sully didn't bother to check the time, but he thought they must have been bushwhacking at least ten minutes when Cary at last stopped moving. Sully and Dez were breathing hard. Poor Raiya was all but wheezing. Sully wondered whether Cary was merely granting them a needed breather.

Until he saw Cal.

He crouched ahead of them in the trees, clothed in much the same outfit Sully had seen him in back at the shop. He was pacing, eyes wild and filled with fear as his mouth gaped as if mid-scream. His hands came up every few seconds to claw at his hair as his gaze snapped this way and that. Searching. Endlessly searching. For what? Cary? Headless Henry?

It wasn't to Cal's posture or attire Sully's attention lingered though. As they drew closer, Sully noticed Cal's neck.

Or rather what was left of his neck.

"What do you see?" Dez asked.

Which, of course, gave Sully the final confirmation. This was definitely Cal not in body but in spirit.

"It's Cal," Sully said.

Dez hung his head. "Oh shit."

It occurred to Sully what Cal might be looking for. His own body. Maybe, depending what more had happened to him after death, perhaps his head.

"I'll go," Sully told Dez. "Stay here with Raiya."

Dez's answer was predictable. "Like hell."

So it was once again all three of them pressed through the trees, scanning the area as they went. In the end, Sully tripped over what he realized was a jean-clothed leg. Tracing it upward to a partially attached head, he quickly put a name to the blood-soaked face. And cursed aloud as he did.

Without a doubt, this was Cal Holdfast.

"Oh hell, no," Dez moaned. A moment later, he was on his phone, dialling in to nine-one-one.

With Dez handling that side of this latest emergency, it left Sully to tend to his own. It—they—stood before him now, both Holdfast brothers, terrified, wounded and traumatized. And somewhere nearby, something dark and dangerous waited.

Sully had no time to waste.

"I'm sorry, Cal," Sully told him. "I didn't mean for this to happen to you."

Cal only shook his head and placed a hand on his brother's shoulder. No, Cal wasn't sorry. After all these years, he hadn't located his brother's missing body part. Instead, he'd found the most important part. His soul.

Cal glanced at Cary, but his gaze darted away just as fast. Unable to look at what had become of his brother. Sully wondered whether Cal had seen Cary's headless remains before his burial. Given his age at the time, Sully doubted it.

Thankfully, there was a way to rectify this.

With no time to waste, Sully focused, opening a doorway to the other side. He couldn't see it the same way he saw the Holdfast brothers, but he knew it was there all the same.

So did they. He knew it when he first felt their surprise, then their relief. Within seconds, Cary's head reappeared, and he took a moment to study the world around him as if seeing it in a new way.

Finally, his gaze settled on his younger brother. If there were ever any question as to whether Cary would recognize this far older version of Cal, it vanished with the grin that broke out on Cary's handsome face. Yes, he recognized Cal all right. Wrapping an arm around Cal's shoulders, Cary turned his attention to Raiya. The smile slipped a little but held on. Not joy now, but gratitude.

"They're ready to cross," Sully told Raiya. "We don't have time to communicate properly, but Cary's looking at you. I think he'd like to thank you for coming to help him."

Cary's nod provided confirmation.

"No need to thank me, Cary," Raiya said. "This is what I do now. I help. I'm only grateful I could see this full circle. Repay me by finding peace and happiness on the other side. And take care of your brother."

Another nod. Cary gave his brother's shoulders a squeeze before both their gazes turned to Sully. In unison, they grinned a nearly identical grin as they gave a wave.

Then they faded away into whatever light awaited them.

Sully felt an intense relief not entirely his own. Once he was certain they were across, he closed the door.

"They're gone," Raiya said. "They're safe now."

"Yes," Sully said.

With the Holdfast brothers crossed over, all the joy of the past couple of minutes vanished too. Now all Sully could feel was darkness and dread.

"They're far safer now than we are," Sully said.

The trees seemed to close in around him—whispering warnings or uttering threats. The crawling sensation of being watched was back in full force, and Sully suspected that in using his ability to open a doorway between the two worlds, he'd created a direct path to himself and his companions.

Whatever darkness haunted these woods was coming.

Movement ahead had his head snapping in that direction. This time, though, it wasn't merely a shadow without a physical presence. This one had snapped a twig.

This was a living human.

Sully spotted a long overcoat and a large hat concealing most of the face. What should have been otherwise identifiable was lost to shadow.

Who it was, Sully couldn't tell. But given their proximity to Cal's corpse, he had to assume they'd played a role in his death—on their own or with paranormal guidance. Either way, Sully needed to see who this was and make sure police had a chance to speak with them.

Easier said than done.

"Hey!" Sully called out. "We need to talk to you!"

The person went ramrod-straight, head swivelling fully toward Sully. If they didn't know they'd been seen a moment ago, they definitely knew now. The moment of panic lasted only seconds. Then the person pivoted in place and fled.

Sully did the only thing he could think to do. He took off after them.

He heard Dez's startled shout from behind. "Sully, stop! *Stop*!"

Sully couldn't stop. He knew only one thing, and it was the need to catch and identify a likely killer—the person who'd taken the life of a man who'd wanted only to bring peace to a long-lost loved one.

A person who might not have been out here tonight but for Sully and Dez's appearance in his store today.

Guilt drove Sully now as much as his sense of justice did. So as the dark figure dashed through the blackening woods, the only choice Sully would allow himself to make was to follow.

CHAPTER 21

SULLY MISSED DEZ'S FLASHLIGHT.

Back to relying purely on his mostly useless phone flashlight, Sully could see little in front of him as he wove a rapid path through the woods.

Dez wasn't following. Dez couldn't follow, not with Raiya to worry about.

Oh boy, was Sully going to catch hell for this later.

But later was later. Right now, he had more pressing concerns to contend with—namely the yet-unidentified figure rushing to escape.

As he ran, the thought flashed through his mind that Cal had suffered a catastrophic neck injury but that his head had remained attached. It wasn't for a lack of trying on the part of the killer. They'd been interrupted before they could finish the job.

The thought gave Sully further impetus to pursue. This was Cal's killer. Had to be. But for Sully, Dez and Raiya showing up, this person would have finished the job and taken Cal's head.

Maybe they'd acted alone. Maybe they'd done it at the psychic urging of an evil spirit. Perhaps it was even a full-on possession. Whatever it was, this person needed stopped. Possessed, influenced or acting alone, they were dangerous. Very dangerous.

So what the hell was Sully planning on doing when he caught

up? Dez was the one trained in defensive tactics thanks to his time with the police. Sully had only been taught a few tricks by Dez and their dad.

Yep, Dez was going to throttle him.

His phone rang, and Raiya's number showed on the screen. It would be Dez except that he was busy on the phone with the nine-one-one operator.

Sully debated not answering, but that would only make this situation worse for him later. Anyway, it was best he be on the line with someone should this whole thing slip seriously sideways.

He answered. "Raiya?"

"What on earth are you doing?" she snapped.

"No choice," he puffed out.

"Don't give me that, boy. You get back here. Catching that person isn't as important as you living through the night."

The crack of a branch up ahead told Sully he was still headed the right direction. "I won't do anything stupid."

"You already have."

"Raiya—"

"Your brother's furious. After everything you've just seen the Holdfasts through, surely you know better than to risk putting yourself and Dez through the same thing."

She had a point. He was tempted to stop and head back, let whoever this was run themselves out. If the police were quick getting here and set up a perimeter in the area, maybe got a plane in the air with heat-sensing equipment, they would catch whoever this was in good time.

The sound of a crash up ahead had Sully thinking otherwise. He drew up short, listening. That had definitely sounded unpleasant, like someone taking a bad fall.

"Hang on," Sully told Raiya.

He listened for additional movement. He heard it, only it wasn't merely the sound of shifting limbs or fabric. It was a pained moan.

A woman's pained moan.

"Stay where you are," Raiya said. "Apparently, Dez set something up on your phones that lets you track each other. We're on our way."

When had Dez done that? Sully guessed it was while he was taking a shower earlier today or during a trip to the bathroom. Just as well. It was the sort of thing they'd talked about doing in the past but had never gotten around to. Pulling up his own map app, Sully indeed spotted two dots on the screen—his own and one marked as "Dez's phone."

It looked like he was going to get his ass kicked sooner rather than later.

Up ahead, a groan transitioned into a scream. Not one of pain but one of terror.

So much for waiting for Dez. Sully ran forward, eyes wide in an instinctive attempt to allow in more light. With only his small beam to guide him, Sully pushed past branches and twists of brambles, nearly twisting his ankle as he came down in an unseen dip in the earth.

Had this been where she'd fallen? He paused again, listening.

Another scream, much closer this time. "Leave me alone! Leave me *alone*!"

He knew that voice.

Carefully, Sully pressed ahead, watching the ground now as much as his surroundings. The earth abruptly fell away ahead—not a cliff by any means, but a steep slope alongside which the ground had slumped away. At the base, Sully saw the coat he'd been chasing. Only this time, he better saw the person wearing it.

Madame Olga. And she wasn't alone.

Looming over her stood a dark, headless figure holding an axe. Silently, it lifted the weapon as if to bring it down against its would-be victim.

"Hey!" Sully yelled.

The ghost paused, axe hanging in the air. Without waiting, Sully focused on the spectre, pushing out against it and sending it backward, away from Olga.

He felt its fury, its hate, its bloodlust. And its attention was now fully on Sully.

Good. Better him than someone else.

"Leave her alone," Sully growled.

The entity started toward him. Sully pushed out again, watching as the entity shot backward under his power.

Raiya wasn't here yet, and the amount of power radiating from the entity was off the charts, but Sully decided he would try to end this before he lost sight of the ghost again. Reaching forward psychically, he began to grasp at the entity.

A burst of lightning-like energy, and the spirit rushed at him, axe raised high. Startled, Sully took an inadvertent step backward. His heel caught on something—that damned dip in the earth—and he fell back on his ass.

Blinking his eyes open, he found himself staring up at the entity. Its axe glistened in the moonlight as the spirit raised it high above its head, ready to swing.

"Sully!" Dez's voice cut the darkness. "Sully!"

The axe stilled. Sully pushed out again, knocking the ghost back. This time, though, it didn't stick around for further battle. Turning to black mist, it drifted off into the night air.

A commotion behind told Sully that Dez and Raiya had found him. Sully was climbing to his feet when Dez, bull-like, charged him, grabbed him by the jacket and slammed him up against the nearest tree.

"What the hell is the matter with you, you idiot?" Dez snapped. "You could have gotten yourself killed!"

"Told you he was angry," Raiya said from behind him.

"I know," Sully said. "It was the only thing I could think to do."

Dez gave him one more shove and released him. "Then you weren't thinking very hard, were you? Moron."

Sully didn't reply. Best not to when Dez was in this state. Instead, he turned his attention to Olga, still lying on the ground at the bottom of the slope. "Are you all right?" he asked.

"Who's that?" Dez asked.

"Olga," Sully told him.

"How the hell'd she end up here?"

Sully had no answer so didn't bother trying for one. With Dez and Raiya next to him, Sully started down to check on Olga who was groaning and clutching her right shin.

"I dropped a pin for police so they can find Cal's body," Dez grumbled as they went. "Once I was told they had it, I pulled yours up and told the operator I was going after you. No point guarding a corpse when I had half a chance at preventing a second one being created. Man, I'd like to bounce you off every tree in this forest."

"Later," Sully said. "Let's make sure Olga's okay. Hopefully, she hasn't broken anything. Getting her out of here is going to be difficult, but I'd like to do it before Henry makes another appearance."

"In that case, so would I," Dez said.

The three of them clambered cautiously down the slope, Dez's flashlight beam illuminating a safer route than the one Olga must have found.

Reaching Olga, Dez stood over her. "Are you armed?"

"What? No, of course not. Why would you ask that?"

"I don't know, maybe because the last place I saw you was five steps away from a guy whose head was halfway removed."

"I didn't do it. I'm a tarot card reader, not a murderer."

Sully finished helping Raiya down the hill and approached Dez and Olga.

"Watch her," Dez said. "I need to make sure she's not carrying a weapon."

Sully kept an eye on her while Dez patted her down. When he finished, he shook his head to indicate he'd come up empty.

"Police are on their way," Dez said. "They'll want to talk to all of us."

Raiya plucked at Sully's sleeve. "Could I speak with you a moment?"

Certain now Dez was in no significant danger from Olga, Sully followed Raiya a few steps away. Her expression read disturbed.

"What's wrong?" he asked her.

"That's the Madame Olga you mentioned?" she said.

Sully nodded. "Yeah. Why?"

"It's not her real name."

Sully chuckled. "You don't say."

"No, I mean, I know who that is."

Sully tilted his head, peering from Raiya to Olga and back again. "Who?"

"It's been a long time, and she's changed her appearance quite a bit, but I know those eyes."

She flicked her gaze back to the woman on the ground. "That's Louise Penske."

CHAPTER 22

DEZ HAD SO MANY QUESTIONS, he didn't know where to start.

The cop part of his brain wondered how much Louise knew about what had happened to Cal. Hell, his thoughts were churning around the likelihood she'd done tonight to one member of the Holdfast family what she'd done to another more than fifty years ago.

History repeating itself.

Dez bit back his questions. Asking them was the responsibility of the responding police. Overstepping would only land him in trouble and, later, in court as a witness. He hated testifying.

Right now, he had other, more pressing concerns—namely getting the hell out of here before Headless Henry made an appearance. But getting out of here was dependent on the state of Louise's health, so Dez focused on that as he knelt next to her.

"Where are you hurt?" he asked.

She sat up a little farther, gritting her teeth as she gripped her lower shin. "My ankle. I don't think I can stand on it. It's either broken or badly sprained."

"Mind if I take a look?" Dez asked.

She shook her head, so Dez carefully pushed up her pant leg to check. Louise's ankle had started to swell, and it was painfully obvious it was indeed either sprained or broken as she suspected.

"Yeah, walking on that's not an option," Dez said.

"Neither is staying here," came Sully's quiet voice.

That had Dez's gaze snapping upward to meet his eye. "Is he close?"

Sully nodded. "He's not right here, but he's close. We need to move."

The police were on their way to the area, taking advantage of a dropped pin Dez had provided them for the location of Cal's body, but he couldn't be sure when they would actually arrive. With a bloodthirsty ghost on the loose, he couldn't take chances. If Sully said they needed to get out of here, Dez intended to get while the getting was good.

As far as Dez could ascertain, while Louise had several cuts and scrapes, she'd suffered no other serious injuries. Dez felt safe in picking her up and carrying her, so with Sully leading and Raiya bringing up the rear, Dez cradled Louise in his arms as they picked their way back through the dense woods.

Dez had intended to keep the conversation to a minimum. Louise had other plans.

"He's dead," she said. "That man is dead."

"Stating the obvious," Dez said.

Perhaps she'd read the twinge of judgment escaping through his tone, because she quickly added, "I didn't do it."

Dez held his tongue, reminding himself any conversation regarding Cal's death would turn him into a key witness.

"I didn't!" she exclaimed.

"All right," Dez said. "I heard you."

"But you don't believe me."

When no one responded—apparently, Sully and Raiya had taken their cues from Dez—Louise leaned up and back to peer past Dez's shoulder. "Do I know you? You look familiar."

Dez didn't know how anyone looked familiar given the lack of light. Louise must have managed a glimpse while they'd been tending to her. They'd had enough light there, after all, for Raiya to put a name to Louise.

"You knew me once," Raiya said. "My name is Raiya Everton. We went to school together for a short time."

The silence that befell Louise spoke volumes. She broke it only after a long moment. "Why are you here?"

"I might ask the same of you."

"You know about him," Louise said. "Don't you?"

'Him' could refer to anyone, but Dez was pretty sure who Louise meant.

"Henry?" Raiya asked. "I know he's still out here, still preying on people. I know he still holds an ungodly amount of power and that he intends to use it to take more lives."

"I didn't hurt that man," Louise said. "If you are what I believe you are, you must know that."

Raiya's turn to fall silent. Dez sensed her thoughts were turning, her powerful senses tuning into whatever universe they poked around in whenever she needed answers.

"If you didn't do it, what were you doing there?" Raiya asked.

"The same thing I'm sure you were doing there. Hoping to lay something to rest."

"I'm not here to lay something to rest. I came to prevent the same thing from happening to someone else. I've failed."

Dez's heart sank, his thoughts trailing back to his and Sully's meeting with Cal. "We all failed. If Sully and I hadn't ended up in his store—if we hadn't got him thinking about Cary and what happened to him—he wouldn't have been out here."

"We can't know that," Sully said. "If it had been you, I wouldn't have given up looking or trying to help you find peace."

An argument Dez couldn't refute.

"Anyway," Sully added, "Cal doesn't blame us. He's at peace now. He's got the answers he needed, and he knows Cary's okay now. They're safe. In the end, that was all he wanted."

Sully's tone belied his words. Attempting to absolve Dez of his guilt wasn't doing much to rid Sully of his own.

"I hear you," Dez said. "But all I wanted was to avoid leaving a trail of bodies behind. Even if Cal was to end up in these woods tonight without any input from us, I wish we could have been there to protect him."

Sully pressed a branch aside, holding it for Dez and Louise. "I know. Believe me, I've had the same thought. He and Cary are at peace, yeah, but I could have given them that without Cal's having to die."

Dez pivoted to hold the branch for Raiya. "Speaking of that dying thing, do you think that's it for Headless Henry this year, then? Is he done until next Halloween?"

"I don't know," Sully said. "I'll tell you one thing I do know though: I could cut the tension in these woods with a knife. If Henry's sated, you wouldn't know it walking in here."

"I have the same feeling," Raiya said. "If he's finished for this year, I'm not detecting it." She cleared her throat. "And that's if he was behind Cal's killing in the first place."

Louise's head snapped in Raiya's direction. "I didn't do it. How many times do I have to say it?"

"At least one more," Dez told her. "The police will have plenty to ask you, especially given your history."

"I resent that," Louise growled.

Dez snorted. "I'm sure Cary had some resentment of his own."

"I know I shouldn't ask," Raiya said. "But are you saying you didn't kill Cary either?"

Louise spoke quickly—perhaps too quickly. "I didn't."

"You were covered in blood, Louise. I was there."

"I don't know how it happened. I don't remember any of it."

"Then how do you know you weren't involved?" Raiya asked.

Louise shifted in Dez's arms. Uncomfortable because of her injury or position, but just as possible the conversation was the cause. "I might not remember the incident, but I know myself. I know I'm not a killer. I told you the truth. I came back here to try to lay some things to rest. I've spent my life going between wanting to recall what really happened and fearing what that could mean.

Maybe I don't want to know the truth. Maybe it'll set me free. All I'm truly certain of is that if I don't find those answers now, it'll be too late."

"Why?" Sully asked.

Louise lifted a hand to rub at her eyes. Wiping at emotion or exhaustion, maybe both. "Because I'm dying."

"Oh no, Louise," Raiya said. "I'm sorry. What is it?"

"Cancer. I had it twice in the past but managed to beat it both times. This time, my oncologist assures me I won't see the same outcome. I've got perhaps one, maybe two good months ahead of me. After that—well, I need to be prepared. It's not just putting my financial affairs in order either. It's this—it's reckoning with my past, with what I might be taking into the next world. If what everyone said about me is true—if I truly did kill Cary—then I need to find a way to make amends before I die. Don't you see? I came to Holy Oak to try to find those answers, thinking perhaps being back in these woods would jog something. If I did indeed recall something I did, I intended to do right by Cary's remaining family. Killing Cal, that would be the exact opposite of what I intended. The last thing I want is to meet my maker with blood on my hands—or, as it may be, more blood."

Dez thought it would have been great if Sully had had the time to ask Cary or Cal to show him what had befallen them. Unfortunately, sometimes a quick crossover was necessary, and this had proven one of those times.

"So do you remember?" Raiya asked Louise. "Being here, has it jogged anything for you?"

A head shake. "No. Everything about Cary's death is a blank. I remember the drive out and being in on Becca and Cary's gag where they were to leave you. As it turned out, Cary and I each suffered a far worse fate for our actions."

"You were never charged though," Dez said.

"No, but I was branded a murderer nonetheless. I was forced to endure all manner of testing and treatments. I was locked away in a psychiatric centre for several months, mentally prodded so often, I began to believe I really had done the things they accused me of. I lost sight of who I was. Then I truly did lose myself. My family turned on me. The grandmother who raised me was targeted by others in town, and she turned on me too in the end. By the time I reached the age of adulthood, I was completely alone, and when I wasn't, I was surrounded by people who believed the worst of me."

Louise rubbed a hand over her face. "I did the only thing I could short of ending my own life. I gave myself a new one. I changed my name, my appearance. I moved away. I changed my entire identity. For years, it was enough—until now. One can only run from oneself for so long. Eventually, those parts you tried to erase catch up. Coming here was my attempt to stop running. I might never know the truth about my possible role in Cary's death, but I know for certain I didn't kill his brother."

And this, too, rang true to Dez. It made sense—far more sense than Louise returning to Holy Oak all these years later and killing a guy who'd been a child the last time she'd seen him.

Of course, this left the obvious question. If Louise hadn't killed Cal or Cary, who had? Which then left the even worse question.

If the killer hadn't been human at all, how much power must Henry have in order to do the deed himself?

And would Sully and Raiya have enough between them to stop him?

CHAPTER 23

So much for avoiding becoming a witness.

Having carried Louise to the edge of the woods where they located a police officer on guard duty, Dez relieved himself of his current burden only to saddle himself with another. With Louise on the way to the hospital in the company of a uniformed officer, that left Dez, Sully and Raiya to answer the necessary questions.

Except those questions would have to wait for someone else to attend. While Holy Oak had a small police detachment to handle run-of-the-mill complaints, major events required the help of specialized units from the city.

"We've got a Major Crimes team responding from Kimotan Rapids," the on-scene sergeant told Dez. "I'm afraid you'll all have to hang tight until they get here."

"Figured as much," Dez grumbled.

He wasn't surprised when he, Sully and Raiya were guided to different spots in the area, near enough for the police to keep an eye on them but far enough the three of them couldn't converse. Until homicide investigators arrived, the local police would need to ensure their witnesses and potential suspects didn't have any additional opportunity to collude. Luckily, none of them had touched the body, nor had they been near enough to have gotten much, if any, blood on themselves. An injury like Cal's would have resulted in a lot of bleeding; whoever was behind it would surely be covered in it.

Unless, of course, the killer was a ghost.

The thought made Dez shudder. Or maybe it was simply the fact he was cold. With just one police vehicle parked on this side of the woods, it was only right for Raiya to sit inside it, leaving Dez and Sully out in the cold.

Dez, seated on a fallen tree at the edge of the tree line, peered over at Sully who had been told to wait on the only bench. Sully met his eye and shrugged. Dez shrugged back. Nothing for it.

An hour passed. Dez found himself stifling yawns more and more often. The thought of crawling into a warm bed was getting increasingly inviting, yet seemed farther and farther away. Depending who turned up and how they saw fit to handle this situation, Dez, Sully and Raiya could be in for a very long night.

Close to another hour passed. Dez had given up sitting in favour of pacing—much to the obvious chagrin of the much-shorter uniformed officer watching him—when a few vehicles pulled up. Dez recognized the van belonging to the Forensic Identification Unit. Behind it were a pair of unmarked cars. One likely belonged to the coroner. Another, Dez hoped, contained members of the Major Crimes Unit.

He felt a burst of relief as Sergeant Forbes Raynor stepped from the car. They knew him well; he and Sully shared the same repugnant biological father.

Forbes took one look at Dez across the short expanse of golf green and heaved a frustrated sigh. "You have *got* to be kidding me."

"You know these folks?" the on-scene sergeant from Holy Oaks asked.

"Sure do," Forbes said. "PIs from town. Harmless—except they do tend to end up in the middle of plenty of cases." Forbes twitched two fingers at Dez, then at Sully, in a come-here gesture. Dez sensed their long night was about to get a little shorter.

"What in the hell are you doing in the middle of my case?" Forbes asked them.

"Believe me," Dez said. "I've been asking myself the same thing."

He let Sully provide most of the rundown, chipping in here and there with a comment or two. Once they'd finished briefing Forbes on their involvement and the events of the night, they paused to let him consider it.

"Can't say I'm familiar with the Cary Holdfast homicide," he said.

"I'm not surprised," Dez said. "You've got a number of years on us, but even you're not old enough to remember that incident."

"Watch it, Braddock, or I'll find a reason to lock you up. One of my colleagues is making his way to the hospital to speak with Louise Penske. Given what you apparently said to the nine-one-one operator about being in pursuit of her, we figured her for a suspect." Forbes shook his head. "I didn't bother checking the name of the caller. Wanted to hit the road and I figured I could check those details once I got here. Once I saw you knuckleheads, I knew I wouldn't need to make any inquiries. Figures it would be the two of you in the middle of all this."

"Speaking of all this," Sully said. "You'll want to be really, really careful. I don't think Louise did this, Forbes. I haven't figured it all out yet, but there's a ghost involved."

"Knew that was coming," Forbes grumbled. "With you here, what else would it be? Please, don't tell me the ghost actually did the deed."

"We don't know yet," Dez said. "We're still in the middle of this thing. Good news is, I suppose, we've only got until tomorrow night."

"Halloween." Forbes rolled his eyes. "Oh boy." He fixed Dez in a stare. "What would you do if I told you to stay out of it? To back off and let us do our jobs? Would you actually do what I say?"

Sully fielded that one. "We can't, Forbes. One man is already dead. He might not be the last. We have to do what we can to stop it before someone else gets hurt."

"About that," Dez added. "You'll want to keep all your people close while they're in these woods. That means you too. So far, to the best of our knowledge, people have mainly been targeted while they've been alone. Don't put yourself in that position, okay?"

Forbes gave him a half-hearted sneer, one Dez guessed was meant to save face. "You want me to come find you to hold my hand if I have to go in there by myself?"

"I won't hold your hand," Sully said. "But I'll keep you alive. Seems like the sort of offer you wouldn't turn up your nose at."

Forbes shook his head as he delivered a dry laugh. "No, put that way, I suppose I wouldn't." He fixed first Sully and then Dez with meaningful looks. "Just so I'm clear, either of you handle the body?"

"No," Dez said.

He nodded toward the marked police car where Raiya sat. "And your friend there? She got anything on her I should know about?"

"Blood? No, she shouldn't. She was with us the whole time, and she didn't touch the body either."

Forbes nodded. "Well, I haven't had time to check the potential suspect, and my colleague hasn't called yet to tell me she has either. You carried her, Braddock, so you could have transfer on you if she had any blood on her."

Dez had had the same thought earlier, though he'd stopped considering it once he became doubtful Louise had done the deed. Of course, that was a conclusion the police would need to reach on their own. "I didn't see anything much on her, but it was dark."

"Exactly. So I guess to be safe, I'll need to take what you're wearing. You got a change of clothes at the room?"

Dez rubbed his face. "A change of clothes is how we met the dead guy in the first place."

Forbes sent a member of the Forensic Identification team with Dez and Sully back to their room to take charge of Dez's clothing. Dez was fine with it. Thankfully, he'd been wearing the items he'd purchased at Cal's store. He would have felt worse about handing over his own clothes. He liked those ones.

Best he could tell, nothing he was wearing had any blood on it. Nor did his hands when he was finally able to check in the light. Hardly a surprise if Louise was telling the truth about not killing Cal.

Sully had gone to wait in Raiya's room, so once the Ident member had gone with a bag full of Dez's clothes, Dez headed a few doors down to check in with the others. Back in his own things, he already felt a little better. He'd feel better still after a shower and a solid night's sleep.

Sully was near the door judging by how quickly he opened it for Dez. "All sorted?" he asked.

Dez nodded. "Not much to sort, but yeah."

Sully stepped back to allow Dez to enter. Raiya was seated on her bed, her face lined with exhaustion.

"We'll get out of your hair right away and let you sleep," Dez told her.

"I think we could all use some after this night. I'll tell you, I haven't had a run like that since … well, to be honest, I can't recall the last time I had a run like that."

"Sorry," Sully said. "We hadn't expected any of this."

"I know. Not your fault. I suppose *I* should have expected it. I knew what I was likely to find when I got here." She met Dez's eye. "No blood on yourself that you could see?"

He shook his head. "Nope. If Louise was lying and she did it, she was miraculously clean of any blood. A wound like the one we saw, there's no way the killer would have avoided getting blood on them."

"I think the police are in for a long night," Sully said. "Just glad we aren't. Until Forbes showed up, I thought we'd be stuck in an interview room giving statements until four in the morning."

"Yeah, lucky us." Dez passed a hand over his face. "Listen, I think we'd better try and get some sleep. Just because we've been given a pass on the statements until tomorrow doesn't mean Forbes won't come up with something else he needs us for."

Sully frowned. "As long as he doesn't need us to save his life. We're in exactly the wrong place to do it."

He and Dez left Raiya's room shortly after. They'd nearly reached their own room when Dez happened to glance down the hall leading toward the rear entrance. There at the end, fixing them with an unnerving stare, stood Rebecca's father, clad in a knee-length robe and little else.

"Good lord," Dez grumbled. "Not again."

Wanting to make sure the man was safe, Dez started toward him. He stopped abruptly as the old man's face twisted into an eerie grin.

"Oh hell," Dez said.

"Did you see him?" the old man asked. And then he laughed.

Dez shuddered.

Sully brushed past him as if to reach the man, but Parker emerged and took Rebecca's dad gently by the arm. "Come on, Leo. Let's get you back to bed."

Leo allowed himself to be guided, but his stare tracked Dez and Sully until Parker at last succeeded in leading him away. Never did the spooky smile leave his face.

"If we hadn't just found a nearly decapitated body, I'd say that right there"—pointing to the spot where Leo Symes had just stood—"is a strong contender for the creepiest thing I've seen tonight."

"Yeah," Sully said. "It's up there, all right." He turned back toward Dez, catching his eye. "I know he's got dementia and everything, but do you get the impression he knows something we don't?"

Dez shivered again. "You could say that. The problem is, whatever it is he knows, I'm not sure I want to."

CHAPTER 24

SULLY STOOD AT THE WINDOW, his gaze turned toward the edge of the green where they'd emerged earlier in the night. It would be difficult to make out the actual spot, even with the scattering of lights along the edge of the green, but the reds and blues of a police cruiser marked the spot.

They'd be there a while yet. The Forensic Identification team would have their hands full between processing the site of Cal's death and attempting to locate the path of the killer. The problem was, Sully didn't want police investigators to find the killer—not if it was who he suspected. Headless Henry wasn't the sort of murderer who could be arrested, nor did it feel as though his bloodlust was sated.

Sully had sent Forbes a couple of text messages to check in and had been relieved when he'd received responses—albeit brief and pointed ones. Forbes was busy, and he was getting frustrated with the lack of answers. Police liked solid conclusions, not paranormal ones they couldn't haul into an interview room for questioning.

If Sully's concern for Forbes and the others wasn't enough, his guilt over Cal refused to quiet. Cal hadn't blamed him, but that didn't mean Sully wouldn't blame himself. And as the night wore on, it seemed guilt and worry were intent on overpowering exhaustion.

"You need to go to bed."

Dez's words had Sully turning from the window. Dez's head was a reddish blur in the darkened room, the details of his expression lost to the shadows. His tone, though, made his concern abundantly clear.

"I can't sleep," Sully said.

"I'm not doing a great job of it either, but I'm trying. You should be doing the same."

"I should be out there."

Dez's shape shifted as he levered himself up onto an elbow. "Doing what? Interfering in a police investigation? They wouldn't let you back in there, and you know it. They've got a job to do. Yours right now is to get some rest so you can handle whatever comes at us next."

Sully pressed the tips of finger and thumb against the inner corners of his eyes. "You're right. I know you're right. Doesn't change what I'm feeling. That ghost is out there somewhere, building himself up to doing something else. He's not done, Dez."

"I believe you."

"I already let Cal down. I can't let it hurt someone else. What if it goes after one of the officers out there? What if it goes after Forbes?"

Dez sat straight up. "Don't you go there, Sully. You didn't let anyone down."

"Don't tell me you don't feel the same. You know you do."

"Doesn't mean we're right. Sometimes good people carry guilt that's not theirs to bear."

Dez had a way of making sense.

"I hear you," Sully said. "I'm still worried."

"Do you have any indication something more is going to happen tonight?"

There was the question, the one Sully had been coming back to again and again as he stood watching the darkness beyond the hotel golf green, endlessly searching for a spectre's dim glow. As they'd passed through the woods earlier, Sully knew they were being watched—stalked even. The feeling had been oppressive and foreboding, and every step he took had felt like passing through a web spun by something evil. But while he'd felt eyes on him, it hadn't evolved to anything sharper or more dangerous. Certainly, no ghostly blades had whistled past his head; no invisible claws had raked his flesh. The threat had been very much present, yet had remained dulled by an immediate lack of intent.

That could change at any time; experience had taught him that. But the same sort of experience had showed him that spirits, even the powerful ones, had limits to their stores of energy. If Headless Henry had delivered the death blow to Cal, the amount of energy it would have taken was off the charts. Even a spirit that powerful must need to recharge after something so violent.

At least, Sully desperately hoped so.

"I wish I'd had time to communicate properly with Cal earlier," Sully said. "He could have showed me his death. It would have answered so much."

"It also would have messed you up," Dez reminded him. "That would have been a really nasty thing to witness, let alone experience firsthand. Call me crazy, but I'd rather go without direct answers if it means you not going through something like that."

Yeah, Dez definitely had a way of making sense.

"Thanks, D," Sully said. "I appreciate it."

"I know you do. Now please, go back to bed and try to sleep, all right? I need you bright-eyed and bushy-tailed in the morning."

Sully chuckled. "Not sure I'll quite hit either mark, but I'll do my best."

He made one final check out the window, playing his gaze over the area the best he could. Nothing showed itself that hadn't been there the last time he checked.

As satisfied as he could be, he crawled back into bed, adjusted his pillow and covers and shut his eyes. As the eventual sounds of Dez's gentle snores washed over him, Sully, too, finally fell asleep.

By the time Sully, Dez and Raiya left their rooms for breakfast, the hotel was buzzing with activity and whispers.

Guests spoke to each other in hushed excitement as several uniformed and plainclothes police officers went to work in the lobby, talking to staff and chatting with a few guests.

Sully had received a text message from Forbes first thing, asking them to come in to provide formal statements as soon as they could. For the time being, Kimotan Rapids Major Crimes members were commandeering a space at the Holy Oak police station, allowing them to remain close during these crucial first hours and days.

Sully wasn't hungry, but he poked down some eggs and bacon from the breakfast buffet anyway. Dez, of course, heaped his plate with most of the items on offer.

Having eaten, Sully texted Forbes to ensure he was at the station. He was.

"Let's get this over with," Sully told Dez and Raiya. "I'd kind of like to find out what's going on with Louise, anyway."

"Me too," Raiya said. She shook her head. "My goodness. The younger me would wonder at the older me saying this, but I feel so sorry for these people. They put me through the wringer that night, but I never wanted any of this for them. So much pain and grief."

Sully lifted his head in time to catch sight of Rebecca Symes as she passed by the entrance to the restaurant. Her cold eyes caught his and narrowed.

Two of Raiya's tormenters had paid hefty prices. Rebecca had managed to rise above all of it. And yet she seemed tormented in her own way by something she had yet to reveal. It couldn't help that her resort was being besieged by law enforcement investigating a murder. Yet there had been plenty enough tension in her manner even before this.

She knew something. Had to. The problem would be getting her to share.

Later. Right now, Sully, Dez and Raiya had their own sharing to do down at the police station. After that, Sully vowed he'd figure out what Rebecca was hiding.

CHAPTER 25

THEY SWUNG by the park on the way to the police station. Sully hopped out and cut a brisk pace through the park, curious to see whether Louise was back at her tent. She wasn't.

It was early in the day, so not everyone was at their stations at the festival. It was possible Louise simply wasn't here yet. It was just as possible she'd been arrested and was being held in custody at the police station. They'd find out which soon enough.

Holy Oak's police department was located inside a small building on Main Street, far enough away from the main businesses as to remain inconspicuous. There wasn't much to the building, as there probably wasn't much to the police department itself. A town this size couldn't boast a very large police force. Located in a one-storey brick structure, it wasn't much to look at, just one door sandwiched between two nondescript windows. Given the size, Sully suspected if the building had any cells, they would be located in the basement. Around here, he couldn't imagine they got much use.

"Can you imagine Forbes cooped up in this place?" Dez asked with a snort. "He must be losing his mind by now."

"Never mind Forbes," Raiya said. "Imagine poor Louise stuck in a cell someplace in that building."

Dez turned from his spot in the driver's seat to face Raiya. "Are we absolutely sure she didn't do it?"

"Did you find any blood on yourself after carrying her last night?" Raiya asked him.

Dez shook his head. "Can't say I did."

"Perhaps that's your answer. For my part, I believe her."

Sully pivoted to meet Dez's eye. "For my part, I agree with Raiya."

Dez shrugged. "Okay then. Good enough for me. Guess we'll find out soon enough what the police believe."

"I'll tell you one thing," Sully said. "We'll have a hard time convincing anyone who isn't Forbes that a ghost might be responsible for this. Even Forbes won't want to hear it."

The three of them slid out of the SUV and made their way toward the building. Inside, they met with an older lady wearing a civilian patch on her shirt. Probably a volunteer, Sully thought.

"Oh, you must be the witnesses from last night." The lady shook her head of grey curls and made a tsk-tsk sound. "What a shame. He was such a nice man. And after everything that happened to his poor family."

Sully did his best to appear uninterested. "I suppose in a town this size, it's safe to say you knew the Holdfast family."

"Everyone knows everyone around here, dear."

Sully could think of a lot more he wanted to ask her, but already the woman was up and making her way toward the back.

"I'll just be a moment," she said as she went. "Wait here."

She returned within the same minute, joined now by Forbes. Sully noted the woman wore a pinched look. He resisted a smile. Forbes had a way of bringing out that expression in people.

Forbes gave them a wave, ushering them behind the counter and toward the employees-only area.

"Come on," he told them. "I'll get you set up with some statement forms. I'll need you to be as detailed as possible. Might be I'll have to ask you to come in to do a video statement at some point, but we'll see how we make out this way first."

Knowing Forbes, he didn't want to waste time with sit-down interviews unless absolutely necessary. He wouldn't see it as such where it pertained to Sully or Dez.

As Forbes led them down a short hallway, Sully leaned in to speak quietly. "What happened with Louise?"

"Very little at this point. She was in the hospital for part of the night. My colleague had a chance to interview her there, and someone from Ident showed up to bag and tag her clothing and check her over for other potential evidence. We found a little blood on her shoes, but nothing on her hands, face or clothing. Between you and me, the evidence shows Mr. Holdfast died where you found him and wasn't moved afterward. Plenty of bleed-out. We've got a blood-spatter expert coming out to take a look as there's a fair bit of spray on the trees. Given that, you can expect a significant amount of blood ended up on the killer as well."

"If it was planned, a smart killer would have worn something they'd be able to remove and conceal," Dez pointed out.

Forbes fixed him with a withering glare. "Thank you, Braddock. I hadn't thought of that." He rolled his eyes. "Of course, I thought about that possibility. But we've searched, we had a dog team come out and search, and nothing. If someone peeled off bloody clothes and dumped them, we've found no trace of them."

He frowned. "Having said that, one major thing bothers me. We've got two murders now involving men from the same family, similar injuries, and the same woman present at each? What are the chances? Granted, the incidents took place more than fifty years apart, but still … I don't know, a big part of me is stuck here questioning how she might have pulled it off."

"But she's not under arrest or facing charges?" Dez asked.

"Not unless something more comes to light. We're not done yet, obviously. Could be we turn up something more that changes things." He crossed his arms snugly across his chest as he leaned on the door frame. "One other thing troubles me though. She changed her name."

"The Madame Olga thing?" Sully asked.

Forbes shook his head. "Uh-uh. I mean, she *really* changed her name. Goes by Poppy O'Connell now. Had it legally changed way back in the seventies. She told my partner she wanted to start over after the whole Cary Holdfast homicide. Guess I can't blame her. She wasn't charged, but given the way she and her family were targeted afterward, she said she felt the need to hide her identity for her own safety."

Forbes leaned toward them. "Makes you wonder, though, doesn't it? Changing your identity is a good way of going into hiding if you're trying to avoid law enforcement." He straightened. "Tell you something else: I'm running checks to make sure there are no similar unsolved deaths at or near any of the places Ms. O'Connell spent time during the past few decades. You never know. Maybe we've got us a serial killer here."

Sully chewed on the inside of his cheek. Maybe Forbes's checks would come to something, but he doubted it. The truth was, the farther they delved into this, the more Sully was convinced Louise Penske—or Poppy O'Connell—wasn't the killer. Not now, not then. The reality of it was far more unsettling. And it wasn't something Forbes would be able to slap a pair of handcuffs on.

"Promise me one thing," Sully told him. "Be careful, okay? Whoever you suspect and however much faith you put in that assessment, don't lose sight of the possibility it's something else behind all this."

Forbes snorted. "You mean Headless Henry?"

Sully ignored the sarcasm as he nodded his response.

"You really believe that's a possibility?" Forbes asked.

"It's me," Sully reminded him. "I believe anything's a possibility."

HAVING GIVEN them separate locations in which to complete their written statements, Forbes left them to it. Within the hour, they'd finished, and within another half hour, Forbes was finished with them.

Leaving Forbes to his remaining tasks, Sully, Dez and Raiya returned to the SUV.

"What now?" Raiya asked.

"I really want to look for that oak tree," Sully said. "But I think maybe we should try to find Louise first."

"You think she's in danger?" Dez asked.

"Not exactly. I am worried about her though. Let's just find her, make sure she's all right."

Forbes would know where Louise was staying, but he wouldn't be at liberty to provide that information. The easiest remaining way to find her would be at the park, but as before, her tent was empty when they checked it. The same sign remained on the outer flap, announcing she'd return at noon. Sully checked his cellphone screen for the time. Ten minutes to.

"Think she'll turn up?" Dez asked.

"We'll find out soon enough." Sully considered finding something to eat in the meantime, conscious of Dez's grumbling stomach. He nixed that plan when a few people began to gather near the tent, seemingly intent on having their fortunes read. Short of butting in line later, it seemed the best thing to do now was stay where he was at the head of the growing queue.

"Why don't you and Raiya go and find something to eat?" Sully suggested to Dez. "I'll wait here for her to return."

Dez was already scanning the grouping of nearby food trucks. "You sure?"

"Not as sure as you are," Sully said through a grin.

Dez glowered at him. "I can go without food now and again, you know."

Sully patted him on the arm. "Why poke the bear if you don't need to? Go eat. If I need you here, I'll call you."

The fact Dez's gaze had zeroed in on the burger stand told Sully he wouldn't be facing additional arguments. "Okay, sold. Coming, Raiya?"

"I'll stay," she said. "You go on."

Dez shrugged and left.

"Guess that means he's done being suspicious of Louise," Raiya said. "I doubt he would have left us otherwise."

"Louise didn't do it," Sully said. "He knows it as well as we do."

"I wonder if she's as convinced."

Sully checked to make sure they weren't going to be overheard before eyeing Raiya. "You think she believes she might have done it?"

"I think she worries about the things she doesn't remember. She was adamant in claiming she didn't do those things, but she also knows she's not in a position to refute it. That's still a burden to carry—especially now that last night happened the way it did."

A commotion from inside the tent drew Sully's attention.

Raiya gripped Sully's sleeve. "She's in there. Something's wrong."

Enough for Sully. Flipping back the front tent flap, he rushed through the small chamber at the entrance to reach the section where Louise did her readings. There she was, on her knees on the ground, using a crutch to try to regain her feet. The other lay just out of reach of her, suggesting a fall.

Sully gained her side, guiding her carefully to standing before easing her into her chair.

"Are you all right?" he asked her. "Were you hurt?"

She waved him off. "I'm fine. Leave me. I'm fine."

Sully took a step back to give her some space. It was then he noticed what he hadn't had the chance to moments ago.

Louise had a series of storage bins placed on the ground inside the tent. The table was bare, her cards, crystals, candles and other items placed haphazardly in one bin. In another, she'd shoved the black tapestries from the walls along with strings of lights she'd had up.

She was leaving.

"What are you doing, Louise?" Raiya asked, her tone making it clear it wasn't so much a question as a gentle accusation.

"You're the psychic," Louise snapped. "You tell me."

"It looks very much like you're running away."

Louise's back went rigid. "I'm about to be wrongly accused of murder for the second time in my life. Maybe worse. Tell me, Raiya, if you were me, what would you do?"

Raiya folded her arms. "I'd stay and make damned sure to clear my name."

Louise returned a humourless laugh. "Would you now? And how would you know? Have you ever been in this situation? Have you ever had to run from your own life?"

"I have," Sully said.

Louise's narrow-eyed gaze flipped to him. "Oh, really?"

"It's a long story, but I had to leave to save my own life. I wasn't off the radar nearly as long as you were, but I had to fake my own death to make it happen."

It had been a dark time, his sole companions most days a dog and a house full of ghosts. He'd suffered through cold and hunger, but nothing had compared to the pain of being so completely without his family.

"I know what it is to fear other people and to have to make harsh choices to protect yourself," Sully told Louise. "I've been there. In the end, the only way out for me was to go topside again and face my fears. Hiding, running—maybe you can do it forever. I couldn't. Figuring out a way to fix things and trusting others to help is the only permanent way out."

"And you're going to help me?" Doubtful, yet hopeful.

"I think you know I can," Sully said. "It's why you called me over when you saw me in the park. You knew I could help somehow. More than that, you knew I'd be willing to try."

Her silence told him he'd hit upon the truth.

"What do I do now?" she asked. "I can't go through again what I went through in the past. I can't do it."

"I don't think you'll have to." Sully lowered himself into one of the chairs facing her. "But I'll need your help too. You told me you knew how to find the oak tree, the one he draws power from. I need you to show me where it is."

Louise dropped her head. "I can't."

"Why not?"

"I don't know how to find it. Not anymore. I went out there, and I looked. But it's as though the forest has changed to protect itself, like it's hiding too. I don't know where to find the tree."

Sully slouched forward, lowering his own chin at this newest defeat. "Okay. Okay, maybe I can—"

"There's someone who might be able to though," Louise said.

Sully lifted his gaze to hers. "If you're going to suggest Rebecca, I've got to warn you, she's not the most helpful person."

"Not Becca. She didn't spend much time in those woods. I was thinking of someone else, if you can convince him."

Sully straightened, brows lifting along with his posture. "Oh? Who?"

"Her father. Leo Symes."

Sully exchanged a glance with Raiya before returning his gaze to Louise. "What makes you say that?"

"He and Becca bought the resort together. I wasn't here, of course, but I kept tabs on the goings-on back in Holy Oak through my grandmother—at least, before she stopped talking to me. Leo was a going concern in real estate in those days. And he loved all the outdoor activities, particularly hunting and fishing. He spent lots of time in those woods. When the opportunity to purchase them came up, he and Becca jumped on it. He wanted it to remain in the family forever. That's what my grandmother said, anyway. If anyone knows their way around those woods, it's him."

Sully shifted. "There's a problem. Leo still wanders around those woods, yeah, but he's got dementia. From what I can tell, it's pretty bad."

Louise tilted her head and lifted a brow. "Dementia?"

Sully nodded, but Louise barked out a laugh.

"What?" Sully asked.

"Leo's got as much dementia as I do. If he's giving that impression, he's got a reason. That old guy is as conniving as the day is long."

"What makes you so sure?" Raiya asked.

Louise's eyes shot to Raiya's. "Because he came to see me at my hotel last night. He told me if I didn't leave Holy Oak now, he'd see to it I never get the chance again."

CHAPTER 26

THERE WENT their afternoon's plans to go tree-hunting, Dez thought as he, Sully and Raiya drove back to the Whispering Winds Resort. If they hadn't already had reason to suspect Rebecca and Leo knew something they had yet to reveal, there sure was evidence of it now.

What it meant, unfortunately, was an additional delay in getting back into the woods. Perhaps someone in town still knew how to locate the Holy Oak, but short of questioning everyone, Leo was their best bet. On the way back to the resort, Sully had put in a call to the local conservation officers to ask if they knew about the tree. But none of the three on staff were from the community, he'd been told, and none had even heard of the legendary tree.

So much for that possibility, so here they were, back to figuring out a way to get Rebecca to talk.

For Dez's part, he had yet to come up with a solution to this ongoing problem. If saving her father from the dangers of the night-time woods hadn't been enough to gain her cooperation, surely nothing would be.

Then again, given Leo's apparent late-night visit to menace Louise, perhaps the danger to him had been overblown.

"What do you make of what Louise said about Leo?" Sully

asked. Apparently, his thoughts were wandering the same paths as Dez's.

"That was weird, all right," Dez said. "If he's making up the whole dementia thing, he's doing a good job of it."

"We have no reason to doubt what she told us," Raiya said. "And given his visit to her and what he said, it really leads me to wonder."

Dez gave it some additional thought before replying. "I mean, dementia isn't necessarily a solid line. People have clear moments and bad ones. Maybe he's back and forth."

"Maybe. I'm not prepared to write off Louise's read of it just yet."

Dez nodded at Raiya's statement. "Me neither. Hopefully, we'll find our answers soon enough."

Speaking of Louise, Dez wasn't sure where she'd end up in all of this. She'd refused to come with them, and she'd likewise avoided any promises of staying put. Dez had done his best to impress upon her the necessity of sticking around; running now would only make her appear more suspect, and that was exactly the opposite of what she'd want. Whether he'd gotten through would become clear if and when Forbes started calling around, asking if any of them knew of her whereabouts.

Louise's choices were beyond Dez's control, and he had more important things to worry about now. His thoughts were turned firmly in that direction as he pulled into a spot in the hotel parking lot and parked. As he had last night, he made sure to pocket his flashlight. He had a sinking feeling he'd need it again before this job was through.

The whirl of activity they'd left behind earlier was gone, the police having moved on to their next tasks and hotel guests probably off to town for whatever Halloween events awaited. It made for a quiet lobby, populated only by a lone woman working the front desk and a man in jeans and a sweater chatting away on his phone while he paced next to one of the large windows.

They'd discussed on the way here how best to handle the situation. In the end, Dez thought it best to confront Rebecca directly. If the police hadn't already questioned her, they would in good time. If she could help Dez, Sully and Raiya end all of this, it could only serve to benefit her—whether she believed in the ghost or not.

Dez took a moment to size up the young woman working the front desk: streaked hair; small earring in her nose; the hint of a tattoo peeking from the top of her blouse along her collarbone.

Dez nudged Sully. "I think you should take this one."

"Why me?"

"Trust me. She'll think you're cute. You're more her type than I am."

Sully rolled his eyes. "Whatever that means."

But he went with it, approaching the desk and leaning toward the young woman as he made the inquiries. Dez watched unsurprised as a light flush coloured the woman's cheeks and a shy smile plucked at her lips.

Raiya sidled up to Dez. "Damn, you're good."

"Sully's kind of hopeless with women," Dez said. "Good thing he's getting married soon. He'd never survive another go-round in the dating scene."

Raiya smirked playfully up at him. "And you would?"

Dez snorted. "Not a chance."

Sully returned a moment later, a slight blush of his own as he tugged Dez toward the door. Raiya followed.

"Don't put me through that again," Sully grumbled. "It was really awkward. I think she wanted to ask me out."

Dez elbowed him. "You should be flattered."

"And you should be flattened."

Dez allowed himself a laugh before getting back down to business. "Find out anything?"

A head shake. "Nothing helpful. Rebecca's in her office, but she's asked not to be disturbed. The lady at the desk told me quietly Rebecca seemed kind of upset. From what I can tell, she's usually pretty guarded. The only time I've seen her emotions get the best of her was when Raiya introduced herself to her back when we first got here."

Dez frowned. "Yeah, usually she just seems like the quintessential ice queen."

"Maybe the police talked to her," Raiya said. "Do you think Forbes would share that much with you?"

"I can ask," Sully said. A moment later, he was on his phone. Thankfully, this was one of those occasions when Forbes picked up. Sully chatted with him for less than a minute. Having asked the question, Sully met Dez's eye with a shake of the head.

Once he'd disconnected, Sully returned the phone to his pocket and gave his attention to Dez and Raiya. "Forbes said he did chat with Rebecca last night, but there wasn't much she had to share. He didn't rule out talking to her again, but he didn't seem as though it was high up his list of priorities. I think he's still stuck on the theory of Louise as a suspect and trying to figure out how she might have pulled it off."

"Figures," Dez said. "The guy always has trouble letting go once he gets his teeth into something."

"So if Rebecca's upset, it's not necessarily about the police questioning her," Sully said. "Which makes me wonder what it is that's got her so shaken."

"It stands to reason she knew Cal," Raiya said. "He was just murdered on her property. Surely that would be enough to upset anyone."

Dez eyed her. "Except this is the same woman who built a business on the same piece of land where her boyfriend was beheaded. Maybe I'm not giving her enough credit here, but she doesn't strike me as the sort to be overly concerned with bad things happening to other people." He switched his gaze to Sully. "We need to get back there."

"How do we manage that? Rebecca's office is only accessible through the door by the front desk."

Dez grinned. "Exactly." He leaned toward Sully. "How about you go turn on that old charm of yours?"

"What charm?"

Dez gave his chin a subtle jab toward the front desk.

Sully's eyes flashed wide. "Come on. No."

"Sull."

"No."

"Five minutes. It's all I need. Just keep her talking for five minutes."

Sully looked so miserable, Dez didn't know whether to laugh or to feel sorry for him. But with no better means of getting a face-to-face with Rebecca, Dez needed Sully on board. The sooner they convinced Rebecca to convince her father to help them find this tree, the sooner they could end this—ideally well before nightfall and the added dangers that would bring.

Sully's shoulders sank. "Fine. Five minutes. If you're not back by then, I'll kill you in your sleep."

Dez chuckled and clapped Sully on the back. "Atta boy."

"Shut up."

With that, Dez made his way across the lobby, finding a spot to wait that would put him within reach of the employees-only door. Then he waited for Sully to work his magic.

SULLY DIDN'T GIVE himself enough credit. It took no work at all for him to capture the young woman's attention sufficiently for Dez to slip past the front desk and through the door, which blessedly was unlocked.

It was a short walk to Rebecca's office, and Dez made it within seconds. No time to spare. He'd spotted the CCTV cameras mounted in the lobby—one above the front desk and one showing the main entrance—and there was no way to know whether someone had been watching. Dez hadn't seen evidence of hotel security; he didn't think this was the sort of place to require that sort of thing, but he couldn't be certain. If he were going to attempt a conversation with Rebecca, best he get things moving quickly, just in case.

He passed no one in the hall, nor did he see anyone in any of the rooms he passed.

Rebecca's office door was shut. Dez rapped and listened for a response from the other side. When none came, he tried again, louder this time. Still nothing.

He tried the knob. Locked. He checked the hallway. Still no sign of anyone. No indication either of any security cameras.

He could back away and leave. That would probably be the smart thing.

But the smart thing would leave him without immediate answers. And a lack of immediate answers would leave him, Sully and Raiya tripping through the haunted woods after dark, attempting to locate a specific tree while avoiding decapitation.

Sometimes, the smart thing wasn't the right thing.

Lachlan had taught Dez a few things. One of them was how to pick a lock. Dez wasn't great at it, but he was improving. Time to put his growing skill to the test.

He timed himself. Nearly two minutes. By the time he heard the click he'd been hoping for, he'd broken out in a sweat. He'd need to practice more.

Still no one around. Dez eased open the door and poked his head inside. "Rebecca?"

He was certain she couldn't be here. No way she would have missed his clumsy scrapings at the lock. If she'd been inside, someone probably would have shown up by now to escort him away.

The office was empty.

Slipping inside and shutting the door behind himself, Dez took a moment to scan the place. He didn't think Rebecca would keep anything useful in here. Certainly, she wouldn't have her teenage diary lying around, describing the night when her then-boyfriend was murdered.

Then again …

Dez spotted the fireplace as he turned back toward the door. More specifically, he spotted what was within the fireplace.

He slipped off his button-down shirt, using it to pick up a fireplace poker. He'd just jabbed a piece of material inside the fireplace when the door opened, revealing a shocked Rebecca.

"What the hell's going on here?" she demanded.

Using the poker, Dez lifted the item from the fireplace—almost certainly the remains of a shirt.

A shirt that was most certainly covered in blood.

"Funny," Dez said. "I was going to ask you the same thing."

CHAPTER 27

Rebecca was in no mood to share. Once the shock passed, she took on a defensive attitude, her eyes shooting daggers and her arms crossed.

"Get out," she said.

Dez raised a brow as he lifted the partially burned bloody shirt a little more. "Given this, I don't think I will."

"I'll call the police."

Dez smirked. "Go for it. I'd love to see you try to explain this." He made a show of considering his statement. "Actually, now that I say it, I suppose the thing to do *is* to call the police. Want me to do it, or were you still planning on calling them yourself?"

Rebecca collapsed into the nearest chair and sank forward, head in hands. Deflated. Defeated. "What do you want?"

"The truth would be a good place to start. Whose blood is this?"

Her head still lowered and eyes hidden, Dez could only imagine the thoughts which must be playing across her face as she gave herself a moment of silence. Looking for a plausible explanation, one he'd buy.

Good luck with that.

Finally, she lifted her head. Her eyes locked onto his. "I had a nosebleed."

She'd done her best to slip the lie past him, maintaining eye contact and keeping a straight face. Unfortunately for her, Dez wasn't born yesterday.

He carefully set the clothing—a shirt, he thought—next to the fireplace. Then he took a relaxed approach, leaning back against the wall. Unimpressed. "Want to give it another shot?"

She fell silent again. Dez took advantage of the moment to pull out his phone. She probably thought he was calling the police—which was, by rights, what he should be doing.

Instead, he brought up his voice recorder app. He'd crossed the line into witness territory already; might as well get his money's worth.

Her eyes flashed wide as she eyed his phone. "Please, don't."

Dez stared back at her. "Give me a reason not to call."

"I'll tell you, okay? Just please leave the police out of this. You don't understand."

Good enough. Dez tapped the record button, careful to keep the screen hidden. By law, he could record without her knowledge, and he'd take advantage if it meant drawing a confession. Even so, he was obligated to provide certain warnings.

"I can't promise you I won't share what you say with the police," he said. "I can't promise you anything whatsoever—except for one thing: if there's a way my brother and I can help, we will."

Rebecca studied him, her eyes locked on his. Searching for reasons to share. Searching for reasons not to.

Dez wished he could contact Sully. Sully probably wished the same by now, stuck in an awkward conversation with a desk agent with a crush. Dez couldn't afford the time, nor did he want to risk this fragile progress he'd made. Often, Sully was the deciding factor for people, his sensitive nature providing natural incentive for those wanting to tell their stories.

Sometimes, though, people didn't need sensitivity to goad the truth from them; they needed a threat. That was Dez's province.

He was certain Rebecca had drawn the same conclusion when, finally, her head drooped once again. "You don't understand."

"Help me to," Dez said.

She drew in a few quiet but deep breaths. Dez watched her shoulders and back lifting with each one.

Her gaze returned to his, her eyes holding not fear now so much as resolve. "I don't know for certain whose blood it is."

A growl started in Dez's throat but died there as Rebecca cut back in.

"But I strongly suspect it's Cal Holdfast's."

Dez resisted the urge to check the recorder. He didn't want to spook her, to give her reason to suspect she was being recorded. Maybe it wouldn't matter now, anyway. She was caught, and she knew it.

Dez tilted his head. "Seems like a solid conclusion to me. Given the amount of blood on this single piece of clothing, it had to be an extremely serious incident. I haven't heard of anything else fitting the bill around here recently." He turned his stare hard as he asked, "Did you kill Cal?"

"No! Of course I didn't."

"But you know who did."

The sheen of tears formed in her eyes, gathering along her lower lashes but managing to stay there as she sniffled back the swell of emotion. "I don't know anything for certain. But my father was wearing that shirt when Parker found him outside last night."

Dez held onto his questions—and he had plenty. Often in an interview situation, silence was your best friend, giving subjects something to fill. He waited, a quiet invitation for her to continue.

She heaved a sigh. "Oh God. Oh God, Dad."

This time, a few tears did come. Dez reached to a nearby shelf where he'd spotted a tissue box. Rebecca uttered a mumbled "thank you" as she plucked a few out and dabbed at her eyes, avoiding rubbing at the mascara coating her lashes. Even now, in the midst of all of this, she was doing a good job of maintaining appearances. The consummate professional.

Her tears once again sucked back, she blinked up at Dez. "What do you want to know?"

"Why would your father have killed Cal?"

"I don't know. I really don't—except for the obvious answer. He's got dementia. He's not himself. He wanders at night, and I don't know what he does while he's out. All I know is he winds up in the woods quite often. He always loved them when he was younger, back when he still hunted and camped. I think the forest still gives him comfort."

Dez couldn't imagine anyone finding those creepy woods comfortable, but to each their own. "Doesn't really answer my question though. I've known people with dementia. Sometimes they got frustrated or angry, and it could make them lash out from time to time. But I saw the injuries to Cal's body. What was done to him took a great deal of force and deliberation. First off, the initial blow appeared to have been sufficient to drop him immediately. And not meaning to get graphic here, but his head was partially removed."

A sob broke from Rebecca's throat. "Oh my God. Oh, Dad, no."

Dez gave her a moment to cry. It gave him time to get his head on straight. He was having a hard time picturing that frail old man being able to generate the power and rage to commit such a horrific and brutal act.

Except maybe he could have—if Sully and Raiya's explanation held. Maybe Leo Symes acting alone couldn't have done it. Add in the power of Headless Henry, though, and the unlikely became possible.

"What happened last night?" Dez asked her.

"I don't know the details. I didn't ask. I couldn't bear it. All I can say is that Parker came to my room shortly before midnight and said he'd discovered Dad was gone from his room. Parker often takes care of him for me, you see. He worked with him since he was young. I suppose in a way, Parker was like the son Dad never had and always wanted."

She sniffled, dabbing again at her eyes. This time, a little mascara smeared. "Anyway, Parker's a godsend with Dad. When he couldn't find him in the hotel, he knew he must have gone outside. Parker, of course, knew Dad would gravitate to the woods, so that's where he went first to check. He found Dad on the green, his clothing, face and hands covered in blood."

"Did you see your Dad?"

Rebecca shook her head. "Not then, no. I couldn't bear to look at him. I suppose I thought if I didn't see him, I could pretend it hadn't happened."

Dez frowned. "But you didn't know Cal had died yet, right?"

"No, not then. Not until the police showed up with questions for me. They wanted to know if I had security cameras that might have picked up anything. I do have them, but they aren't hooked up to record. Anyway, when the police mentioned what had happened to Cal, I knew then for certain."

She shifted in her chair, recrossing her legs in the opposite direction and propping her elbows on her topmost knee. "I had asked Parker earlier to get my dad cleaned up and to do something with the clothing. Once I learned what had happened, and once I was certain the police were gone, I had Parker bring me the clothing. You can see what I did with them."

"You attempted to destroy evidence."

Rebecca's eyes narrowed. "He's my father. If it were your father, what would you do?"

This time, Dez was the one falling quiet. It was a question he'd asked himself privately every once in a while when they came up against situations like this. As ever, there were no easy answers.

"What are you going to do?" Rebecca asked.

Another question with no simple answer.

"I don't know," Dez said.

His phone buzzed with an incoming call. He checked the screen to find Sully's name on the caller ID. No surprise there. He had to be going nutty wondering what Dez was doing.

Dez couldn't pick up the call, but Sully's name provided the reminder Dez needed. There was no doubt they'd need to inform the police about Leo's role in Cal's death, and ordinarily Dez would be making the phone call now.

They had yet to touch on the other key issue though.

"Do you think your father killed Cary?"

Dez's question had Rebecca's startled gaze snapping to his. "What?"

"Makes sense to ask. The two deaths share pretty clear similarities, plus what are the chances they involved two brothers? And not to overlook one other significant detail: your father purchased the property on which Cary was murdered. Some might argue it gave him a means to ensure any evidence was destroyed or well-hidden. Come on, Rebecca. You've got to admit it's pretty suspicious."

Rebecca gripped her armrests so tightly, her knuckles began to whiten. "You want me to believe my father killed before? That I've spent my entire adult life living and working with a murderer? Not only that, but the person who killed my high school boyfriend?"

Dez didn't break eye contact. "I think somewhere deep inside yourself, you've been asking yourself the same question."

Rebecca seemed to fight for breath as though she'd been punched in the gut. In a way, she had. Because the truth was, even if Leo was found not criminally responsible for Cal's death due to dementia—if he did, in fact, have it—he would have had no similar excuse regarding Cary's death.

"I know you're having a rough time here, but I need to ask you one more thing you won't like," Dez said. "Headless Henry."

"Oh good lord, you can't be serious."

"I am, actually. Your father saw him shortly before I brought him back here. I don't know whether it's his mental state or whether he's always seen these things, but he did see something out there. There's a good chance whatever it is, it played a significant role in the deaths of the Holdfasts."

"You're saying a ghost killed them?"

"I'm saying there's a really good chance a ghost played a major role. If so, your father wouldn't be entirely to blame." Time to ask the big question. "What do you remember about the night Cary was killed?"

"I don't want to talk about it."

"I think we've passed that point, don't you?"

Rebecca's head drooped. Dez gave her a moment, hoping when she next spoke, she'd finally break her silence.

She did.

"I've never talked about that night. I told the police I didn't see anything until it was over."

"It wasn't true?"

She shook her head. Again, she fell silent. Again, Dez waited her out.

Finally, she lifted her eyes to his. "I didn't see the thing happen. I really didn't. After we left Raiya, we ran off. We were laughing, dumb kids that we were. It was dark, and we weren't paying close attention to anything but getting far away from her."

"A dick move."

"It was. I acknowledge that completely. As I said, dumb kids."

"Then what happened?"

Her mouth worked as though she were chewing on the inside of her lower lip. "We were running fast, and we lost sight of each other. One minute, Cary and Louise were next to me. The next, they weren't. I began to call out to them, but I stopped. A feeling came over me like someone was there watching me. I always thought I must've imagined it, but I'm sure I saw the shape of a man. It was dark. Whether I really saw it or not, I can't say. Whatever it was, he had no head."

Dez tamped down the excitement. Finally, he was getting someplace. "Did he approach you?"

"No. He was there, and then he wasn't. Moments later, I heard Cary yell. It only lasted a moment, and then it was over. I ran toward the sound, thinking maybe he'd taken a fall. At first, I couldn't find him. When I did, I saw Louise kneeling next to him. He was on the ground, covered in blood. Louise was also covered in blood. That's when I saw the shadow again. No head."

A quiet moan escaped Rebecca's throat. "Something was in the thing's hand. An axe, I think. He took Cary's head. He took it, and then he disappeared."

She shook her head as if trying to dislodge the memory from her brain. "I ran. I ran faster than I knew I could run. I don't remember much of that next period of time. My memory is fuzzy when it's there at all. I think I was screaming. I don't know. Somehow, I made it back to the road, though it felt like I was out there forever before I found my way. Parker happened to be driving past, and he picked me up, drove me back home."

"Parker Decatur?"

Rebecca nodded.

"What was he doing there?" Dez asked.

"He was apprenticing with my dad at the office, and he'd been working late. He lived in the countryside, and he was driving home for the night when he happened upon me. Thank God for Parker. He really took care of me that night, getting me calmed down a little and back home again. He's been such a great help to my family."

"Why didn't you share this with the police?"

"I thought I must've imagined it. Either that, or I was going crazy. I told my father about it. He told me to keep it to myself, said it couldn't have happened that way. Ghosts didn't exist. And then I saw what happened to Louise, how she was talked about afterward. I thought everyone must be right, that she had killed Cary. If so, what I thought I'd seen had to most definitely have been a hallucination of some sort brought on by the trauma of seeing what I'd seen."

She straightened, thumbing a tear from the corner of her eye. "At least that's what I've told myself all these years. It was easier, I suppose, than letting myself believe something dark walks these woods. And it was easier than putting myself in a position of having the town think I was crazy too. I had plans to go into business with my dad once I was out of school. He wanted to leave real estate and open a resort. He thought it would be a great thing for me to go in on it with him. If my reputation took a hit, it would have seriously damaged my family's credibility and our standing in the community—and therefore the success of any future projects. Do you see?"

Dez saw, all right. He saw how ambition had given Rebecca an excuse to avoid doing the right thing. If he had a dime for every lousy bigwig who made similar choices, sacrificing truth and honour for money and power, he'd be richer than they were.

He left it unsaid. Shame flickered on Rebecca's face as Dez regarded her in silent judgement. She knew already how she came off in all of this. If she hadn't been aware, she would have come forward years back.

Rebecca slumped back in the chair. "I read about your brother, you know. I looked him up. According to what I saw, his abilities have been taken seriously by at least some people in positions of authority."

Dez nodded. "Plenty of times, actually. Sully and I, this is what we do. We solve the problems no one else can." He tilted his head as he regarded Rebecca. "I can't tell you how this ends. I can't promise your dad gets out of this without going to jail. What I can promise is that if there's something evil in those woods, we can stop it. And I can promise that if your father was dragged into this by some evil thing, you and he will find out the truth. If nothing else, you'll come away knowing he isn't as evil as the deeds would make him appear."

"That's supposed to make this better?"

Dez shrugged. "You're the only one who can answer that."

He leaned in a little. "We need to stop this, Rebecca—for your dad, for you, for everyone in this town. Ask him to help us find the Holy Oak. We think if we can find it, we can stop the ghost in his tracks before he does this again."

Rebecca heaved a sigh. "After all of this, I can't ask him to go back out there."

Dez's heart sank. He didn't want to keep arguing, but he'd have to. This was their best chance. Maybe their last chance.

But Rebecca wasn't done. "Parker. Parker knows how to find the tree, I think. If he goes with you, would that be good enough?"

Dez smiled. "Good enough for me."

CHAPTER 28

Sully's frustration at being left out of the conversation with Rebecca vanished as Dez filled him in while he, Dez and Raiya stood waiting in the lobby for Parker.

"I can't believe you actually got her to tell you all that," Sully told Dez.

Dez gave him a cocky half-grin. "Hey, I'm damn good at my job, Sull. You know that."

Sully checked the time. Mid-afternoon. Still several hours of daylight remaining, which gave them plenty of time to locate the tree and get this sorted before nightfall. "Okay, I know you're good, man, but not what I was getting at."

"I convinced her of the truth. She's out of options. Her father's already on the hook here. Even if we can't get him totally off it, we'd be able to provide some peace of mind—never mind the fact we can keep this crap from happening again."

Parker was a long time coming. Dez had begun to sprawl out on one of the plush lobby seats when Parker finally turned up.

"Sorry to keep you waiting," he said. "Poor Leo's in quite a state today. I wanted to wait until his medication kicked in. He's sleeping now. And Rebecca's staying near, so everything should be fine for a bit."

"Did she fill you in on what we discussed?" Dez asked.

"I believe so," Parker said. "Although I wouldn't know if she hadn't told me all of it, I suppose."

"We should get going," Sully told him. "I can give you the rundown on the way. I'd like to get moving before it starts getting dark out."

Parker gave a humourless chuckle. "Given what's been happening, I would too."

SULLY HAD EXPECTED they could walk from the hotel to the tree, but Parker told them it was a short drive.

"It's been a long time," he told them as they made their way to the parking lot. "I sure hope I still remember how to find it."

Sully did too. If Parker couldn't locate the Holy Oak, they were going to have a hell of a time.

Sully and Dez had talked about how best to handle the whole debacle involving Leo and the clothing in the fireplace, and they'd decided they had to let Forbes know—eventually. For the time being, they'd opted to keep Leo this side of custody in case they needed him. In the meantime, Dez would remain on guard in Rebecca's office, ensuring no further tampering with evidence.

Sully expected a tongue-lashing from Forbes over delaying this new information. It couldn't be helped. Solving a murder investigation was a huge deal, but preventing further murders was a bigger one. With no other clear solutions, Sully was relying on finding the tree. After that, he would figure out the rest.

They had yet to disclose to Parker all that Dez had discussed with Rebecca, and it turned out they wouldn't be talking about it on the drive either. It seemed a better idea to take two vehicles; Parker would need to get back to the hotel before long, and Sully might need to remain behind at the tree. If they couldn't get a handle on the ghost this afternoon, Sully would have no choice but to wait until nightfall. If they were right about the ghost drawing energy from the tree, no way Sully was going to leave it unguarded.

With Parker taking the lead in his vehicle, Sully and Raiya followed in Dez's SUV. They went most of the way to the main road before Parker took a turn onto a narrow dirt path sandwiched between thick stands of trees.

Sully grimaced as he steered. "Man, I hope this doesn't scratch up Dez's paint job."

Raiya made a humming noise. She seemed a thousand miles away, and Sully wasn't sure whether he should cut in.

In the end, he did. "Did you know Parker when you lived here back then?"

She glanced at him as though she'd briefly forgotten he was here. "Oh. No, not really. He wasn't in school with us. As Rebecca mentioned to Dez, Parker was working with Leo already. And I didn't get to know too many people outside of school before we moved away."

She shrugged as her gaze returned to the scenery out the window. "Well, anyway, it's a good thing he's here. Living in the countryside, I suppose he'd have a better idea how to find things like this. Lucky for us."

"Lucky is right. I just hope the woods haven't changed all that much since he was a kid. If they have, even he might not be able to find the Holy Oak."

Parker's vehicle continued on for a ways, until the pathway narrowed to the point it would soon become impassable. Sully was starting to worry about how they would get out of here again when the path opened up onto a field on one side. Parker turned into the open space and parked. Sully pulled up next to him.

"The rest of the way is on foot, I'm afraid," Parker told them once they'd met up outside their vehicles. "It was hard to get to the old tree even when I was a boy."

Sully peered at Raiya. Her anxiety was clear, and without asking, he knew. She'd been here before. This must be where she and the other kids had parked that horrible night.

He leaned toward her, speaking in hushed tones. "You okay?"

She nodded, her expression not matching the movement. "I'd really like to get this over with."

"I hear you," Sully said.

Parker led them from the field back toward the path they'd been driving. While it appeared wide enough for a vehicle at this spot, the path closed in not far ahead. Sully had the impression of the trees acting as foot soldiers defending their king, closing ranks, keeping out opposing forces.

The thought did nothing to relax him. One glance at Raiya told him her thoughts might well be travelling the same path.

"Rebecca told me you believe her father might be responsible for these attacks," Parker said as he led them along the path. "You don't truly believe that, do you?"

"You tell us," Sully said. "As I understand it, you're the one who found him covered in blood. What about you? What did you see?"

Parker stopped, wheeling on Sully, a surprising amount of anger in his ordinarily quiet eyes. "I saw a man whom I've known my entire life—a man who's never been remotely violent—who is clearly suffering from a severe mental condition. If he did do anything, he has no idea. And how do you know he didn't merely find Cal? Blood can get on a person for any number of reasons, you know."

"My brother found pieces of Leo's clothing in the fireplace," Sully reminded him. "An awful lot of blood for it to end up there innocently."

Parker's mouth worked as though he were attempting to think up a response. "Well, all I'm saying is we really don't know what happened."

"Fair enough," Sully said. "And it'll be up to the police to figure it out. I'm just asking you because Rebecca said you've been working with Leo pretty much your entire adult life. You'd be in the best position to know what he's capable of."

"Precisely. And I can tell you he isn't capable of murder—most certainly not the kind of hideous violence that's befallen the Holdfast brothers."

"So why destroy evidence?"

"Because of what you're suggesting. Whether or not he did anything wrong, the state of his clothing makes him look guilty."

"What about Headless Henry?" Sully asked. "What if the ghost was involved somehow?"

Parker started walking again. "Is that what you believe?"

Sully fell into step behind him. "I'm still trying to get my head around it. You lived in this area your whole life. You might've seen things or experienced things others haven't."

"Well, I can't say I've ever seen a ghost. I don't entirely discount the stories, but an invisible presence can't behead a man surely."

"Maybe not," Sully agreed. "But a ghost might be able to influence a physical presence to do it for him."

"I wouldn't know of such things," Parker said. "And I mean no offence, but I really don't care to discuss it—especially in this place."

Sully exchanged a look with Raiya. Raiya shook her head. She wasn't eager to discuss Headless Henry in this place either. Quite often, talking about a ghost led them right to you. And until they located the tree, they needed all the time they could buy.

Best, then, they keep their conversation to a minimum on that point. Sully returned to Parker's relationship with Leo. "You started working with Leo after high school?"

"In a manner of speaking. I left school early. My father died young, and I had to take care of my family. I was delivering groceries for the local store when Leo made me an offer. Said he liked the cut of my jib. My dad worked at the bank, so he had frequent dealings with Leo as a realtor. Leo offered to take me under his wing and show me the business. He trained me from the ground up, got me started writing up listings. Eventually, I was showing properties to clients and even getting them started on making purchases. And when Leo sold the business and purchased the resort property, he brought me along with him. I've as good as been a part of the family."

"You owe him a lot," Sully noted.

"I do. He's been like a father to me. So yes, I do know him well. And I know he didn't do what you suppose he did."

Sully had known a great many people who'd said the same thing about their own loved ones—even the ones who were definitely guilty of murder. Most killers weren't the coldblooded, soulless types they made true crime podcasts about. Most had a human side —a good side, even. They had people who loved them, and perhaps more importantly, they had people they loved.

In all those cases, the existence of love in their lives hadn't been enough to stop them committing evil deeds. Everyone, after all, had a shadow side.

"He sounds like a good man," Sully said.

"He is. What's happened to him is very unfair."

"Someone we talked to told us Leo is making up the dementia, that he's using it to hide bad things he's up to."

Parker spun around again. "You've been speaking to that woman, haven't you?"

Sully played it out. "What woman?"

"Louise Penske. Someone at the festival called the hotel to warn Rebecca that Louise was masquerading as a tarot reader. Rebecca was indisposed, so I took the call. I went down there myself to check, and yes, I did indeed see the resemblance. If Louise told you that, she's as much a liar as she ever was."

Sully pressed ahead. "She said Leo showed up at her hotel and threatened her."

Parker growled low. "She's lying."

"You sure about that?"

Parker was silent a long moment. Finally, he fixed Sully with a stare and said, "I am. I was there."

Sully stared back. "You were?"

"Well, Leo can't very well drive himself anymore." Parker crossed his arms. "I hadn't planned on sharing any of this, but the truth is, I didn't want to upset Rebecca. I went to Leo instead and told him Louise was back. Leo's first instinct was to protect his daughter. That meant having a word with the woman who killed Rebecca's high school boyfriend and getting her to leave town. I don't know how much you know about dementia, but Leo has great moments of clarity where I see the man I've always known. This was one of them. It isn't just about Rebecca, you see. Leo was very close to the Holdfast family. He wanted Rebecca and Cary to be married. Cary's folks were great friends of Leo's, all of the same ilk, so to speak. Likely this is information you don't need, but there were plans for the Holdfasts to go into business with Leo, to buy up shares in the resort. When Cary was killed, everything fell to pieces with the Holdfasts, and those plans went away. But Leo always did his best to support the family all the same. So yes, when he learned Louise was back, he wanted her gone."

"A good man," Sully said again. He wasn't so sure however. It might have been decency behind Leo's actions, or it might have been the work of an opportunist. A partnership with another up-and-coming local family in the Holdfasts. Recruiting Parker, a young man down on his luck who would be happy to take on grunt work in exchange for pay and opportunity. Maybe Sully was being cynical. Maybe he wasn't.

"He was the best." With that, Parker resumed his search. "So that's further proof he couldn't have killed Cary and Cal. They were too important to him. Anyway, he didn't mean anything by what he said to Louise. As I told you, he's not a violent man by nature."

Sully said nothing. Nature or not, he wasn't ruling out the possibility Leo had carried out the murders. Not until he had proof of his own.

Leaving the conversation there for now, they pressed on through the woods. As they shifted farther forward, the trees seemed to close around them even more, branches snagging at their clothes and exposed flesh.

Sully was struck by one other thing, something he hadn't noticed in the section of woods near the resort.

Silence. Complete and utter silence. No birds. No footsteps from deer or other woodland creatures. Not even a breeze. It was as though they'd stepped into a soundproof bubble.

Raiya leaned nearer Sully, speaking in a whisper. "We're close. Stay on your guard."

Sully nodded. He felt it too. It wasn't just the trees closing in now but something more. Something darker.

"I believe we're almost there," Parker said. "It's been a long time, but this is starting to feel familiar."

Sully took a moment to centre himself, putting up what guards he could around himself. He felt the thrum of warm energy against his chest where the wooden amulet rested. Whatever Raiya had done to it, it seemed to be working.

Thank God for that.

Pushing forward, Sully kept his eyes peeled for figures or movement. Nothing showed, and he wasn't convinced it would. Not quite yet. While he sensed dark energy swirling around them, it hadn't yet concentrated itself into a form he could see or fight. He thought maybe it was simply the forest guarding itself he was picking up on.

Then a more disturbing theory occurred to him. The entity was thinking. Watching them and considering its best move. Two strong psychics with the auras to show it—that had to be a concern, even for a ghost this strong.

Sully hoped the Holy Oak was close. He had some considering to do himself, and he'd need to reach the tree to do so.

Then, finally, Parker pushed a branch aside and stopped. "There it is."

Sully took a few more steps, positioning himself so he could look over Parker's shoulder. "That's it, all right."

There could be no doubt. The tree was huge, its trunk thick and solid, its countless branches gnarled and bare. No, on second thought, the trunk wasn't so solid after all. About ten feet up, a large split had formed, the sort which must go deep within the tree's core.

Sully peered upward from there, studying the branches high

overhead. Most of the trees around here had lost the bulk of their leaves, but many held on to a few.

Not the Holy Oak. Not a leaf to be found, no sign it had held any at all this year or during any recent year.

"It's dead," Raiya said. "I hadn't expected it to be dead."

Dead, yes, but it was still emitting energy like a nuclear power plant. Sully felt it humming around him, reaching for and encircling him as though it meant to pull him in.

"Steady, Sully," Raiya said. "I feel it too. I don't know how a dead tree can possess energy like this."

But Sully did. He'd learned the hard way strong ghostly energy could possess not just the living but the dead. If Headless Henry had concentrated his energy here, the tree had become like a power station, one supercharged battery for him to use as needed. All he had to do was feed it on occasion, adding to its stores what he removed.

This tree held secrets and memories of its own. Sully's task was to uncover them.

Before Headless Henry manifested and attacked.

"I've never communicated with a tree before," he said.

"You can do that?" Raiya asked.

Sully shrugged. "It's energy from a ghost, so maybe." He met Raiya's eye. "Only one way to find out."

Gently pressing past Parker, Sully stepped up to the trunk. Lifting a hand, he twitched his fingers, working some added warmth into them. Placing his fingertips against the rough bark, he drew in a breath and held it, focusing.

He was only slightly surprised when the vision started, sweeping him from this world and into another.

CHAPTER 29

The land had been in his family for three generations. As far as he was concerned, it would remain with his family for generations to come.

The problem would be convincing others of that.

The Bruce family had laid claim to the property, using their positions in the town's upper echelon to purchase what wasn't rightfully theirs. Times were hard, even harder for an ex-soldier who'd seen the things he had. He'd returned, having served, to his home, only to discover he no longer had one. Adam Bruce had used his considerable influence, and no doubt his equally considerable wealth, to have Jonas Simon declared dead. Once a crooked judge had made the declaration, Bruce promptly purchased the property.

Now, the place Jonas had grown to love—the only thing in the world he truly did love—was no longer his to return to.

Well, to hell with that.

For a time, he lived secretly on the outskirts of his property, using the woods of his youth to conceal himself. He hunted and warmed himself by a fire only by moonlight and hunkered down by day.

But the days were getting colder, winter rapidly approaching. In this unforgiving climate, it was only a matter of time before his human frailty exposed him.

He hadn't yet decided what to do about it when circumstance decided for him.

The Bruce family wasn't large by the standards of the day, but Adam Bruce had three strong and capable sons with the attitudes to match. Charming and brutish in turn, they held the town and the surrounding area in sway, managing to get their own way simply by being who they were.

Jonas knew them, first as teenagers prior to his years away. They had been pompous then, and they were even more pompous now.

As he discovered late one night, they were prepared to back their attitudes with action. And they would hold onto their property and their wealth by any means. Even through bloodshed.

HE'D BEEN EXISTING on borrowed time. He'd known it since his return.

The sun was setting, the day brutally cold for October. Jonas had been forced to light a fire early to warm himself and to cook the deer he'd taken near the property's northern border.

It hadn't been dark enough, and as the Bruce brothers entered the clearing, Jonas knew the smoke from his fire had breached the treetops.

He stood to meet the threat. He expected an argument, accusations of trespassing and poaching, threats to summon the town constable.

No arguments ensued, no accusations levelled, no threats made. The Bruce brothers had come for a fight and nothing less.

Jonas had been taken unawares. His rifle and his axe were out of reach on the opposite side of the fire.

The Bruce brothers were younger than him by a decade and more. And they were stronger, their bodies untouched by the impacts of combat or cold. They set upon him without a word, and though he gave it his best, he was no match for the three of them together.

They left him battered and bleeding, a crumpled mess next to his dwindling fire. Now, the accusations and threats did come, uttered through sneers and taunts. Their family owned his land now, they said, and there was nothing he could do about it. Leave and stay gone, or he'd get worse next time. He was, after all—as they took great delight in reminding him—

already dead in name. They could kill him, and no one would even know he was gone.

They took his rifle, made a show of aiming to shoot him in the head. They left without taking the shot, their repugnant laughter diminishing with distance. The Bruce brothers were many repulsive things, but they were no killers.

Unfortunately for them, Jonas was.

HE'D TAKEN his first life in battle, his stomach turning as he watched the life dim and disappear in the man's eyes.

Jonas was trained, but nothing readied a man for that first kill. Only, far from the trauma suffered by some of his fellow soldiers, Jonas found he could tolerate the memory quite easily. Perhaps the hardest thing for him to contend with was the concern which came from the knowledge he didn't feel as the other men did.

As those around him fell in battle or grew war-weary, Jonas's cool demeanour became a boon for his commanders. Having grown up hunting in the woods, Jonas knew how to stalk prey and to do so with great stealth. And free of feeling for those he killed, he was well-suited to the tasks of an assassin.

He used the dark as a tool, his skills as weapons. He never took his rifle, and while he carried a pistol, it rarely left its holster. He favoured a blade—a knife for quiet work, an axe for when things got messy. If there were such a thing as past lives, Jonas thought he might have been an executioner, back when treason led to heads rolling.

He not only learned how to kill, he was good at it. The way some were born to carpentry or blacksmithing, Jonas was born to deal death. Like anyone with a well-honed skill, he came to appreciate his ability. And he came to enjoy it.

The way he'd once stalked deer for meat, he now hunted humans for pay. He revelled in the power that came from putting himself right behind another man, the knowledge his presence had gone undetected. And he thrilled to the moment when his blade met flesh and eyes wide with shock, pain and fear found his.

In the days that followed the attack by the Bruce brothers, Jonas took his time, planning as he recovered. Picturing out the coming days, the things he would do, got him through, warming his blood when he got cold and dulling his pain when it throbbed.

Little sparked a wronged man's soul like thoughts of revenge. And little fed him like the act of taking it.

He took them one at a time.

The first one, the middle brother, he came up on while he urinated beyond the barn as the sun's last rays flickered through the wind-lashed trees. Jonas had grinned into his face as the younger man's mouth worked beneath Jonas's hand.

Once the blood had spilled, once the life had fled the Bruce brother's eyes, Jonas stood to leave.

And had stopped.

This wasn't a kill by a paid soldier, after all. This was personal. A message needed to be sent.

The executioner within called to him. Certain offenders were once, long ago, beheaded in the name of justice. Such deaths served not only to punish the wrongdoer but to warn others against doing wrong themselves. To let the yet-uncaught know what awaited them.

And so as the day ended and the night set in with a biting cold, Jonas took the man's head. Tucking the gruesome prize beneath his arm, he found a place to hide.

He stayed there long enough to hear the screams of the others as they found their dead family member. Only then did he melt back into the darkness of the woods where he would await his next opportunity.

WITHIN THE FOLLOWING WEEK, the other two Bruce brothers met similar grisly fates. Jonas watched. He waited. He crept. And finally, a thrill leaping in his chest, he sprang.

As with the first brother, he took the heads of these two, returning with each to the spot where he hid.

For a few days, he kept the heads as a hideous trophy, lining them up next to each other, even sleeping next to them. Sightless, white eyes stared into the darkness, tongues lolling, flies taking advantage for their own ends.

His last target was to be Adam Bruce himself. One last head to add to the collection. There was Adam's wife, of course, but Jonas drew the line there. He'd never killed a woman. Some lines should not be crossed. Anyway, he saw no excitement in it, in taking the life of someone he regarded as weaker than he was. True hunters desired a challenge, and he was to his core a hunter.

Anyway, with her sons gone, she didn't wish to stay in the house. Late at night, Jonas had lingered outside the house, listening to the couple argue. She wanted to leave. She didn't want to stay one more day on the property where her sons had died so horribly. Jonas Simon was still out there somewhere. Even if the current manhunt finally succeeded in locating him, his presence would be felt here by her forever.

She'd leave. With Adam dead, his wife would go and never return. And the property would again belong to Jonas. Who else would wish to live here when the very mention of his name brought shivers of fear to those in the community?

On the night he was to go for Adam, Jonas decided it was time to rid himself of his trio of trophies. They were beginning to smell, even the cold temperatures failing to prevent nature and time having their way.

The question of what to do with them was answered as Jonas recalled the great tree. The Holy Oak, his parents had called it. Massive and twisted, the old oak had a gaping crack partway up its trunk. Jonas thought it might just be large enough to conceal his trophies.

He'd climbed the tree as a youngster, its heavy knot of branches carrying him well up into the forest canopy. He'd imagined what it must be like to fall, but never had the tree betrayed him. It provided him his first glimpse into what it was to go unseen, the world going on below him with no idea he was present. Rarely, he'd discovered, did prey look up.

Upon learning of his many visits to the Holy Oak, Jonas's father had told him of the tree's history. The land on which they lived was once the site of executions, one large branch used to string up the convicted or the lynched. From it, they'd dangled, twisting in the wind until someone saw fit to cut them down.

Far from scaring Jonas away from the tree, the story had only served to further intrigue him. The next day, he'd made a trip across the property and deep into the woods, all but running until he stood beneath the Holy Oak. There, he'd stared up at the branch, perhaps eight feet from the ground. For the first time, he took note of a trio of worn grooves in the wood. Caused by rope and the weight dangling below. Had to be.

The young Jonas placed his hand upon the bark, willing the tree to give up its secrets. He couldn't explain it, but it was as though he could feel the tree's energy, as if in its way it spoke to him. Jonas had always had an affinity for the woods, had felt comfortable there. It wasn't the house to which he was attached. Rather it was the woods that surrounded it. This tree seemed to stand at the heart of it all.

Now as he stood beneath the Holy Oak, the heads of the Bruce brothers bundled within a sack, it was like coming home all over again. Yes, there was the opening he had thought about, perhaps ten feet up the wide trunk. Plenty large enough to receive three skulls and more. And yes, this tree would gladly accept them and conceal his secrets for him. It would protect him as he would protect it.

As he deposited the heads within, the tree seemed to thrum with energy. How it knew, he didn't understand, but it did. Having played a role in the taking of lives so many times in its past, it had come to revel in its task, just as he had come to enjoy his. In this way, he and the Holy Oak were one.

Having fed the tree the heads, Jonas left it behind.

He had business with Adam.

THE TOWN FOUND JONAS FIRST.

They were waiting, concealed around the Bruce property in much the same fashion as Jonas had when he'd hunted the brothers.

Perhaps it was fitting. The rational part of him knew what he'd done was wrong, that surely it would come back to bite him one day.

He'd become overconfident, had come to believe nothing bad could befall him on the property he considered home. So it was with a great sense of shock that he was set upon and trussed up.

He was equally surprised to learn the townspeople also knew of the tree, of its history. A fitting place to execute a murderer, said one.

The intention was to string him up, to let him dangle by the neck from the branch. Adam had other ideas. An eye for an eye, he said. Jonas's axe had been seized from him during his capture. Now Adam wielded it, forcing Jonas to kneel before him.

Where were the heads, Adam demanded to know. But Jonas would take the secret with him to what he accepted would be his death. In this, at least, he still held power. The heads had fed the tree, and in death, the tree would feed Jonas. He was sure of it. Alive or dead, he would come for Adam—him and all others who dared to trespass on Jonas's land.

He grinned at the thought. Kept grinning even as Adam swung the axe at his neck.

THEY BURIED *his body in an unmarked grave near the tree. His head they stuffed between branches on the Holy Oak, letting the bugs, birds and weather have their way over the coming days.*

Jonas, though, wouldn't allow such a desecration. This land was his strength, and the tree, chief among all things here, was his core. He found if he concentrated, he felt the tree's spirit in ways he hadn't before. It fed him, gave him power. Power to move things even though he had no physical form any longer.

It took time, but he soon managed to place his own head within the tree, down where the others lay. Instantly, he felt better. He felt powerful.

His work wasn't done, and now he had a way to do it.

ADAM BRUCE DIED under mysterious circumstances a year later. All Hallows' Eve, a year to the day after Jonas had drawn his last breath. As with his sons before him, his head was never found.

The town named for the great tree whispered of a spectral man, dark and headless, prowling the dark woods near town. They thought perhaps the Holy Oak held a secret, but none were so brave as to venture there.

Adam's widow abandoned the cursed place after his death and left the area altogether. No one knew where she went, though all agreed it was best she go. If Jonas still walked, bent on destroying the final remnants of the Bruce family, best she not be here. Perhaps the ghost of Jonas Simon would be sated knowing the property was his.

And he was for a time. Free to wander the woods as he wished, fear keeping away interlopers, he felt peace for the first time since his youth.

But as the years passed, peace gradually went with them. The house he'd grown up in fell into ruin and the forest changed as all forests do. Only the Holy Oak remained strong and unchanging, guarding its secrets even as Jonas himself did.

The heads remained, nothing now but bits of flesh and hair over bone. The Bruce family, together forever in death. The men who'd lynched Jonas that day claimed to have smelled something sickly wafting from the tree, but none had had the courage to look. And so Jonas's trophies remained safely ensconced in the Holy Oak. He expected they always would.

As long as they did, the tree would remain strong—a king amongst a forest of loyal and fearful subjects. And if the tree remained strong, so too would Jonas.

And so he walked. He watched. He waited. He crept. And when he happened upon a foolhardy soul who dared to trespass on his land, he sprang. There was power in fear, in violent death. And there too was fuel for his beloved tree. Fuel for himself.

The Holy Oak and the surrounding forest would be here forever as long as Jonas himself remained. To take one was to finish the other.

This was his land. His home. His very essence. It always would be. He would make it so.

If not through fear, then at the edge of his axe.

CHAPTER 30

SULLY'S EYES FLASHED OPEN, a gasp catching in his throat.

He started hacking, and he doubled over, hands on knees, as he tried to keep from vomiting.

Raiya's hand was on his back. "Are you all right? I was about to try to draw you out. It seemed you were having trouble breathing."

"Happens sometimes," he ground out and promptly set off another round of coughing.

"What happened?" Parker asked.

"I saw it," Sully told them as he straightened. "I saw how this tree holds energy. It's the heads. Headless Henry's real name is Jonas Simon. He puts the heads inside."

Parker's eyes shot toward the trunk as he stepped away from it. "In the tree?"

Sully nodded. "That big crack in the trunk up there. He puts them inside."

"Oh, good lord," Raiya groaned. "How awful."

Sully redirected his gaze to her. "Anything from Dez?"

"Nothing yet. Why?"

"I need him down here. I have to get into that tree."

Raiya blinked up at the crevice. "In there? You can't be serious."

"Totally serious. I think we have to remove the skulls to cut into his power."

Raiya wrinkled her nose. "I don't like the sound of this."

"Believe me, neither do I. But I think this is the answer. He's deeply connected to the tree. We take one, we take them both. That's what I was shown."

"Okay," she said. "I'll call. You just keep your eyes and other senses peeled."

Easily done. Now that they'd found the tree, the vibrations in the immediate area were like a mini-earthquake inside Sully's consciousness, shaking him from the inside out. He nearly laid a hand against the tree to steady himself. He remembered before he did so, backing away and seeking balance beneath another tree instead. It was better but far from ideal. Nothing around here was going to right him, not unless he could first right the balance here.

He wasn't looking forward to what he'd need to do to pull it off.

Raiya was scrolling through her contacts, presumably searching for Dez's number. Sully fought past the press of negativity, needing to impart a message to Dez through Raiya.

"Tell him to look for a chainsaw."

"A what?" Parker's tone was one of shock. Something else was there too though, something Sully couldn't put a finger on.

"I need to get inside that tree," Sully said. "Either that or take the whole thing down."

"You can't do that."

Sully canted his head as he regarded Parker. "Why not?"

"This tree is a part of the area's history. It's been here at least a few hundred years. It could stand for hundreds more."

Sully peered up at it again. "It's ancient, all right. But it's dead, Parker. Normally, I'm totally with you. My mom's a huge plant person, and she taught us how important nature is and everything. This isn't about that. The Holy Oak hasn't only soaked in loads of dark energy, it's a storehouse for it. I'm hoping if I can remove some of it—in graphic terms, remove the skulls inside it—the tree won't hold the same energy. But it was a hanging tree too, okay? I'm pretty sure those things leave scars on trees just like on humans, buildings or objects. Maybe I can save what's left of it. I want to try. But if I can't, we need to be ready."

"How do you know all this?"

"It's what I do. I connected with the energy inside the tree, and I saw its past. I saw the ghost's past. It wasn't pleasant. Far from it. It needs stopped, Parker, and this is how I know to do it."

Maybe it was the substance of the conversation. Maybe it was simply their presence here. Whatever it was, the energy around the tree changed. What was vibrations and pressure before turned to jabs and fire.

It was strong enough and pointed enough, even Parker seemed to notice. He blinked heavily, his eyes drooping shut as he stumbled back against the tree.

"Parker?" Sully said. "You okay?"

He didn't respond. Sully rushed to his side. The sharp sensations grew stronger.

Placing a hand on Parker's shoulder, Sully redirected wide eyes to Raiya. "Tell Dez we might need an ambulance here. Ask him to check my pin."

She looked up from her phone screen, her own eyes saucers as they met Sully's. "I can't. I've got no signal."

Sully pulled out his own phone. The message on the screen made it painfully clear.

No service.

"Oh hell," Sully groaned.

Panic wasn't an option. Headless Henry—no, Jonas Simon—was manifesting.

Sully yanked out Dez's SUV keys and tossed them to Raiya. "Take Parker and get back to the SUV. I'll hold Jonas off."

"Sully, no."

"Go! Now!"

Raiya stepped forward and took Parker by the arm, helping him away from the tree. "Come with me, Sully. We're stronger together."

"I need to—"

"I won't leave you. Not like this." She managed a smile. "Your brother would kill me."

Sully took a couple of seconds to study her expression. She wasn't kidding about not leaving without him. She'd stay, and that meant Parker would stay. Getting Parker to safety was his priority. Ensuring Raiya was protected was another big one.

Sully opened his map app and tapped to drop a pin. Though he had no reception, he hoped his phone would record the location anyway, allowing him to share it once he re-entered the range of a signal.

"All right," he told Raiya. "Let's go."

They didn't get far.

Sully was bringing up the rear, ensuring Raiya and Parker got out before him, when he felt something slam into his back. Nothing physical, although it almost felt that way. This was something else, like what had happened to him the other night when he'd taken the blow to the head and lost himself to a ghost's memory.

He fought with Jonas, battling him for control. But this close to the source of Jonas's power—of his evil—there could be no win for Sully. He needed Dez, and Dez wasn't here.

As he felt himself buckling beneath Jonas, he knew instinctively what would come next. The night wouldn't end until someone else was dead.

He fell to his knees, head swimming. He had next to no time left before he disappeared behind Jonas's dark power. Just enough to urge Raiya and Parker onward.

"Run!" he yelled. "Go!"

For a moment, Raiya stalled. Sully worried she'd argue and remain behind. It must have said something about his appearance that she didn't, that she instead turned and ran, tugging Parker with her.

Sully held on as long as he could, giving Raiya and Parker a head start. Or maybe it wasn't Sully at all. Maybe this was Jonas granting them time, letting them gain some ground. For him, the pleasure in hunting was the hunt itself.

As the sounds of footfalls and snapping branches grew more distant, Jonas lunged forward inside him. And Sully was forced back and down until he'd lost control. A passenger inside his own vehicle.

One being driven by a murderer.

CHAPTER 31

Dez had a bad feeling. Granted, it was virtually impossible not to given the current set of circumstances, but this was different.

Something was wrong.

He'd tried Sully's phone twice, Raiya's once. No answer at either, each heading straight to voicemail.

Only two reasons that would happen. Either they were both on the phone at once—not likely—or they were out of range. The latter was the probable scenario, and it wasn't unexpected given the heavy trees in the area. Explanation or not, Dez couldn't shake the chill creeping over him. Whatever was going on, it wasn't a good thing.

The ex-cop part of him knew he needed to stay and guard this evidence until they were ready to alert the police. The brother part of him knew he needed to get out of here right now.

The brother part won out. He called Forbes.

"Don't be pissed," Dez said. "But Sully and I turned something up you're going to want to see."

"Do I really want to know about this?" Forbes asked.

"Just get over to the resort," Dez told him. "As soon as possible. I need to get out of here, but I don't want to leave this unguarded.

Please. If you can't get here right away, send a patrol officer. I'm in Rebecca Symes's office."

"What the hell's going on?"

"I don't know. But whatever it is, it's bad. I need to find Sully, but he's not picking up his phone. Neither is Raiya."

"What are they doing exactly?" Forbes asked.

"That, you definitely won't want to know."

"Where are they?"

Dez tugged a hand through his hair. "That's what I need to find out."

JONAS SNEERED as he stalked through the woods on the tail of his prey. A dark thrill coursed through him, setting the heart of his current vessel to pounding.

This vessel was different—a lot different from the last one. This one held the sort of power Jonas normally only felt pulsating through the great oak on All Hallows' Eve night. At one time, someone as strange and powerful as this man might have been burned at the stake or hanged as a witch. Even in Jonas's own time, this man might well have met his end at the Holy Oak itself.

Times had changed. Jonas knew it. He understood many years had passed since he'd last drawn breath, and some things that had been crimes in his day were no longer.

Lucky for him. In control of this body, he thought he might be able to do anything.

Right now, that anything involved catching and killing the man he was chasing.

Parker. That was his name. Jonas had learned that much when he first possessed him many years back, the night when he had taken the young man with the denim jacket.

Parker had been a willing accomplice, having entered the woods with murder in his own heart. It had made it only too easy for Jonas to take charge, to lend his own considerable hate to that of the young man he was possessing. Together, they had caught up with their prey, and Parker had delivered the death blow with an axe he'd brought with him for that purpose.

Jonas had thrilled to Parker's wrath, to his bloodlust. And he'd enjoyed it all over again only recently, when Parker had tracked and killed the man Jonas knew was called Cal.

What Parker's problem was with the pair of them, Jonas could only guess at. He hadn't stopped to explain, killing each of them wordlessly while clad in a dark cloak worn above his head in a way that made him look as though he were headless. Jonas might've found the whole thing insulting were it not for the obvious impact the costume had elicited in Parker's victims.

Terror. Now there was something Jonas could get behind.

He was certainly enjoying it now, hearing the screams from Parker ahead as Jonas slowly but surely closed the distance between them. The woman was quiet. If she were equally afraid, she wasn't vocalizing it.

It didn't matter. Jonas sensed her power, nearly as strong as the young man he was possessing right now. But as much as he thought that perhaps he should kill her too, he had decided he wouldn't. He had never crossed that line, killing a woman. He didn't think he would need to start now.

He said nothing, no need to call out or threaten. They knew he was coming.

RAIYA TUGGED PARKER ALONG, desperate to put as much distance as she could between herself and Sully.

Leaving him had been the hardest thing she'd had to do in a while, running contrary to every instinct she had. But Sully had been right. She couldn't fight this ghost on her own, and neither could Sully.

They needed help. They needed to break down the power coming from that tree.

That meant getting Dez down here as quickly as possible. And they couldn't do that if the ghost found them.

Parker was panicking. Raiya understood the threat better than most, but she was a little surprised Parker seemed to as well.

"Try to calm down," she told him. "You need to help me find the SUV."

"We can't let him find us. He'll kill us. I know he will."

There would be time for questions later. Raiya needed to focus.

The moment wasn't lost on her, this meeting of past with present. The last time she'd been in such a situation, she'd been a terrified sixteen-year-old. Now, although she had to admit she was frightened, it hadn't reached the stage of terror. She was confident in herself. She was confident in Sully. He wouldn't kill her, not even under the power of the spirit possessing him.

At least, that was what she told herself.

She'd come a long way since her teenage years. If she hadn't known it before, she was keenly aware of it now. She wouldn't only survive this day, she would ensure Parker did too.

"We're not going to make it," Parker cried, the words catching in his throat as a sob sounded. "He'll catch us. He'll kill us."

Perhaps Raiya would need to talk to him after all, if only to calm him down. She had some idea about the direction they needed to go, but Parker was the one who truly knew how to get back.

"I understand this is terrible situation," she said. "But what makes you so sure we're going to die?"

"Because he's killed before. Don't you see?"

"I know that young man very well. He's no killer." Playing dumb, pretending she didn't know about the possession. Admitting to what was really happening would do nothing to calm Parker.

"It's not him! He's not himself. It's Headless Henry! He knows what you plan to do to his tree, and he'll kill you before he lets you do it."

Raiya changed her mind. Maybe conversation with Parker wasn't such a good idea after all.

"Keep moving," she said. "Focus on finding the vehicles. The sooner we do, the sooner we get out of here."

"We don't have time!"

And then they didn't.

The crash of branches behind them had Raiya whirling in place. She threw herself to the side as Sully flung himself at them. He had in his hand the pocket knife Sully carried. It wasn't large, but even small blades could do horrible damage.

Sully—or rather the ghost possessing him—was focused on Parker. Raiya took advantage, launching herself at Sully's back and seizing him around the neck by her arms.

A guttural sound was wrenched from Sully's throat as he grabbed at Raiya's arms with his free hand, stumbling backward as he did.

"Parker, run!" Raiya yelled.

No problem there. Parker did as told, flinging himself through the trees as he ran as fast as his legs would carry him.

So much for chivalry.

Raiya was rammed backward against a tree hard enough her lungs rattled. She coughed, and pain radiated up her spine, but she didn't let go.

Sully wrenched himself around, trying to toss Raiya off his back, but still, she refused to let go.

Another couple of steps back. Another collision with a tree. Another twist to try to throw her off. This time, she couldn't hold on, and she found herself sprawled out on the ground.

He was coming at her, possibly to kill her.

She couldn't allow it. She wouldn't. Whatever happened now, Sully would have to live with.

That's when she spotted the branch, large and heavy looking. She scrambled forward and grabbed hold. As he lurched toward her, she heaved herself to her feet, wielding the branch.

One problem with possession: it wasn't always easy for the dead to control the living. Sully was young, limber and quick, but only when in control of himself. The ghost wasn't quite so adept.

As he came for her, knife at the ready, Raiya stepped quickly to the side, swinging the branch as she did. It connected with a sickening thud, nailing him hard on the back of the head. He went down, but she didn't stick around to find out more about his condition.

She paused long enough to scoop up the knife. Then, following the approximate path Parker had taken, Raiya ran for her life.

CHAPTER 32

DEZ HAD CONVINCED Rebecca to allow him to use her car. The problem was, he had no idea where he was going.

That changed the moment his cellphone rang.

Raiya.

He picked up immediately, just as he was about to unlock Rebecca's car. "Tell me everything's okay."

"I can't."

Oh hell. "Sully?"

"I don't know. He's possessed. I had to hit him with a branch so Parker and I could get away. We're driving back. I had to leave him to save Parker."

Dez's heart sank. "Okay. Okay, we'll figure this out. Get back here, and I'll head out and look for him. Does he still have his phone on him?"

"As far as I know. Depends on reception though. We didn't have any until we were closer to the vehicles."

"Are you taking both vehicles with you?"

"We are. Parker's in his, and I'm in yours. Sully tossed me the keys once he realized things were going south."

Dez blinked heavily, brain spinning around this latest information. Another day, another nightmare. "All right, listen, I've got

Forbes down here now, so he's taking charge of Rebecca's office and everything in there. She's lent me her car, so I'll start driving and meet you. Just show me where you parked, and I'll find Sully."

"No, stop. You need to listen. Parker showed us to the tree. You'll need to cut into it and get those skulls out. The tree itself is dead, but those heads and whatever nasty stuff is connected to them are keeping the tree fuelled with energy. You need to get them out to power this guy down. See if Rebecca has a chainsaw or something like that you can borrow. You might need a rope too. There's a crack in the tree big enough to drop skulls inside, but it's a bit higher up. By the time you get those things together, Parker and I should be at the resort again. Then I'll head back with you."

"No, Raiya. It's too dangerous."

"Exactly my point. You're not going alone."

Dez jogged back inside the hotel, intent on locating Rebecca. "I won't be alone. Sully's there. He won't hurt me."

"I'd like to think so too, but he's not himself. He's really not. He's in there, but this ghost is strong. When I say we need to get him powered down, I'm not putting it lightly. Until we do, Sully's a real threat to anyone who crosses his path—even you. We can't put him in a position to do something he won't be able to live with."

As much as Dez hated to admit it, Raiya was right. They had been in a situation like this more than once. Dez knew firsthand how possessions could go. He and Sully had nearly killed each other a couple of times thanks to overly strong spirits riding one or the other of them.

"I hear you," Dez said. "Come back, and we'll get this figured out."

He disconnected and promptly found himself staring into Forbes's face. "What's happening?"

Dez debated for a moment how much to share before accepting he could use all the help he could get. "Sully's in trouble. Can you help?"

Forbes groaned. "As much as I hate his brand of trouble, I guess I'm going to have to."

Dez and Forbes waited in the parking lot until Raiya and Parker returned. It didn't take long.

"The Holy Oak isn't right on resort property," Parker explained. "There's a section of property next to it that's still Crown land. It's on there."

"Let's go," Dez said.

They opted to take two vehicles. Best to allow people to leave if necessary without stranding those left behind. Dez drove his SUV with Raiya as passenger; Forbes, who had a patrol officer guarding the office until the forensics crew arrived, drove his own.

Dez was surprised when Parker dropped into his back seat.

"You're coming back with us?" Dez asked him.

"I'd rather not, but I'm the one who knows best where to find the tree," Parker replied.

Dez cast him a glance in the rearview. "Thanks, man. I appreciate it."

He then passed Raiya his cellphone, first using his face to unlock it. "Tap into my map app, would you? See if you can find Sully's marker on there."

Raiya did as requested, but her head shake told Dez she'd come up empty. "Nothing. Sorry. The reception out there is really bad."

"Always has been," Parker said. "We always warn wild campers not to count on their cellphones. Probably all the trees."

Dez wasn't sold. Lots of trees stood around Whispering Winds, yet the reception there seemed decent enough. The reason was likely something else. Spirit activity messed with electronics; massive amounts of spirit activity screwed up that and much more. If Sully was right, and the entire wooded area was poisoned by this entity and the big oak it had taken over, Dez wouldn't be at all surprised to find no reception anywhere nearby.

They'd need to wait until they reached the tree to find Sully.

At least that was what Dez hoped.

Parker led the way. They parked at the edge of a field, then climbed out of their respective vehicles and met up at the back of Dez's SUV. From the hatch, Dez removed the items Rebecca had found for him in Whispering Winds's maintenance shed: a gas-powered chainsaw and a length of arborist rigging rope. With all the trees in the area, the resort thankfully had those items readily available. His flashlight was already inside his coat pocket. The daylight was already beginning to wane; by the time they got deep into the woods, it would all but vanish.

Parker watched, anxiety tensing his face and shoulders, as Dez placed the rope coil over a shoulder and hefted the chainsaw. "You're going to cut it down?"

"I don't know yet," Dez told him. "I won't know anything for sure until I get there. Want to lead the way?"

Parker eyed him. "He won't let you do it, you know. He'll kill you first."

He was starting to remind Dez of Leo. This time, Dez had an answer to the warning. "Not if I kill him first."

"I'm not sure you can."

"If it's down to him or Sully, you'd better believe I can."

Discussion over for Dez. He made sure Parker knew it too as he levelled a purposeful stare at him. "Let's go. Now."

Parker eyed him another second or two. Maybe he recognized the threat posed by Dez himself, because he finally turned and started off into the woods.

They wound through the forest in a line, Parker leading the way and Raiya in front of Dez where he could stay alert to her body language and make sure she was safe. She was tense, though she'd so far stayed silent as to what she was experiencing. She'd speak up if a threat became a full-blown danger. Until that moment, Dez was focused mostly on one thing.

He kept his phone out, his screen showing his map app as he prayed to see the dot representing Sully pop up somewhere. But it never did, and as they headed deeper into the woods, Dez's own position eventually stalled out too as the message at the top of his screen advised he had lost signal.

They were on their own.

PARKER LED them to the hulking, twisted tree that was the Holy Oak, then stood back, arms folded tightly across his body as if protecting himself.

His fear was obvious, but Dez didn't have the time or inclination to make him feel better. He had a job to do.

Cut into the tree's core, pull out those missing skulls. Then, if all went to plan, Sully would have a chance at battling Headless Henry and ending this nightmare forever.

Dez stepped to the side of the tree and eyed the large gap overhead. Yeah, no question, it was large enough to stuff a human head inside. Depending how hollow the tree was inside, those skulls could be way down inside.

Patting himself down to double check the flashlight was where it should be—it was—Dez handed the chainsaw to Forbes.

"Hang onto this for me for a minute," Dez told him. "I'll climb up to that big branch up there. It looks plenty sturdy to hold me."

"That's the hanging branch," Parker said quietly.

Dez flipped wide eyes to him. "Seriously?"

"They hanged people from there."

Dez started up at it. Yeah, now that he was studying it more carefully, it had that look to it, all right. "Oh man."

He shook off the chill. Nothing for it. He needed to get up there. Sully was counting on him.

Dez cast Raiya a glance as he ensured the rope was snug around his shoulder. "Getting anything?"

She shifted from one foot to the other. "Too much."

"What about Sully? Anything there?"

She shook her head. "No, but I'm not concerned it's because he'd come to any physical harm. He's possessed, so his essence has been weakened. Do what you need to, and I'm sure I'll find him."

Good enough. Dez turned toward the tree, preparing to climb.

"You shouldn't do that," Parker said.

Dez ignored him. A broken branch a few feet up would act as a makeshift foothold. He was testing it for strength when Parker spoke again.

"You *really* shouldn't do that."

This time, Raiya gave a small squeak.

Dez spun back toward them, noting as he did that Forbes dropped the chainsaw and drew his sidearm, levelling it at Parker.

Parker, who was holding a knife to Raiya's throat.

CHAPTER 33

"PUT DOWN THE KNIFE, PARKER," Forbes growled.

Parker stared down the gun but shook his head, ducking farther behind Raiya. "I can't do that."

"He wasn't asking," Dez growled.

"Let me handle this, Braddock," Forbes muttered. Then, to Parker, "I wasn't asking."

Parker jutted his chin toward the Holy Oak. "You need to leave that tree alone."

"Maybe I'm not making myself clear," Forbes said. "I'm with the Kimotan Rapids Police Department, and I'm ordering you to put down the knife and step away. Do as I say, and this ends well for you."

"It won't end well for any of us if you don't leave now."

This was going nowhere fast. "We're ending it by cutting into this tree," Dez said.

"I can't let you do it." Parker pressed the edge of the blade against Raiya's throat. She tensed further and drew a sharp intake of breath.

"I swear to God, Parker," Dez snarled. "You hurt her, I hurt you."

"Yes, but she gets hurt first."

A good point. The question now centred on how serious Parker was in his threats.

Dez guessed his thoughts were playing out in his expression because Parker jumped back in. "You think I won't? You think I'm not capable of hurting her? I will, you know."

Dez studied his face, his eyes. There was panic there, yes. But there was something else there now too. Resolve. And behind that, steel. The kind-eyed Parker was gone. If Dez didn't know better—if he didn't know the ghost was occupied with Sully—he'd think he was facing the soul of Headless Henry now.

"What are you saying, Parker?" Dez asked.

"You all think you're so smart. Everyone has always thought so little of me. Good ol' reliable Parker, they'd say. He'll help. He'll do whatever you ask. And I did, you know. I've always given so much of my time, my effort, *myself* to help Leo. Right from the time I was a boy, back when he first took me on, I've done everything I could to make him happy. All I've ever asked is to be treated fairly."

Dez hoped Forbes wouldn't cut in. They were on the edge of something here. Something big. "Leo didn't treat you fairly?"

"None of them did. Not one. I did right by Leo. I always did. My own father died young, and Leo was there to help. He was like a father to me, and I thought, in his way, he viewed me as a son. But then Cary Holdfast came along. All his charm and swagger, and he swept Rebecca right off her feet. Leo too. Leo and Cary's father were great friends, and they were taken with the idea of Cary and Rebecca marrying one day. Consolidating their families' wealth, going into business together. Well, if they joined up, where did that leave me? I'll tell you where: right where I started out. With nothing. Cary would take my place at Leo's side, and I'd be nowhere. So I planned. I waited for the right opportunity. And when I heard of their plan to frighten Raiya in the woods, I knew my moment had come."

He gave a nervous giggle. "I wasn't alone. Henry, he's been my strength when I thought I'd have none. I didn't think I could go through with it that night. I had my costume sorted, figuring if I was seen, people would blame the ghost. Only, when it came to it, I was afraid. Henry made me strong. He helped me do what I needed to do."

"And Cal?" Dez asked. "What harm did he do to you?"

Parker snorted. "I devoted my life to Leo. I took on all the grunt work, the thankless tasks he or Rebecca assigned to me. And as he aged and started to lose his marbles, I took care of him. I did all of that. Again, I thought, well, Leo won't live forever. Surely he'll remember me in his will."

His expression darkened. "And then he asked me to help him finalize his will. I read it, you see. Rebecca, as expected, is to inherit almost everything. Almost. The rest—a couple of properties in town—was to go to someone else. Can you guess who?"

Dez didn't think it took a genius at this point. "Cal."

Parker gave a slow nod. "At first, it made no sense to me. So I asked. Leo reminded me about how close he was to the Holdfast family. Told me how much they'd suffered. Cal needed a hand, he said, what with his being stuck with that little clothing store in town. Cal had his family's house, of course, but he'd never sell it. So Leo wanted to help him. To help *him*. Nothing for me. Not one red cent. So, yes, when the opportunity arose, I went after him. Didn't quite get a chance to finish when Louise Penske turned up. I barely got away unseen."

Forbes took a few small steps to the side, angling for a better position. "You let her take the blame for Cary's murder. And you would have allowed it again with Cal."

Parker snorted. "Please. Everyone believes she's crazy. Louise herself believes it. She's never served time for killing anyone. She wasn't likely to be forced to now."

"What about Leo?" Dez asked. "You tried to pin it on him. You told Rebecca you found him wandering the woods and that he was covered in blood. You gave her Leo's clothing to destroy."

"He *was* wandering. Leo wanders as a matter of course. It was an easy thing to exchange my shirt for his. I no longer had my Henry cloak, so I used a dark sheet instead. It gaped open at the wrong moment. So yes, I needed to come up with something fast once I saw the blood. Leo happened to be nearby. Look, I care about him, but like Louise, he wasn't going to serve time. Not in his condition."

"How do you know that?" Forbes asked. "Quite a chance you took with someone you profess to care for."

"You'd truly lock away a man with dementia?" Parker asked. "If so, you're more heartless than I am. Anyway," he added with a shrug, "after what I discovered in that will—after all I gave that man—perhaps it's only right he should give me something in return. If not an inheritance, then my freedom."

"Where are the cloak and the sheet you wore?" Forbes asked.

Parker was silent on this point. Dez thought he knew why.

"They're in the tree, aren't they?" Dez asked.

The slight flash in Parker's eyes gave him his answer.

"And Cary's head?" Dez said. "You put it in there too?"

Parker's answer surprised him. "Nope. I ran like hell. I didn't even finish slicing it off. Found out later it was gone. I can think of only one explanation for why it might have ended up where it did."

Dez did too. The explanation didn't involve a living human at all.

He'd find out soon enough—once they managed to end the threat to Raiya.

"That's enough now," Forbes said. "Put down that knife, right now."

"No. She's coming with me, and you're going to stand there and not move. You do, and—"

Parker broke off in a sharp wheeze as Raiya drove an elbow into his gut. He barely had time to double over when she brought down her heel on his instep. Parker howled in pain and released both her and the knife.

Dez and Forbes rushed forward, Forbes providing cover with his sidearm while Dez put Parker to the ground on his belly.

Forbes plucked a set of cuffs from his belt and handed them to Dez. While Dez snapped them on, cuffing Parker's wrists behind his back, Forbes read him his rights for murder.

Standing, Dez faced Raiya. Despite the tension of the ongoing situation, a grin broke out on his face. "Holy hell, lady, that was awesome."

She beamed back. "Hey, a lady's got to know how to protect herself."

"And protect us guys at the same time. Well done." He returned his attention to Forbes. "All good?"

Forbes finished clipping his sidearm safely back in its holster. "Would've preferred to get all of that in an interview room, but hey, I'll take what I can get." He nodded toward the tree. "Let's get busy saving our brother, huh?"

Dez answered with a quirk of his lips. "Absolutely."

CHAPTER 34

Jonas sensed something was amiss well before he could do anything about it.

This was the problem with possession. He'd been thrilled when he learned how to take over a human body, enabling him to protect his property in ways which would have required far too much energy as a spirit.

But there was a tradeoff. As a spiritual entity, he could travel anywhere on his property in next to no time. In the blink of an eye, he could go from the Holy Oak to the field where, long ago, his house had stood. Another blink, he could be at the spot where they'd buried his corpse or where he'd taken one of his last victims.

But in a human body, he could go only as fast as the mortal form would allow. Flesh, blood and bone—they might be strong in the physical sense, but they were weak and slow compared to spirit.

It was what he was stuck with as the feeling struck him like a punch to the gut. The interlopers were back, and this time, they'd brought help.

He smirked. Just as well for them. They'd need it.

Jonas moved as stealthily as he could through the trees. The body he occupied was youthful and strong, and it was also light enough to manipulate quietly.

The man's psychic power should have lent considerable power to Jonas's own, only it wasn't. For some reason, Jonas couldn't hold it, couldn't use it. As far down as he'd pushed the soul connected to this body, it remained strong, in control in a way Jonas couldn't touch.

To hell with it. Even if he couldn't hold control of the mental aspect, he had the physical. It would be enough.

He made it most of the way back to the tree before he thought perhaps he was wrong. He heard the witch before he saw her.

"He's coming," she said.

She'd appeared familiar to him earlier. Now he knew for certain who she was, the memory taking him back several decades to a particularly delicious kill. He'd let her live that night, sticking to his code regarding females.

Now, he thought he should have reconsidered.

Nothing for it. She knew. The witch was connected to the spirit world just as Jonas was, just as the young man he possessed.

The Holy Oak stood tall and twisted ahead of him. Its long, winding branches formed their familiar web above his head, raining down energy over him.

He crouched low. From beneath the jacket he currently wore, he produced his axe. He'd learned to avoid leaving it in or near the oak; the tree simply attracted too many hunters, and the last thing he wanted was to lose his weapon of choice. He kept it near his grave, safe and sound. This axe had been with him since his living years. It would remain with him throughout his eternal death.

Ahead, a short sprint away, stood a shorter, stockier man in his forties. He stood in a way that suggested he was unaware of Jonas's position. Then Jonas saw the gun on his hip.

A policeman.

Jonas would need to be quick.

Lifting the axe to his side so it was ready for a quick, debilitating slice, Jonas rushed forward.

A shout came from overhead. "Forbes!"

The short man whirled, but Jonas's attention travelled elsewhere.

To the huge, redheaded beast of a man coming down on him from within the branches of the Holy Oak.

Jonas deked left, but there was no escape as he was grabbed and tackled. He'd held on tight to the axe, and he prepared to use it now, to get in whatever blows he could as the man-beast's movements slowed with apparent shock.

But before he could deliver a blow, the short man was there too, adding his own weight and grip, pinning Jonas's axe hand to the ground.

Jonas ground out a wail as he writhed against the men. Then he was being flipped onto his belly, his arms wrenched behind him.

"His hands," the big one panted. "Tie his hands."

"With what?"

"The rope, Forbes! Get the rope!"

The smaller one released him, for all the good that did. The man-beast had the strength of two, and he seemed to know how to use it to its best advantage as he pinioned Jonas's vessel's hands behind his back. Next thing Jonas knew, the shorter man was back on his knees next to him, looping a rope around his wrists and pulling it tight.

"Come on, Sully," the big one said. "I know you're in there. Fight him. Come on, Sull, I need you back here. Fight!"

Jonas had been about to leave the body behind, useless as it was proving. Now, though, he paused. The young man he possessed was important to these people. Maybe he could use it to his benefit.

"He's mine," he snarled. "Go to hell."

It was the witch who answered for the group. "You first." Then to the big man, "Turn him."

Jonas struggled but got nowhere fast as the large man obeyed. Then the witch was there, kneeling over him.

"You will leave him, Jonas Simon, or you will suffer."

He sneered up at her. He quit grinning as she removed something from around the young man's neck. Jonas had felt it there, burning. Not enough to trouble him greatly, but he'd been aware of it all the same.

Now, though, it took on a new threat.

The witch rubbed it between her palms, muttering something Jonas couldn't make out. Still mumbling what seemed to be an incantation, she leaned forward and pressed the wooden cross to Jonas's head.

Fire. White hot fire like a branding iron. He thought it must be burning straight through flesh and bone and brain. Coming straight for his soul.

He screamed. Kept screaming until he could take no more.

With nothing more to be done, he fled the body.

Not the area though. No, these people would pay. And their heads would stay here forever inside his tree.

SULLY SLUMPED, barely conscious, against Dez's leg.

Dez watched him for a few seconds, hand against the back of Sully's head, hoping. "Is it over?" he asked Raiya.

She shook her head. "Not yet. You need to finish it."

Dez didn't need to ask what she meant. He launched himself back at the tree and up, up to the branch from which Parker said they'd hanged people.

"Should I untie him?" Forbes asked from next to Sully.

"No," Raiya said. "Jonas is still around. We need to make Sully as useless to him as possible. We don't want him getting back in there."

"What if he comes after one of us next?" Forbes asked. "I don't know what to do about it."

"That's why Dez is up there now, doing what he's doing."

Speaking of that ... "Forbes," Dez called down. "Chainsaw."

Forbes jumped into action, grabbing the tool and lifting it up.

Dez grasped it and brought it up next to the trunk, a foot or two below the large gap overhead. With luck, he didn't need to climb farther; hopefully, the skulls were here, right in front of him.

The things he had to think about.

This was one of those chainsaws with the pull cord, but blessedly, it operated better than the one his dad used to own. Two yanks and it roared to life. He pressed the blade to the tree, wincing to protect his eyes as the wood chips flew.

Something hard collided with his back, driving him forward. He caught himself, keeping both from falling and from coming too near the blade. What had hit him he didn't know. He knew only he couldn't stop.

"Leave him alone!" Raiya yelled. "You leave him, Jonas!"

Another slam. This time, Dez nearly dropped the chainsaw. He glanced down long enough to see Sully staring back at him, wide-eyed. Whatever was beside Dez, it wasn't good.

It didn't matter. He needed to do this, needed to do his part to end this. He had to protect the others, to keep Jonas from taking Sully again.

Another impact, this one to Dez's head. His knee buckled. This time, he had to release the chainsaw with one hand to hold onto the tree.

Sully roared. "Leave him!"

Something in the air changed. Whatever had been behind Dez was gone.

It wouldn't be for long, but with Sully back in action, Dez went back to work.

Sully stared up at Dez, watching for Jonas's return. Sully had flung the ghost from the branch, had watched as Jonas flew backward, vanishing between the trees ahead.

But he'd be back, just as strong and as angry as before.

"Raiya," Sully said.

"Keep an eye on your brother," she said. She started with an incantation, whispered under her breath. Sully couldn't understand her, but he wasn't really trying to either. His focus was fully on Dez, on the anticipated return of Jonas.

The chainsaw whirred back to life as Dez got both hands back on it. It sliced back into the dead tree, bits of wood flying everywhere.

Raiya was moving, taking her nearer the tree. Sully decided she was muttering protective enchantments of some type. He didn't know much about the whole Wiccan thing, but as long as it worked, he could live with not understanding it. What he did understand was his own ability, and right now it was screaming at him that the danger was back.

The shadow appeared again behind Dez. This time, something dull and metallic flashed into view.

The axe.

No.

Sully pushed out, sending Jonas flying once more. The axe, about to cut into Dez, vanished.

"Hurry, Dez," Sully mumbled. "Please."

Sully was exhausted. Being possessed, fighting against it, had taken a huge pile of energy. He had little left, but whatever there was belonged now to Dez.

Dez finished one slice, pulled the chainsaw blade free and went in for another cut.

Jonas again. This time, the axe appeared before the shadow itself did. Sully caught it mid-swing, shoved it aside. Kept shoving until the entity was pushed fully back again.

Second slice made overhead. Dez kicked at the wood, shifting it. Kicked again. This time, a big chunk of the trunk broke away and fell toward the ground.

Dez dropped the chainsaw. First shaking tension from his hands, he then pulled out his flashlight and used it to peer inside. The wrinkling of his nose told Sully what he'd found.

"I've got hair here, guys," he called down.

He reached inside—just in time for Jonas to come back at them.

This time, though, he didn't come at Dez. He came at Sully.

Sully expected a blade. What he got were fingers clenching his throat, forcing him back against the ground. Strangling him.

His air was cut off immediately. His hands still bound, he squirmed against the forest floor, struggling to get away from the entity, working to gather the focus needed to kick Jonas away again. But he was so damned tired. And Jonas, possessed of the sort of manic energy born of a genuine threat to his existence, was stronger than ever.

As unconsciousness began to pluck at Sully's brain, he heard Dez scream his name. Raiya, though, yelled back at him, "No, Dez! Do your job! It's the only way! Hurry!"

Sully was nearly lost to reality when, finally, something released. It began with a small weight, then another. Then one more.

The fingers released. Sully wheezed in lungs full of air and immediately began hacking. But he had oxygen.

More than that, he had a chance.

Cracking open his eyes, he spotted the shadow ahead at the base of the tree. Next to a trio of decayed heads. More probably remained inside the tree, but what Dez had already managed to do was enough.

Psychically, Sully reached out for Jonas. Jonas, panic radiating from him, took a step back, then another.

He was going to flee.

Sully focused, needing to stop the ghost before it got away. Except he found he didn't need to. Jonas shot backward, but he bounced off of something, shooting him back toward Sully once again.

That's when Sully realized. Raiya hadn't been working a protective enchantment. She'd been sealing a circle, enclosing the dark spirit inside with them.

Sully felt a grin form. It only served to worry Jonas more.

He had every reason.

Sully grabbed hold of him, ensuring every horrible bit of him was ensnared. The evil power he'd fed the tree now badly weakened, there was nothing left for Jonas to cling to as Sully held him and opened a doorway to the other side.

"It's understandable to want to protect your home," Sully told him. "But not the way you did it. You're headed for a new home now—one I doubt you'll enjoy much."

And then Sully sent him over. Something beyond the door seized hold of Jonas, pulling him the rest of the way. Then Sully closed and sealed the portal.

"You feel that?" Forbes asked. "Something's different. It's lighter somehow."

Sully did feel it. Of course he felt it. With Jonas gone, the woods were clear. The silence lifted too as, somewhere nearby, an owl hooted.

A thud as Dez jumped back to the ground. Sully waited until Dez's form loomed over him. Certain he was now safe in doing so, Sully finally gave into unconsciousness.

CHAPTER 35

DEZ WAS HOVERING. He tended to hover whenever Sully ended up in a bad situation.

"I'm fine," Sully told him again as a paramedic checked him over at the open rear door of an ambulance. When or how it had gotten here, to the edge of the field where they'd left their vehicles to locate the Holy Oak, Sully didn't know. Thankfully, there was little for a paramedic to do other than tend to a few cuts and scrapes.

Dez held his tongue. He'd continue to hold it, Sully knew, until they were someplace more private. It wasn't strictly Sully's physical health Dez would be concerned with.

A variety of police vehicles had arrived as well, including the forensic van. Those people would have their hands full in the coming days, running whatever tests needed done to identify the various heads and conduct whatever other investigation needed done. Sully was happy to leave it to them. His part in this, as far as he was concerned, was done. The woods were safe now, and so would be anyone venturing inside them—safe from the paranormal world, at least.

Forbes made his way over as Parker, seated in the back of a marked police car, was finally driven away.

"Should make for an interesting suspect interview," Forbes said. "At least it will be if he repeats even a little of what he told us before." He shrugged. "He'll have a hard time managing it if he denies it later on. I'm told a dog team found the bloody sheet stuffed in a hollow at the edge of the woods by the golf green. I'd expect we'll find some of Parker's own DNA on there alongside all of Cal Holdfast's."

"Guess this lets Louise Penske off the hook," Dez said.

"Guess it does. Leo Symes as well, although I'm not sure he'll be overly aware of it."

"Do you think he actually has dementia or is he faking it like Louise suggested?" Dez asked.

"I definitely don't get the impression he's faking," Forbes said. "From what I hear, Louise had some reason to dislike Leo after that run-in with him. Regardless, the whole dementia thing is for someone else to worry about. All I know is he didn't kill anyone or take part in any murders."

"I know one other thing for sure," Sully said. "Rebecca will feel a whole lot better knowing that."

"What about you?" Forbes asked. "You doing okay?"

Sully stuffed his hands in his pockets and nodded. "Fine."

"Tell you one thing," Forbes said. "Glad I get to book the killer for a change. Most times you turn up, I don't get to make an arrest at all."

THE FOLLOWING MORNING, Sully, Dez and Raiya packed up their things and prepared for the return trip to Kimotan Rapids. They were loading up their vehicles when Rebecca appeared.

"I've taken the liberty of refunding your stays," she told them. "It was the least I could do."

Sully was a little surprised. They had, after all, been instrumental in getting her longtime employee and friend locked up for murder.

Rebecca must have taken note of his expression because she added an explanation.

"Mr. Braddock here told me yesterday you two suspected my father of murder. He suggested I had to have had my suspicions too. I didn't deny it because, truth be told, he was right."

Her gaze moved vaguely to the right, drifting toward the approximate area where the Holdfast brothers had met their violent ends. "All this time, a part of me wondered, I suppose. Maybe he'd bought the property to cover up for something terrible he'd done. Maybe he hadn't wanted me to end up with Cary after all. I didn't know. For the sake of my own sanity, I didn't go far down that rabbit hole."

She shook her head as if ridding herself of a memory. "I suppose I won't ever know for certain why he bought it. He'd say it was purely because the land came at a good price, but I don't know. I think it's just as possible he bought it to cover for what Parker did. Parker apparently believes my dad owes him something. What he doesn't understand is my dad already repaid him a hundred times over."

Rebecca closed the distance to them, shaking each of their hands. She saved Raiya until last.

"I can't say this enough. Thank you for everything, Raiya. And I'm truly, truly sorry for being so rotten to you back then. You deserved better."

She didn't await a reply, simply turning and making her way back inside her hotel.

THEY HAD one more stop to make before leaving for home.

The Holy Oak Halloween festival was done, the crowds dispersed and, sadly for Dez, the food vendors gone. The remaining booths were now being torn down and packed away—among them Madame Olga's tent.

They found Louise inside, packing away her things in a far more orderly approach than the last time they'd been in here.

Upon spotting them at the entrance, Louise's brows lifted behind her large glasses. "Well?"

"I thought maybe the police would have made you aware," Dez said.

She shook her head. "I haven't talked to anyone from the police since sometime yesterday."

"I think they're pretty swamped," Dez reasoned. "I don't think they'll mind us telling you, in that case. You're off the hook. Parker's confessed to killing both Cary and Cal Holdfast."

Louise stared at him for a long moment. A fortunate thing she hadn't yet removed the chairs since she collapsed into one a second later, bursting into tears as soon as her butt met seat.

Sully exchanged a glance with Dez before returning attention to Louise. "You okay?"

She managed a rapid nod amid the emotional burst, but speech was out of the question. They gave her the time, along with a couple of tissues Raiya extracted from a small package she carried in her purse. Louise took it with a shaky hand and a quick "thank you," before wiping at her eyes and blowing her nose. Another minute or two, she'd calmed enough to talk.

"I don't know how to thank you," she said. "All this time, all these years, I've wondered. And now … I don't actually know what to do now without this hanging over my head. It's like someone gave me my life back."

She dropped her head and gave it a shake. "Imagine that. I get my life back right when I'm getting ready to die."

"I'm so sorry, Louise," Raiya said.

But Louise only shook her head again. Using the armrests to lift herself to her feet, she took a step toward Raiya. "Don't be sorry. I'm not. I'm ready to be done with this life. I'm tired. Not just from being sick and having to fight it over and over and over—although that's a big part of it. It's everything else. It's carrying the weight of guilt. It's being alone all the time. It's having to hide who I am, where I've been. You've made so much of that go away, all of you, and I'm grateful. So, so grateful. But I'm ready to be done with the rest. Do you understand?"

Raiya nodded. She closed the distance to Louise and took her hand. "I do. I only wish—"

But Louise wasn't done. "What we did to you all those years ago, it's part of what I've carried. It was a horrid thing to do, and for what it's worth, Raiya, I'm sorry for my part. To tell you the truth, I suppose I was jealous of you. At that age, you long to be special. I wanted to be a witch without knowing what that even meant. When you came along, I saw in you all the things I wanted to be myself. I suppose my treatment of you sprung from that."

She made a small sweeping gesture with her free hand. "I guess I found a way to be what I wanted to be—even if I don't truly have a gift the way you and Sullivan do."

Raiya smiled. "I don't know. I believe, in a way, we all have a gift. It's not just about whether we're particularly psychic or not. It's about finding our purpose in life."

Louise quirked her lips. "I'm not sure I ever have."

Raiya gave her hand a squeeze. "Well, one thing you have done: you've helped me find peace with my past, just as we did for you. Maybe that's enough."

Louise met Sully's eye. "You help the dead cross over. What's waiting for me?"

"I don't know," Sully said. "I don't get to see beyond this world. What I can tell you is I've never crossed over a good person who didn't leave behind the most incredible sense of peace and joy."

A small smile lit Louise's face. "For the first time in my adult life, I actually feel like I have a chance at that, rather than an extended stay in hell."

She blinked away a fresh round of tears as she gazed at Raiya. "I know I have no right to ask, but when the time comes, if it's not too much to ask, would you consider …" She trailed off, a flush crossing her features.

Raiya answered anyway. "When the time comes, you call me, and I'll be there."

Louise hugged her. "I was wrong, you know. It's not the witch thing that makes you special. It's you. Just you. Thank you."

She released Raiya and peered at Sully and Dez. "Why don't you let me buy you all something to eat before you leave?"

Sully looked to Dez, figuring it would be a big yes.

He figured wrong and found himself fighting a laugh as Dez replied.

"Thanks, Louise, but if it's all the same, I just want to get the hell out of this damn town." He peered at Sully. "Incidentally, bud, if you decide to get married here, I'm not coming."

"Don't worry," Sully replied. "If I never come back here again, it'll be too soon."

ACKNOWLEDGMENTS

There's rarely a day that goes by in which I don't pinch myself at least once (figuratively, not literally, to spare myself the bruises). Being able to write books as a full-time job amounts to the realization of a childhood dream—one I never thought I'd achieve.

In 2022, I was able to hand in my notice, ending a two-decade career as a newspaper crime reporter. The decision was a difficult one, not just because I was giving up a job with a set wage and benefits, but because I truly loved and found value in what I did. But at the end of the day, I knew I was ready for a new adventure.

The support of my family and friends was crucial in getting me to this point, and I can't say thank you enough to all of you who might happen to be reading this. I've never once felt anything less than blessed in the people surrounding me. So to my parents, my brother, my sister-in-law, my nephew and niece and their significant others, my aunts and uncles, my cousins, my wonderful BFF, my former work crew (at the paper and extended media world as well as in the policing and justice system in which I spent so much time), and to so many others in my life, please know how much I appreciate your support.

To my editors, Hannah Sullivan and Bambi Sommers, a huge thank you for all your help in making my books all they can be. The same goes for my stellar team of advance readers. Your eagle eyes and your suggestions have made the books—and me as a writer—stronger.

To my Sully's Spirits group, thank you for being there to bounce ideas and cover designs off of. You folks have an amazing eye, and your honesty is always, always appreciated. Thank you for helping me to get things right. Speaking of getting things right, thank you to Gerry Morin for answering questions I've had about Indigenous language and culture when the topic has arisen in my books. I can't express how thankful I am for your wisdom.

A big thanks to folks in the writing community—my mom, my good friend J.C. Paulson and Gail Bowen, among many others—for giving me so much wonderful advice when I was fumbling toward my first published book. Huge thanks as well to my former colleague Andy Cooper for pointing me toward self-publishing podcasts and courses which really got me going.

And last, but absolutely not least, to my newsletter subscribers, social media followers and my fabulous readers in general, thank you so much for reading what I write! I appreciate so much the many wonderful and kind comments and messages over the years I've been doing this. When I started, I didn't know what to expect. You've made me feel so welcome, so cared for, so blessed. My heart is constantly warmed by your words, and I can only endeavour to do the same for you.

In what sometimes feels like a world filled with darkness, you are all a reminder there is still so much light—if only one remembers to look.

So thank you.

For those interested, I'm constantly working on a collection of short stories featuring characters from the city of Kimotan Rapids. While the city and the people in it are completely made up, I strive to make them feel real—for you and for myself. The collection—*Haunted: The Ghosts of Sullivan Gray*—delves deeper into characters' backgrounds and hopefully explains a bit more about Sully, Dez, Tracker Jack and others. The collection is free to newsletter subscribers. You're free to sign up and then unsubscribe—although if you stick around as a subscriber, I'll update you whenever there's a new free short story added or new books coming out to buy or read through Kindle Unlimited. Just click this link (if you're reading this as an e-book) or visit my website, hpbayne.com, and follow the link you'll find there to get the book.

All my best to you, and thanks again!

ABOUT THE AUTHOR

Fascinated by ghost stories and crime fiction, H.P. Bayne has been writing both in some capacity since her youth. As an adult, she spent more than two decades as a crime reporter, a career which provided her with a detailed knowledge of crime and those who walk in that world. Raised on a farm on the Canadian Prairies, H.P. enjoys reading, portrait drawing, travel and spending time with family and friends.

For more information, visit H.P.'s website at hpbayne.com.

ALSO BY H.P. BAYNE

Wray Mallory

Hell's Gate

Book of the Dead

A Song for the Dead

The Sullivan Gray Series (best read in the following order):

Black Candle

Harbinger

The Dule Tree

Crawl

Hollow Road

Second Son

Spirit Caller

Sullivan Gray box sets:

The Sullivan Gray Series Box Set 1

The Sullivan Gray Series Box Set 2

The Braddock & Gray Case Files (can be read in order or as standalone novels):

The Edge Creek Light

The Haunting of Thornview Hall

The Wynne Witch

The Blake Ghost

Dead Man's Lake

The Hanged Man

Twitch

Ghosts of Christmas Past

Mr. Grin

The Cursed

The Haunting of Blythe Theatre

The Wakefield Haunting

Ghosts of Riverview

House of Mirrors

The Haunting of Sutton Hill

The Attic Room

The Durlow Dollhouse

The Kilburn School Haunting

The Holy Oak Haunting

The Braddock & Gray Case Files box sets:

The Braddock & Gray Case Files Books 1 - 4

The Braddock & Gray Case Files Books 5 - 8 (coming soon)

Tracker Jack Winter

The Vigilante

Printed in Dunstable, United Kingdom

78550832R00150